Julian Critchley has been a Tory MP for twenty-five years in two incarnations. He sat at the feet of Mr Harold Macmillan, Lord Home, Mr Edward Heath, and trod on the toes of Mrs Margaret Thatcher. He escaped office, and has not been knighted for long and silent service. (Mrs Thatcher, when the honour was tentatively suggested, cried, 'Never!') He has taken up writing instead, mainly but not exclusively about politics. He has written regularly for every good newspaper and several bad ones. His last three books, *Westminster Blues, Heseltine: The Unauthorised Biography* and *Palace of Varieties*, have all been bestsellers. Here, he turns his hand to fiction. 'Why should Jeffrey Archer have all the good tunes?' asks Critchley. Why indeed?

Hung Parliament

An Entertainment

Julian Critchley

HEADLINE

First published in 1991
by Hutchinson,
a division of the Random Century Group Ltd

First published in paperback in 1992
by HEADLINE BOOK PUBLISHING PLC

10 9 8 7 6 5 4 3

ISBN 0 7472 3836 7

Phototypeset by Intype, London

Printed and bound in Great Britain by
HarperCollins Manufacturing, Glasgow

HEADLINE BOOK PUBLISHING PLC
Headline House
79 Great Titchfield Street
London W1P 7FN

The little lady has a fetish,
She goes to bed in mink.

Louis MacNeice, 'Autumn Journal'

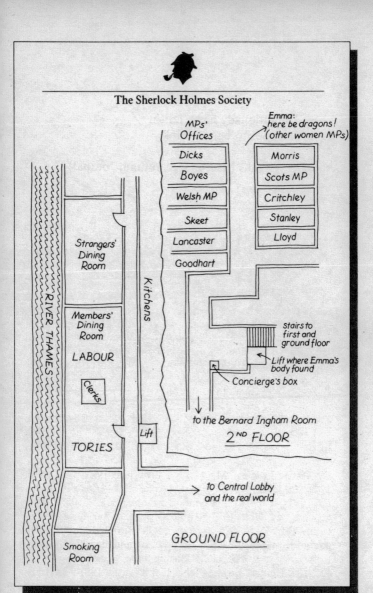

The Sherlock Holmes Society

MPs' Offices

Dicks
Boyes
Welsh MP
Skeet
Lancaster
Goodhart

Emma: here be dragons! (other women MPs)

Morris
Scots MP
Critchley
Stanley
Lloyd

Strangers' Dining Room

Members' Dining Room

LABOUR

Clerks

TORIES

Kitchens

Lift

RIVER THAMES

stairs to first and ground floor

Lift where Emma's body found

Concierge's box

to the Bernard Ingham Room

2ND FLOOR

to Central Lobby and the real world

GROUND FLOOR

Smoking Room

Joshua Morris's sketch map of the House of Commons

Principal Dramatis Personae

CATFORD, The Rt Hon Kevin Albert; MP (C) Arnos Grove 1970–, PC (1979); s of Albert Catford; *b* 29 Feb 1932; *Educ* Westbourne Park Secondary Mod and Lon Univ; *m* 1962, Mavis Banham; *Career* Nat Serv Intelligence Corps; oppn spokesman Indust 1976–79, parly sec Tport 1979–81, sec of state for Trade and Indust. 1981–85, sec of state for Tport 1985–87, mem Inst of Econ Affrs; chartered accountant and company dir; *Books* Margaret Thatcher; a woman to watch (1977), Love in the Mist (fiction, 1984), The Decline and Fall of the Upper Classes (1989); *Style–* The Rt Hon Kevin Catford, MP, House of Commons, London SW1 0AA

CURRIE, Edwina; MP (C) S Derbyshire 1983–; *b* 13 Oct 1946; *Educ* Liverpool Inst, St Anne's Coll Oxford (MA), LSE (MSc); *m* 1972, Raymond Frank Currie; 2 da; *Career* teacher and lectr 1972–81, head dept of business studies Bromsgrove Sch 1978–81; city cncllr Birmingham 1975–86; memb: Birmingahm AHA 1975–82, Birmingham Community Rels Cncl 1979–83; chm: Birmingham Social Servs Ctee 1979–80, Central Birmingham Health Authy 1981–83, Housing CTee 1982–83; memb Select Ctee on Social Servs

1983–86, vice pres Fedn cons Students 1984–85, gen advsy cncl BBC 1985–86, pps to Sir Keith Joseph Sec of State for Educn 1986. Parly under sec DHSS, min for Womens Health 1986–88; *Recreations* family, swimming, domestic arts; *Clubs* Swadlincote Cons (Derbys); *Style–* Mrs Edwina Currie, MP; House of Commons, London SW1 0AA

DEAN, Sir (Arthur) Paul (Kt 1985); MP (C) Woodspring 1983–; s of Arthur Dean; *b* 14 Sept 1924; *Educ* Ellesmere Coll, Exeter Coll Oxford (MA, BLitt); *m* 1, 1957, Doris (d 1979), da of Frank Webb, of Sussex; m 2, 1980, Peggy *née* Parker; *Career* WWII Capt Welsh Gds, ADC to Cdr 1 Corps BAOR; former farmer; CRD 1957, resident tutor Swinton Cons Coll 1958–62; asst dir CRD 1962–64; Party candidate (C) Pontefract 1962, MP (C) N Somerset 1964–83, front bench oppn spokesman Health and Social Security 1969–70, Parly under-sec DHSS 1970–74, chm Cons Health and Social Security Ctee 1979–82; memb: Commons Servs Select Ctee 1979–82, exec ctee Cwlth Parly Assoc UK branch 1975–, Commons Chm's Panel 1979–82; second dep chm House of Commons and dep chm Ways and Means 1982–87; first dep chm Ways and Means and dep speaker; formerly: memb Church in Wales Governing Body, govr BUPA, chm Cons Watch-Dog Gp for Self-Employed; dir: Charterhouse Pensions, Watney Mann and Trueman Hldgs; govr Cwlth Inst 1981–89, pres Oxford Univ Cons Assoc; *Clubs* Oxford Carlton (pres); *Style–* Sir Paul Dean, MP; House of Commons, London SW1 0AA

FISHER, Mark; MP (Lab) Stoke-on-Trent Central 1983–; s of Sir Nigel Thomas Loveridge Fisher, MC, *qv*, by his 1 w Lady Gloria Vaughan, da of 7 Earl of Lisburne; *b* 29 Oct 1944; *Educ* Eton, Trinity Coll Cambridge; *m* 1971, Ghilly (Mrs Ingrid Hunt), da of late James Hoyle Geach; 2 s 2 da; *Career* frmr prncpal Tattenhall Educn Centre; frmr documnty writer and film prducr; contested (Lab) Leek 1979; memb: Staffs CC 1981–85, Treasy and Civil Service Select Ctee 1983–86, BBC gen advsy cncl 1987–, Cncl Policy Studies Inst

1989–; dep pro-chllr Univ of Keele 1989–; oppn whip 1985–86, shadow min for Arts and Media 1987–; *Books* City Centres, City Cultures (1988); *Style–* Mark Fisher, Esq, MP; House of Commons, London SW1 0AA

GRUNTE, Sir Ralph Redvers (Kt 1980), MP (C) Warwickshire South 1974–, s of Percy Haines; *b* 8 Dec 1930; *Educ* Sutton Coldfield GS; Univ of Birmingham; *m* 1960, Marjorie Grunt, No chdn; *Career* motor trader and garage owner; pres Midland Motor Traders, 1970–74 dir Harry Greenway plc, tyre distrbrs, Steve Norris and Sons; Rotarian; del to the Cncl of Europe and the Western European Union 1974–80; vice chm Party's Europe Cttee; *Style–* Sir Ralph Grunte, MP; The Copper Beeches, Arden, Warwickshire (2345 54321)

HAILSHAM OF ST MARYLEBONE, Baron (Life Peer UK 1970); Quintin McGarel Hogg; KG (1988), CH (1974), PC (1956); s of 1 Viscount Hailsham (d 1950) by his 1 w Elizabeth, da of Judge Trimble Brown, of Nashville, Tennessee, and widow of Hon Archibald Marjoribanks (4 s of 1 Baron Tweedmouth); disclaimed both Viscountcy and Barony for life 1963; 1 cous of Sir John Hogg, TD, *qv*; *b* 9 Oct 1907; *Educ* Eton, Ch Ch Oxford; *m* 1, 1932 (m dis 1943), Natalie Antoinette (d 1987), da of Alan Sullivan, of Sheerland House, Pluckley, Kent; *m* 2, 1944, Mary Evelyn (d 1978), o da of Richard Martin, of Kensington; 2 s, 3 da; *m* 3, 1986, Deirdre, er da of Mrs Margaret Briscoe and late Capt Peter Shannon; *Heir* (to Viscountcy and Barony of Hailsham, UK cr respectively 1928 & 1929, only) s, Hon Douglas Hogg, MP; *Career* served WWII Rifle Bde; barrister 1932, QC 1953; MP (C) Oxford City 1938–58, St Marylebone 1963–70; first lord Admiralty 1956–57, min Educn 1957, lord pres of cncl 1957–59 and 1960–64, lord privy seal 1959–60, min Science and Technology 1959–64, ldr House of Lords 1960–63 (dep ldr 1957–60), lord chllr 1970–74 and 1979–88 (3 in precedence in Cabinet); chm Cons Pty Orgn 1957–59; rector Glasgow Univ 1959; editor Halsbury's Law of England

(4th edn) 1972–; fellow All Souls Oxford 1951–58 and 1962–; Hon DCL Oxford, Hon LLD Cambridge; FRS 1973; *Style*– The Rt Hon the Lord Hailsham of St Marylebone, KG, CH, FRS, PC; The Corner House, Heathview Gdns, London SW15 3SZ (071 789 3954/788 2256)

HARVEY, Charles Witherspoon MP (C) Long Melford June 1987–; s of Charles Dorrington Harvey; *b* 8 Dec 1952; *Educ* Edgeborough, Charterhouse, Pembroke Coll Oxford; *m* 1980, Miriam Joseph; 2 da. *Career* merchant banker; parly sec to the Min Tport 1989–; *Style*– Charles Harvey, Esq, MP; 30 Onslow Square, London SW1 (071 546 3125)

HESELTINE, The Rt Hon Michael Ray Dibdin; PC (1979), MP (C) Henley 1974–; s of Col R D Heseltine; *b* 21 March 1933; *Educ* Shrewsbury, Pembroke Coll Oxford; *m* 1962, Anne Harding Williams, 1 s, 2 da; *Career* Nat Serv Welsh Gds; contested (C): Gower 1959, Coventry N 1964; MP (C) Tavistock 1966–74; oppn spokesman Tport 1969, parly sec Miny Tport June-Oct 1970, parly under-sec Environment 1970–72, min Aerospace and Shipping (DTI) 1972–74, oppn spokesman Indust 1974–76, Environment 1976–79, sec Environment 1979–83, sec of state for Def 1983–86; dir Bow Pubns 1961–65, chm Haymarket Press 1966–70; Assoc Cons Clubs 1978, (vice-pres 1978), Nat YCs 1982–84; *Books* Where There's a Will (1987), The Challenge of Europe: Can Britain Win? (1989); *Style*– The Rt Hon Michael Heseltine, MP; House of Commons, London SW1 0AA

KELLETT-BOWMAN, Dame (Mary) Elaine; *née* Kay; (DBE 1989), MP (C) Lancaster 1970–; da of late Walter Kay; *b* 8 July 1924; *Educ* Queen Mary's Sch Lytham, The Mount Sch York, St Anne's Coll Oxford; *m* 1, 1945, Charles Norman Kellett (d 1959); 3 s, 1 da; *m* 2 1971, Edward Thomas Kellett-Bowman, MEP, JP, *qv*; 3 step s, 1 step da; *Career* farmer; welfare worker London, Liverpool; called to the Bar Middle Temple 1964; contested (C): Nelson and Colne 1955, SW Norfolk 1959, 1959 by-elections, Buckingham 1964 and 1966;

memb Press Cncl 1964–68; alderman Camden Boro 1968–74, chm Welfare Ctee 1969; MEP (EDG) Cumbria 1979–84; *Clubs* English Speaking Union; *Style–* Dame Elaine Kellett-Bowman, DBE, MP; Slyne Grange, Slyne, nr Lancaster LA2 6AU

KERR, Emma Betty; MP (C) Corve Dale June 1987–; *b* 21 June 1959; *Educ* Birmingham High Sch, Univ of London; *m* 1980, Barry Kerr, no chdn; *Career* journalist (Woman's Own and She) and political research assistant (Sir Ralph Grunte, MP); Memb Home Affrs Select Ctee. *Style–* Mrs Emma Kerr, MP; 56 Beatty House, Dolphine Square SW1 (071 865 9986)

LANCASTER, David Arbuthnot; MP (C) Nottingham South 1983–; s of Percy Lancaster; *b* 19 Jan 1952; *Educ* Carlton GS, Leicester Univ; Unmarried; *Career* chartered accountant; ex-chm Nottingham City YCs; memb Monday Club; Select Ctee on the Environment; vice-chm All Party Anglo-Mexican Group; *Style–* David Lancaster, Esq, MP; 32 Quex Rd NW6 (071 435 8734)

LANGFORD, Samuel Mark; MP (C) Ongar June 1987–; *b* 1 April 1940; *Educ* Billericay Sch, Chingford Poly; *m* 1983, Dawn Scragg; 2 da; *Career* car salesman and motor trader; dir Gaming Machines plc, The Gorman Institute; chm Essex YCs, Friends of St Andrews; memb Home Affrs Select Ctee; *Pubns* 'Some of My Best Friends', a Conservative Political Centre pamphlet; *Style–* Sam Langford, Esq, MP; River View, Dagenham (2356 76234)

MacGREGOR, Rt Hon John Roddick Russell; OBE (1971), PC (1985), MP (C) S Norfolk Feb 1974–; s of late Dr N S R MacGregor, of Shotts; *b* 14 Feb 1937; *Educ* Merchiston, St Andrew's Univ, King's Coll London; *m* 1962, Jean Dungey; 1 s, 2 da; *Career* univ admin 1961–62; former chm: Fedn of Univ Cons & Unionist Assocs, Bow Gp; first pres Cons and Christian Democratic Youth Community, with New Society and Hill Samuel (dir 1973–79); special asst to PM 1963–64, CRD 1964–65, head of ldr of oppn's Private Off 1965–68, oppn whip 1977–79, lord cmmr Treasy 1979–81, parly undersec Trade and Indust with responsibility for small businesses 1981–83, min state Agric Fishers and Food 1983–85, chief sec Treasy 1985–87, min of Agric Fisheries and Food 1987–July 1989, sec of state for Educn July 1989–; *Recreations* opera, gardening, travel, conjuring; *Style–* The Rt Hon John MacGregor, OBE, MP; House of Commons, London SW1 0AA

MACLENNAN, Robert Adam Ross; MP (Lab until 1981, when joined SDP) Caithness & Sutherland 1966–; s of Sir Hector Maclennan (d 1978, sometime chm Advsy Ctee on Distinction Awards, an obstetrician & gynaecologist, and twice Lord High Cmmr to the General Assembly of the Church of Scotland), by his 1 w, Isabel, *née* Adam; *b* 26 June 1936; *Educ* Glasgow Acad, Balliol Coll Oxford, Trinity Coll Cambridge, Columbia Univ NY; *m* 1968, Helen, wid of Paul Noyes, and da of Judge Ammi Cutter, of Cambridge, Mass: 1 s, 1 da, 1 step s; *Career* barr 1962; cwlth affrs sec 1967–69, pps to Min without portfolio 1969–70, additional oppn spokesman Scottish Affrs 1970–71. Def 1971–72, parly undersec Prices and Consumer Protection 1974–79, memb Commons Public Accounts Ctee 1979–; oppn spokesman on For Affrs 1979–80; SDP spokesman Agric 1981–87, on Home & Legal Affrs 1983–87; ldr of the SDP 1987–88; Democratic spokesman Home Affrs 1988–; *Recreations* theatre, music, books, 2800 square miles of constituency; *Clubs* Brooks's; *Style–* Robert Maclennan, Esq, MP; Hollandmake, Barrock, Caithness (084 785 203); 74 Abingdon Villas, London W8 (071 937 5960)

MAJOR, The Rt Hon John; MP (C) Hungtingdon 1983–, PC (June 1987); s of Thomas Major (d 1963), actor (real name Abraham Thomas Ball), and his 2 w, Gwendolyn Minnie, *née* Coates (d 1970); *b* 29 March 1943; *Educ* Rutlish; *m* 1970, Norma Christina Elizabeth, da of Norman Johnson (d 1945); 1 s, 1 da; *Career* sr exec Standard Chartered Bank plc to 1979; assoc Inst of Bankers; MP (C) Hungtingdonshire 1979–83; pps to Min of State, Home Office 1981–83, asst govt whip 1983–84; Lord Cmmr of Treasury 1984–85; parly under-sec of state DHSS 1985–86, min of Social Security 1986–87, chief sec to the Treasury June 1987–July 1989, foreign sec July 1989–Oct 1989, Chancellor of the Exchequer Oct 1989–1990, Prime Minister and First Lord of Treasury 1990–; *Style–* The Rt Hon John Major, MP; 10 Downing Street, London SW1

MORRIS, Joshua George; MP (C) Shropshire West June 1970–; s of George Evans-Morris; *b* 7 Sept 1930; *Educ* Broughton Hall, Shrewsbury, Queen's Coll Oxford; *m* 1960, Fay Greene (d 1982), 3 da, 1 s, *Career* journalist and author; delegate Cncl of Europe and the Western European Union 1979–83; pres Sherlock Holmes Soc of Gt Britain; *Books* inc The Young Margaret (1986), A Short Life of Nigel West (1987); *Style–* Joshua Morris, Esq, MP; 23 Broad Street, Ludlow, Shropshire (0584 872222)

RYDER, Richard Andrew; OBE (1981), MP (C) Mid Norfolk 1983–; s of Richard Stephen Ryder, JP, DL, and Margaret MacKenzie; *b* 1949; *Educ* Radley, Magdalene Coll Cambs; *m* 1981, Caroline, o da of Sir David Stephens, *qv*; 1 s (decd), 1 da; *Career* political sec to Rt Hon Mrs Margaret Thatcher 1975–81; PPS to: Fin Sec Treasy 1984, Sec of State Foreign Affrs 1984–; chm Cons Foreign and Cwlth Cncl 1984–89; govt whip 1986–88; Parly sec MAFF 1988–89, econ sec Treasy 1989–; *Style–* Richard Ryder, Esq, OBE, MP; The House of Commons, London SW1 0AA

SOAMES, Hone (Arthur) Nicholas Winston; MP (C) Crawley 1983–; s of Baron Soames, GCMG, GCVO, CH, CBE, PC (Life Peer), d 1987, and Hon Mary, DBE, *née* Spencer-Churchill, da of late Sir Winston Churchill and Baroness Spencer-Churchill; *b* 12 Feb 1948; *Educ* Eton; *m* 1981 (at which wedding HRH The Prince of Wales was best man), Catherine, da of Capt Tony Weatherall, of Dumfries; 1 s

(Arthur Harry David, b 1985); *Career* served 11th Hussars; extra equerry to HRH The Prince of Wales; Lloyd's insurance broker; *Clubs* White's, Turf, Carlton; *Style*– The Hon Nicholas Soames, MP; The House of Commons, London SW1 0AA

THATCHER, The Rt Hon Margaret Hilda; PC (1970), MP (C) Finchley 1987–; yr da of late Alfred Roberts, grocer, of Grantham, Lincs, and Beatrice, *née* Stephenson; b 13 Oct 1925; *Educ* Huntingtower Primary Sch Grantham, Kesteven and Grantham Girls Sch, Somerville Coll Oxford (MA, BSc; hon fellow 1970); *m* 1951, Sir Denis Thatcher, (Kt 1989) company director; 1 s (Mark), 1 da (Carol (twin), radio journalist, presenter (freelance) with LBC); *Career* former research chemist; called to the Bar Lincon's Inn 1953 (hon bencher 1975), contested (C) Dartford 1950 and 1951; MP (C); Finchley 1959–74: Barnet, Finchley 1974–1983 and 1983–87; jt parly sec Miny of Pensions and National Insurance 1961–64, memb Shadow Cabinet 1967–70 (spokesman on: Tport, Power, Treasury matters, Housing and Pensions), chief oppn spokesman educn 1969–70, sec of state Educn and Science (and co-chm Women's National Commn) 1970–74, chief oppn spokesman environment 1974–75, leader of the Opposition Feb 1975–79, prime minister and First Lord of Treasury (first woman to hold this office) from 4 May 1979–Nov 1990; minister for the Civil Service Jan 1981–; freedom of Borough of Barnet 1980; hon freeman of Worshipful Co of Grocers 1980; freedom of Falkland Islands 1983; Donovan Award USA 1981; FRS; *Style*– The Rt Hon Margaret Thatcher, c/o Dickins and Jones, London W1

WORTHINGTON EVANS, Peter Jackson; MP (C) Edgbaston West 1983–; s of Campbell Evans; b Sept 12 1960; *Educ* Sparkbrook Sch, Univ of Keel; *m* 1984, Shirley Worthington; 1 s; *Career* pub rels offr; Pig Marketing Board; chm Sparkbrook YCs; memb YC's nat ctee; ass govt whip 1990–; *Style*– Peter Worthington Evans, Esq, MP; 34 Litchfield Avenue, Edgbaston (0987 56432)

1

An observant motorist driving northwards over Westminster Bridge at night might wonder why a small lantern burns in the tower of Big Ben higher up than the illuminated clock face itself. He could not fail to notice the great bulk of the Palace of Westminster on his left, its lights ablaze like those of an ocean liner, and the people standing or sitting on the terrace. The light tells London that the House of Commons is still sitting: the Palace itself, with its thousand rooms and thousand politicians, to say nothing of as many cooks, clerks and bottlewashers, has all the confidence of a *Titanic* bound for New York on a far from maiden voyage. So it seemed on the evening of Monday 7 June 199–.

In the early hours of the following morning, Tuesday 8 June, a prominent woman Conservative MP, whose face had been long carried into every home in the land, was to be found dead in what the Sergeant at Arms said gravely were 'unusual circumstances'. However unusual they may have been, the fact remained that the news of her death was not made official until noon on Tuesday, several hours after the murder had been committed. For much of that morning, while rumour spread as to the victim, who was thought by many to be Mrs Edwina Currie, the authorities published no statement of any kind. However, at midday the Leader of the House, John MacGregor, made a statement to the journalists of the parliamentary lobby. He was speaking in the Bernard Ingham Room. 'It is true,' said MacGregor, looking like a solemn Scottish fifth former, 'that an Honourable Member has been found dead. It was not, as we all now know, Mrs Edwina Currie.' He paused at this point. 'It was a case of mistaken identity. I am very sorry to say that the victim was Mrs Emma Kerr, the Member for Corve Dale.' At this the ears of the lobby pricked up. Had not the lovely Emma been described by Mr Robin Oakley of *The Times* only yesterday as 'the Tory Party's sweetheart'?

'The police,' continued MacGregor, 'are carrying out exhaustive inquiries into the circumstances surrounding Mrs Kerr's untimely death. I have no further information to give at this time. Rest assured that, as soon as I have, I shall inform the public.' Pressed for more information by the journalists present, John MacGregor said he thought an arrest was imminent. The Leader of the House, after making reference to the assassination of Sir Spencer Perceval in 1812, concluded his remarks by saying, 'A colleague has been helping the Met. with their inquiries.' At first he refused to give the name of 'the colleague', but after taking advice he went on to explain hurriedly that this observation did not necessarily mean that the culprit was an MP ('Only Harrods employs more people in London in one large building than we do'), but that a

Member of Parliament would be helping the Metropolitan Police in its attempt to solve the mystery. That MP was, of course, Mr Joshua Morris.

The Leader of the House concluded by paying a tribute to Mrs Emma Kerr. 'Mrs Kerr was a young woman with many friends and a splendid future.' At this point Ron Barton, the lobby correspondent of the *True Brit*, was heard to comment, 'Too many "good" friends and more of a past than a future.' Barton was a horror but a good tabloid journalist. Had he not been, when working for the *Sun*, Mr Kelvin Mackenzie's best man?

On Monday 7 June Joshua Morris, twenty years a Tory MP and twenty years a backbencher, parked his secondhand Rover in the Members' underground car park and made his way up the escalator into the Palace of Westminster. Two large men with mirrors stuck on sticks had inspected the underside of his car for Semtex. They had found nothing. Leaving the garage, Joshua recalled that a friend called David Walder, long since dead, had once said that the wall next to the escalator should be covered with photos of women MPs in their underwear. Poor David, thought Joshua, it was his remorseless sense of humour that killed him. He died laughing in '78.

Joshua hung his mac on a peg in the Members' cloakroom, nodded towards an attendant whose task in life seemed to consist only of copying, in laborious longhand, the names of all those who spoke in the day's debate, glanced at the tapes of the PA, 'Prime Minister says "perhaps" to closer European integration', and climbed two flights of marble stairs on his way to the Members' Lobby. Recently Joshua had noticed that the climb was robbing him of his breath. It was just after two, and Joshua, who had driven down the M1 from his home in Shropshire, wanted a salad and a cup of coffee. It was too late for a proper lunch. He stopped, however, in the Members' post office in the Lobby to collect his mail. He took the large bundle, tied in a knot which was meant to come loose at the flick of his wrist but rarely did, into the tea room. Having helped himself to a piece of pie, the sort which had one Cyclopian eye made from half an aged egg, he sat alone at a table and began to open his post.

Most MPs leave the opening of their post to their secretaries, who weed out the hate mail and the unsolicited letters in large brown envelopes and, later in the day, present the remainder for perusal and reply. Joshua Morris, however, had several reasons for opening his own. Hate mail amused him, so long as it did not carry a West Shropshire postmark. He would tear open the cheap envelopes and read only the first sentence – often written in green ink. 'You are an effing nigger-lover . . .', 'Hanging is too good for you', etc. These missives, over which the unbalanced had taken immense trouble, would then be tossed smartly into a nearby bin, where they lay unread, smoking with frustration.

The bulk of Joshua's mail came from his constituents in Shropshire West. The topic of the month was abortion. Letters from the 'pro-life' lobby outnumbered those from '*Guardian* women' by three to one. Sometimes there were postcards carrying the vividly coloured pictures of the aborted. More encouragingly, there were two cheques for media services rendered and an invitation from the editor of *The Times* to write what the letter called 'an occasional column'. He would take the place of Clement Freud. Joshua had once striven hard for political promotion, a time many years ago when his journalism consisted of worthy leader-page articles entitled 'Whither NATO?' More recently, as his hopes of advancement had died away during the long years of Mrs Thatcher's none too golden rule, he had adopted a lighter touch, mocking, not always gently, the pretensions of his more successful colleagues. He had once been described, by Tony Howard on Radio 3, as 'a political mocking bird', but few Tories listened to Radio 3.

Towards the bottom of his pile of post, tucked away between an unsolicited copy of *Concrete Quarterly* and the *UK Press Gazette*, was a blue envelope in a familiar hand. The top left-hand corner was marked 'personal'; an injunction which might not have been obeyed by a careless or hard-pressed secretary. The letter was from Felicity, Joshua's mistress. He put the letter in his inside pocket, to be read later in the privacy of his office.

Joshua Morris was sixty, the age when one starts to feel younger at lunch than at dinner. He was half a stone overweight. He had four children, not all of whom were in gainful employment. He had lost neither his hair nor his zest for life. Recently he had been told at a party by an ancient female celebrity that he was a handsome man. 'I used to be,' had been his reply. 'But you are,' she had insisted. 'You look like a Roman emperor.' 'Which one?' Morris had asked. 'An evil one,' had been her cheerful reply. Morris had been delighted by this exchange. Could he one day persuade John Major to send him to the Lords? Mrs Thatcher would have sent him to the hulks. They had not seen eye to eye.

Joshua had once sat for a seat in south London, which he was later to lose. A quarter of a century after he sat for Shropshire West, the prettiest part of a

5

county famous for its Tories and its sheep. He was considered to be something of a loner, the possessor of a sharp pen and an occasional wit. His friends said he was charming; his enemies – and in politics few are without enemies – thought him shallow. In truth he was idle. He was no zealot in a Party of zealots. He was literate, and made a living writing funny books and serious articles. He was the Chairman of the Sherlock Holmes Society of Great Britain, a tribute to his interest in crime. His Party colleagues were more interested in punishment. He thought himself not clever enough to write poetry, but admired greatly Houseman, Larkin and MacNeice. His reputation as a sleuth had been made while still at Oxford in the early 1950s when he had unmasked the killer of the college chaplain. (It had been his wife.) His romanticism he hid beneath a predictable blanket of cynicism. He was regarded as fun, but not by Mrs Thatcher, who had never considered him to be 'one of us'. Joshua was relieved to hear it. In the great leadership contest of November 1990 he had voted first for Michael Heseltine, then for Hurd. But he was happy with Major, far happier than he would have been had Margaret stayed.

Joshua ate his pie but left the egg. Its accusatory stare reminded him of someone. He was joined by Peter Worthington Evans, a member of the Government whips' office. Evans was a youngish man, somewhat half-heartedly on the make. He lacked a sense of humour, which could well have been the explanation for his one unpublicised, but privately well-known mistake. As a senior whip with responsibilities to the Royal Household, he had once had the task of writing a daily account of politics, which was delivered each evening to the Queen, who read it while she was dressing for dinner at Buckingham Palace. His other role was as sheepdog to a flock of fellow Tory MPs, in which capacity he would sometimes be obliged to write curt notes of protest to the dilatory or faint of heart. It so happened that one day he mixed up his envelopes: the Sovereign received a card which read, 'Where the hell were you at eleven o'clock last night?', the recalcitrant MP a bland and misleading account of Mrs Thatcher's universal popularity. The incident had been hushed up – at the cost of many a blind eye turned towards one MP's inattendance – but the story had spread none the less.

Peter Worthington Evans was know, even to his face, as 'Worthy', a nickname that fitted him like a handmade shoe. He was nondescript in appearance, with fair hair and a taste for costume jewellery so pronounced – waistcoat chains, bracelets and the rest – that he rattled as he walked. He was entirely without a sense of fun. In an attempt to please, he now launched into a well-told story about Edwina Currie's first political appearance at a Party conference in Blackpool, where she turned up on the rostrum waving a pair of handcuffs. She had threatened to stay put until hanging was restored. As the applause of the Party faithful rose to a crescendo, the Party's Chief Agent, a man who had, in his time, seen everything, remarked, 'We've a right one 'ere.'

Joshua acknowledged the story politely (he rather liked Edwina) and sipped from his cup of vile coffee. He noticed the Prime Minister, John Major, enter the tea room, flanked by his parliamentary private secretary, the burly and bespectacled Graham Bright. Major sat quietly at a table. How times had changed, thought Joshua, and for the better. Mrs Thatcher's occasional forays into the tea or dining room had been made when her popularity was unusually low. She would sit herself down at one of the larger tables while her PPS, Peter Morrison, who had the air of a gentleman butcher, set about inviting colleagues to sit next to her. In the halcyon days he would have had no trouble but, towards the end of her reign, the trawl had often proved less than rewarding. After she had lost Nigel Lawson, the pundits claimed that the one-time Iron Lady was suffering from metal fatigue, a condition which in no way diminished the intensity of her opinion or the rapidity of her tongue. Joshua recalled watching the young Emma Kerr, newly elected, sitting rigidly to attention, her eyes unblinking as if she were undergoing a religious experience. He had caught the word 'resolution'; clearly the then Prime Minister was standing no nonsense. She had been wearing her blue, mused Joshua; an invariable sign that the nation was in for a good thrashing.

Joshua had welcomed Mrs Thatcher's resignation. In 1975 she had said publicly that the Tories did not like their leaders staying in office beyond ten years, but 1985 had been and gone with no sign whatever of a graceful withdrawal. The events of November 1990 had been traumatic; since her rejection, 'Lady' Thatcher, as she now was, had become a threatening presence, rarely seen in the House but often heard outside it. Her friends at Westminster, wrapped in their cloaks, gathered in the corners of corridors like so many Florentine conspirators. The general atmosphere, however, had changed for the better; the irredentists might nurse their grievance, but the bulk of the Party felt a lightening of the load.

Emma Kerr was pretty enough to bring out what passed for the paternal instinct in the more elderly of her colleagues. The Father of the House did not let a day go past without kissing her decorously on both cheeks (he had served once on the Council of Europe where he had picked up the habit); Sir Rhodes Boyson had been seen kissing her hand, a strange courtesy on the part of that jovial, side-whiskered figure. When Emma had first risen to her feet at the weekly meeting of the '22, the committee open to all Tory back-benchers, and had made a nicely worded plea in favour of tolerance, Sir Tufton Bufton had to be helped from the room by the whip on duty. He had been heard to exclaim, as the door closed behind him, 'Damn fine woman'. They could well have been his last words. He died of heart failure later that evening. The resultant by-election had been won by Labour.

Emma Kerr had been elected in 1987. She was by far the youngest woman Tory MP and was, as yet, unscarred by the hatreds that rive the small band of Tory women MPs. She had not, as once had Edwina Currie, suggested to the newspapers that her sisters were a dullish lot. Nor had she said as much as Emma Nicholson, whose views as to the heaviness of the other women's thighs had been misreported by the *Sun*. Emma Kerr was well liked and enjoyed the warm admiration of her male colleagues as well as the praise of the redoubtable Dame Elaine Kellett-Bowman, the shop steward of the women MPs. It had not gone unnoticed that Alan Clark invariably removed his dark glasses on Emma Kerr's entry into the tea room. Emma was the Party's piece of crumpet. She was not as witty as Dame Janet Fookes, as magisterial as Dame Elaine or as dotty as Teresa Gorman, but who cared? What was more, Emma had taken to sitting in the smoking room, a male preserve. Even Nicholas Budgen, a thrifty Tory, had been known to buy her a drink. She was not regarded as being especially bright. ('Not so much the *Political Quarterly*, more like *Penthouse*' was the view of the acerbic journalist, Ed Pearce) but she was pretty enough – a little like a young Joan Collins, but with red hair – to appeal to a posse of knights both of shire and suburb.

According to Andrew Roth's *Guide to MPs*, Emma was happily married to a Midlands accountant, but few had glimpsed the lucky man. She lived during the week on the river at Dolphin Square in a small flat paid for by her Parliamentary London Allowance. At the cry of 'Who goes home?' she never had to wait long beneath the canopy in New Palace Yard for a taxi. Invariably a black ministerial Montego would draw up beside her, into which she would vanish at the bidding of some lubricious junior minister.

Joshua asked Worthy Evans if *la belle* Emma was having it off. Evans went pink in the face. 'We are the souls of discretion in the whips' office.' Then he added with a touch of pique, 'There's more than one string to her bow.'

'Twang,' cried Morris cheerfully. 'I must fly.'

At two-thirty the division bells rang to announce that the Speaker was at prayers, an ill-attended four-minute ceremony during which the House chaplain prayed fervently that the nation's leaders be granted wisdom. Joshua went upstairs to his office in the Upper Committee corridor south where he opened Felicity's letter of love and, after reading it through a couple of times, fell asleep in his regulation armchair. Thank God for the siesta. It was Welsh questions that day and Joshua could slumber, guilt free. After questions, the Commons would go on to debate the Report and the Third Reading of the Broadcasting Bill. The House was debating a new clause to the Broadcasting Bill which would, if passed, oblige the BBC's Board of Governors to include four political nominees, two Tories, one

Labour and one Liberal Democrat. This would give the political parties a greater 'overview' of the BBC's programmes. The politicians thought it a good idea; the broadcasters most firmly did not. The Government Chief Whip, Richard Ryder, had issued a three-line whip, the strongest summons to attend. There could be votes at any time during the hours of five till ten. What was worse, the ten o'clock rule, which should bring proceedings to a halt, would be suspended and the business continue long into the night. A three-line whip meant that it was virtually impossible to find a Labour pair – that is, an uxorious Socialist MP with whom one could safely depart. The imprisonment of MPs in the Palace always put great strain on the Members' dining room, Morris reflected. Well, he would dine early, at seven-thirty, the latest time he could expect prompt service. The hazard would be the predictability of his companions. It threatened to be a long night.

The telephone rang in his office. It was the World Service of the BBC wondering if he would give an interview about Mrs Thatcher's attempts from the back-benches to sabotage her successor's policies? Joshua said he would.

David Lancaster had come down to the House that day from the studios of the 'World at One', where he had crossed swords with Jim Naughtie. Lancaster was a BBC producer's dream, a news editor's delight. He held views and he held them strongly. A bishop had only to speak up on favour of the poor, an Irishman in favour of the unification of Ireland or a Zulu against apartheid for Lancaster to volunteer to say his piece. His speciality was outrage. Although he had been in the House for only a few years, his polytechnic accent

11

and instant availability threatened the pre-eminence of other MPs whose knighthoods past and prospective had been, and would be, awarded for services to the media. Bores to a man, they all felt their roles under challenge from the bull-throated newcomer.

Lancaster was a large, heavily built youngish man whose retreating hairline and walrus moustache made him look like David Hart. He had not expected to win his Nottinghamshire seat. He had begun the election campaign as an executive in a provincial public relations firm, but by polling day the agency had folded. Had he not won the seat by a whisker after two re-counts (Tory majority 234), he would have been on the dole. However, the Chairman of the East Midlands Young Conservatives had fallen neatly upon his feet. In place of £13,000 a year and the use of a Ford Fiesta, Lancaster found himself the possessor of the magic initials 'MP' and a salary of £28,000, to say nothing of a larger sum in expenses. He was resolutely right-wing and determinedly unmarried. He had, according to his Central Office CV, two hobbies: the collecting of silver vesta boxes and of books about Margaret Thatcher. He had a first edition copy of George Gardiner's *Margaret Thatcher: From Childhood to Leadership* signed by both author and subject, and a desk covered with Thatcher mugs. Had he ever been invited to take part on BBC's 'Mastermind' he would have chosen Grantham as his special subject. He knew the dull Lincolnshire town backwards. He could name the streets that divided the Roberts's shop from the schools Miss Roberts herself attended. He knew the birthplace of Alderman Alfred Roberts. He was also a keen cottager.

To the innocent, a 'cottager' might suggest a life spent spinning on the Arran Isles, or even on a Dorset heath; to the far from innocent it is the name given to those seeking out young men in public lavatories in the hope of masturbation. Tom Driberg, the Labour MP for Barking, who died some years ago, had devoted his life to the practice. Like his distinguished predecessor, David Lancaster lived dangerously. Unlike Driberg, his tastes were not famous. Lancaster wanted to get on. Although one of nature's category 43ers, he took a stern line when it came to criminal misbehaviour. A firm hand was just what his Nottinghamshire Party executive committee craved, and a firm hand was what he gave them. He was due to appear on TVS, filmed the previous afternoon at the Queen Elizabeth Conference Centre, to call for the return of the birch. Lancaster was not a whips' favourite. He was too dour and his views were tediously predictable. He would never get office; but he did vote at the time and place required of him. Peter Worthington Evans thought him a shit, an umbrella term of abuse, unspecific, but in his case satisfactory. So, too, did Joshua Morris.

The mid-afternoon hazard of life in the Commons is the mass lobby, the entry into the Central Lobby of the banner-bearing classes. Green cards requesting an interview clutter up the pigeon-holes in the Members' lobby, and the uniformed attendants, ex-SAS men, patrol the corridors of the building, summonses in hand. One such veteran ran Lancaster to earth in the reference room of the library where he was reading back numbers of the *News of the World*. Another spotted Edwina Currie in the tea room where she was sitting with friends. Someone was telling how Sir Peter Emery, the MP for Honiton and as massive as a Yorkshire Alderman, had barked out the words 'Earl Grey' at the Irish girl behind the counter whose task it was

to dole out tea and buns. 'Maureen' had been her eager
if uncomprehending response.

Edwina herself was the subject of a wary, if reluctant, admiration. Her claim, made on the floor of the
House, that among a wife's many duties was providing
her husband with 'a steamy bed' had made some
cringe; others, less inhibited, had never doubted that
she did. Joshua claimed that, steaming or not, she
would never have stopped talking; others noted that
she had a pert attractiveness and a good mind. She had
the ambition of a Michael Heseltine, but the whips,
grave men all, were not upbeat about her chances of
returning to office. Had she come out for John Major
it might have been different, but Edwina had nailed
her colours to Michael's mast. And there was always
the problem of finding a senior minister confident
enough to take Edwina under his department wing.

Edwina took her green card, glanced at it and
groaned. A Derbyshire Pakistani wished to enlist her
in the cause of a Muslim Kashmir. She abandoned her
cup of Indian tea and made for the Central Lobby,
that marketplace where patronage is returned for sup-
plication, MPs are wreathed in smiles and constituents
are taken on one side in order to be reassured. She
could give Ahmed ten minutes only; at five she was
due upstairs at a meeting of the Party's Food and
Agricultural Committee.

Sir Ralph Grunte ('the "e" is sounded, dear boy, as in
Brontë') boarded the lift outside the Members' dining
room. Once the slow-moving doors had closed upon
him, Grunte, safe in his isolation, pressed the button
and farted noisily. With a little bit of luck, he thought,
I will travel the two floors on my tod. As luck would
have it, he was joined on the first floor by a patrolling

Commons' messenger, pink telephone slips in hand. At least no one broke silence.

Grunte, who suffered from an irritable bowel, a painful condition which he shared with Sir Kingsley Amis, was a man of bad habits. Polluting the lifts of the Palace of Westminster was only the smallest of them. Ten years ago, a slimmer Grunte had been parliamentary private secretary to a cabinet minister, but the second rung on the ladder of promotion had eluded him. Self-indulgence had turned him into the shape of a Williams pear, which was not inappropriate as he had served time, along with many other MPs of all parties, in the *Weinstuben* of Strasbourg. He had ended many a 'free' dinner with a large glass of poire William, the Alsation eau-de-vie. He had served for a time as an unelected member of the European 'parliament'. A keen Thatcherite when it mattered, he had long striven to become richer. His Roller ('Grunt 1') was lodged safely on the fourth floor of the Members' underground car park; and his wife lodged safely in his Warwickshire home. He spent most of his time, not always *en garçon*, in a small but comfortable flat in Lord North Street. He was standing for election that afternoon for the chairmanship of the Party's backbench Europe Committee, the ballot for which would take place in committee room twelve at five o'clock.

For the last few days Grunte had sat in his office, No. 60 Upper Committee corridor south, topping and tailing a hundred letters to colleagues, soliciting their support. Grunte's view on Europe and Britain's role within the Community were robust to the point of inanity. In Warwickshire, Grunte flew the Union flag from a pole in his garden in order to tell his neighbours that the Member was in residence. The village referred to him unamiably as 'the old sod'. In private he talked cheerfully of 'the frogs' and even of 'wogs'; in public his opinions echoed the bleak nationalism of the Party's neanderthals. He had once refused publicly to dine with the French ambassador at his residence on the grounds that he did not like his food 'mucked about'. This sally had been greeted with joy by the tabloids.

His rival for the chairmanship that afternoon was Sir Anthony Meyer, who in November 1989 had gained notoriety as the stalking-horse candidate against Mrs Thatcher, an offence of *lèse-majesté* for which he had been de-selected by his curmudgeonly Party activists and smeared by the tabloid press. Thus the two men had nothing, save for their seniority, in common. Grunte was very fat. He wore striped 'regimental' ties (it was claimed he bought them all from a boutique on Waterloo station), and had once sported grey shoes. He owned a chain of Midlands garages. 'A Fair Deal with Grunte' could be glimpsed, along with furry animals, along the rear windows of Solihull Cavaliers. Meyer, an ex-foreign Office 'intellectual', was thin and conventionally dressed. He was often to be seen, even at Westminster, in the company of his wife. The fact that two such different people as Grunte and Meyer could co-exist in the same Party was remarked upon by the duller political correspondents as proof positive that the Tory Party remained a broad church.

Grunte was the favourite to win the contest. Under Margaret Thatcher, the Party had come to abandon the Euro-enthusiasms of Edward Heath, and John Major had taken care not to rekindle them too obviously. Besides, Meyer had not been forgiven by many Tories for having had the temerity to put the Leader to trial by vote. Even so, the Party whips were not too happy at the prospect of Grunte in the chair. That afternoon the Chief Whip, Richard Ryder, had called

16

for Grunte's personal file, which along with 371 others
was kept safely under lock and key. Whenever challenged as to their existence the whips denied all knowledge of files, but exist they most certainly did. They
were meticulously kept up to date. The Chief himself
kept the key upon his silvered ring. His secretary, a
handsome woman in her thirties, who had served more
than one chief whip, brought Ryder the brown folder
with the word 'Grunte' slashed at an angle across the
cover. She held it delicately, between finger and
thumb. She had once shared a lift with Grunte. Ryder
switched off his telephone, untied the dark blue tapes
and began to read.

'Ralph (not Rafe) Grunte. Born December 1930.
Son of Percy Haines, a motor mechanic. Changed
name on his marriage to Marjorie Grunt in 1960.
Elected to Parliament in the Conservative interest for
South Warwickshire in February 1974.' A bad year,
thought the Chief Whip. His eye caught the words 'not
ministerial material' written in ink by Michael Jopling,
who had been Chief Whip in the early 1980s. Somewhere else David Waddington had written in an
unsteady hand the word 'unsound', the word which,
together with 'shit', echoes like the clang of a cell door
in the mansions of the Tory Party.

Grunte's division record – that is, the number of
times he had answered his Party's call to vote – was
among the five poorest in the Party. Yet he was always
trumpeting his loyalty, thought Ryder. And Grunte
was fit enough; fat, but usually cheerful. Why on earth,
he wondered, was the sod ever knighted? He turned
the page to find that Grunte had received the honour
at the hands of the Queen in 1980 in the second of
Margaret Thatcher's lists. Francis Pym could not then
have been a member of the scrutiny committee: only

later had he become the eye of the needle. Grunte had, it seemed, raised the sum of £100,000 from commerce and industry as a contribution towards paying for Mrs Thatcher's private office while in opposition. Later, Grunte had tried strenuously for membership of the Privy Council, an honour which would have permitted him to put the words 'Rt. Hon.' before his name. He had canvassed widely, but had been thwarted by the intervention of Willie Whitelaw, a copy of whose curt note to 'All it may concern' was attached. It included more than one reference to his dead body.

Pinned to the final sheet was a photograph in an unsealed envelope. Ryder removed it. It was in colour and showed a pair of hairy buttocks and two pairs of legs. The bedhead was made of carved wood, and above the lovers' heads was a cuckoo clock. Beneath the soles of four feet were two pairs of underpants, His and Hers. 'Abroad on Parliamentary business,' murmured the Chief. The photo had been mailed to the then Chief Whip and the Chairman of the Party in 1981. Other copies had landed on the desks of Mike Molloy of the *Mirror* and Kelvin Mackenzie of the *Sun*. They had caused hilarity and had been passed round the newsrooms of both papers, but they had not been published. There was no clue as to the identity of the man, save for a typed caption with the words, 'Tory MP on the job. Watch this space.' The editors had waited, and then, with no sequel to hand, filed the 'pix' away for future use. Who knew? and had not something similar happened to Commander Courtney, another Tory MP, in the 1960s, sent by courtesy of the KGB?

Michael Jopling, however, had recognised the hotel bedroom. It had once been his. Without any doubt whatever it was Room Eight at the Hotel Gutenberg,

situated near the cathedral in the old town of Strasbourg. The picture on the wall was of Napoleon III;
the bed curtains which hung down from a gilt-wood
crown were covered by Imperial bees. There was only
one hotel in France which commemorated the Second
Empire, and that was the Gutenberg. It even had a
portrait of the Emperor and Empress in its foyer. And,
as for the bees, had they not buzzed as 'Joppers' himself tried to sleep, tossing feverishly after a dinner of
fish in cream sauce and pork knuckle, washed down
by the somewhat acid *vin du pays*?

In the photograph, a calendar on the wall showed
the date to be *27 septembre 1981*. Although no one
could put a face to the arse, Jopling thought it must
be Grunte's, and the more fetching pair of legs those
of a Belgian interpreter called Monique Selvier, the
one who had danced naked on a table one night at the
Crocodile. Most convincing evidence of all was the
sight of two men's grey shoes peeping out from under
the bed. Ryder, whose Oxfords were as black as the
Balliol boat, or a Cheltenham candidate, winced with
displeasure.

Among the other papers in Grunte's personal file
was a letter from the Commons' fees office, the department responsible for the payment of MPs' salaries and
expenses. It complained of Grunte's apparent over-
charging on his car expenses. MPs with large motor
cars (left-wing Tories called them 'motor cars', moder-
ates 'cars' and Thatcherites 'motors'), that is over
2,300cc, could charge 61p a mile, a figure arrived at by
the AA as the true running and capital costs. Grunte
sat for a seat in Warwickshire and lived in Arden. In
fact, he had two other houses and used to boast that
the 'gold plate' was kept in Norfolk. His monthly
expenses had averaged, over a twelve-month period,

nearly £1,000, made up of frequent journeys to and from Warwickshire and an unverifiable amount spent on constituency mileage, that is on parliamentary business within South Warwicks. As Grunte was known to be an infrequent attender at constituency functions and spent most of his time at his flat in Westminster (when not abroad), the figure seemed curiously high. Tim Renton, Ryder's immediate predecessor, had sent the letter on to Grunte without comment; Ryder noticed that the more recent claims had fallen by nearly half the amount.

Ryder took a letter from another envelope. It was dated April 1987, and was from a firm of London solicitors. It was written on behalf of a client, a famous West End wine merchant who had failed to persuade Sir Ralph to pay his bill. The sum was for over £10,000 and detailed the wines sent to Grunte's house near Sandringham. Ryder, who bought his wines from the *Spectator*'s Wine Club on the recommendation of Auberon Waugh, was a man of modest taste who aspired to nothing higher than a decent Burgundy: his disapproving eye followed the list of great names which Grunte had appropriated – Le Montrachet by Laflaive, Corton-Charlemagne by Laflaive and a variety of *vins d'Alsace* by Trimbach and Hugel. He supposed the bill had been settled eventually. Then there was a bill from a West End jeweller notorious for the sale of gew-gaws of the kind lovers bought for their less sophisticated girlfriends, and a note from the refreshment department of the House complaining of an unsettled account. Sod Grunte, thought Ryder, who had enough on his hands as it was: Margaret Thatcher was making trouble on the backbenches, interest rates were too high and Labour was, once again, ahead in the polls. The Chief Whip re-tied the confidential file and returned it and the key to his secretary. 'Horrid man' was her only comment. What a choice for the chairmanship of an important committee. The winner would never be off the air, incessantly asked for his opinion on Government policy towards Europe – Meyer, almost a Federalist, or Grunte, who despised all foreigners, save possibly rich Republicans. At least Meyer was intelligent and civilised. Either way, the views of the bulk of the Tory Party would be unrepresented.

Ryder looked down the list of his appointments for the day. At four forty-five he was expecting a visit from a backbench MP on behalf of the No Turning Back Group. And had there not been something in *Today* that morning about a pending court case, a little matter of paternity? It had to do with the daughter of an Asian newsagent in Barking. Oh God, thought Ryder, the older they are the worse they behave. I was better off at the Treasury.

2

Emma Kerr had sat prettily in the Chamber to listen to the speeches from the front bench on the Broadcasting Bill. Now she made her way across the Members' Lobby en route for the Europe Committee election upstairs. As she stopped to take a letter from an attendant, she was accosted by the lobby correspondent of the *True Brit*, Ron Barton, a tiny man of under five foot with bad breath and the habit of sucking the stub of a pencil. He was known as the poison dwarf. 'Did you enjoy your meal at Bibendum?' he asked. Emma coloured and said yes. Charles Harvey, a junior minister, had taken her there to dinner the previous week. They had laughed as he had implored her not to let him leave his ministerial red box behind in the restaurant as poor Dick Crossman had once done. Still, thought Emma, it was no crime to dine with a Minister of the Crown, however junior.

'You must take me there one day on your expenses,' she added, flashing the smile that had done for poor Tufton.

'Love to,' said Ron Barton. 'Be in touch.'

Emma hurried on through the swing door into the library corridor, pushing past a group of Scots journalists. Damn, damn, damn, I shall have to be more careful in the future. And Harvey always shouted so, and complained about his wife. But he was fun, and the food at Bibendum had been bloody good.

Charles Harvey had been made Parliamentary Secretary at the Department of Transport after the '87 election. He was thirty-nine and was married with three daughters. Andy Roth, from whom there are few Westminster secrets, described him in his compendium as 'gingery, intense, right-wing, Catholic and very, very ambitious. Owes more to Jack than to Charles Kennedy.' The *Mail* had once described him as 'fun-loving', but at least, as Charles Harvey himself had said, he was not yet 'balding'. Harvey had the gloss of an Old Carthusian, the charm of a chat-show host and the persistence of a Jack Russell. The political correspondents all said that he was an up and coming man, abrasive and once close to Mrs Thatcher. When he had learned that he was 'close to Mrs Thatcher', Charles Harvey had explained to Emma (they were in bed) that he had only spoken to his one-time leader on three occasions: at a Party Conference in Brighton he had bought her a drink at a party given by Granada TV. 'How is the constituency?' he had been asked. Harvey had tried to tell her but had been interrupted by Jeffrey Archer. The second time was when Mrs 'T' had paid a state visit to the Department of Transport. She had subjected Paul Channon to what a legal correspondent might have called a hostile cross-examination. When it came to Harvey's turn to perform – five minutes on traffic congestion in London – she had commanded him to speak up. He had done so. The third occasion was when Harvey had introduced her at a constituency annual dinner. He had laid it on thickly, praising her to the skies. He was nervous and had drunk a glass too many of Mateus Rosé. He had concluded, somewhat foolishly as he later recognised, by saying that she was Grantham's most famous son. Mrs Thatcher had taken him aside after the function was over. 'Isaac Newton was Grantham's most famous son. I am its most famous daughter.' She had laughed; Harvey had laughed even harder. Still, the political correspondents had been right: Harvey was a devoted admirer of all Prime Ministers – and, they agreed, 'a coming man'.

At five o'clock sharp, forty or so Tory MPs crowded into room twelve to vote for a new chairman of the Party's Europe Committee. The voters, who had been handed their ballots by the Party whips, marked them, folded them carefully and dropped them into the ballot box. The atmosphere was unsolemn. Nicholas Budgen could be heard joshing Grunte ('come on, Grunt, now's yer chance for greatness'), Sir George Gardiner, Margaret's long-serving standard bearer, looked more than usually miserable and Anthony Meyer slipped in and out, unnoticed. Their votes cast, the MPs left the room without waiting for the result: it would be posted later that afternoon in the whips' office.

Edwina Currie returned to her room to write a piece for the *Mail*. At a pound a word for 600 words there are few easier ways of making a living. The features editor had rung to ask her to write for the following day's paper – 'Why we need more women in Westminster'. In private, Edwina, who had recently been worsted on 'Any Questions' by Clare Short, had had occasion to feel that there were more than enough of them already. David Lancaster, who had voted for Grunte ('He's a fat sod but better than the other one'), fell in with Sam Langford, a heavily-built one-time docker. They were bound for a meeting of the Party's Media Committee in order to discuss the anti-Conservative bias of the BBC – a discussion that was to be 'kicked off' by Sir Norman Tebbit himself.

Sam Langford, the MP for Ongar, bore the name of a famous, old-time American black heavyweight boxer – Sam Langford, the Boston Tar Baby. This irony was wasted on him. Essex's tar baby was lily white and proud of it. He was, not to put too fine a point upon it, a racist. His enemies called him, but never to his face, 'tar baby'. He was in his early fifties and had been returned at the General Election four years before. He wore purple pinstriped suits and kipper ties.

The marshes of Essex were populated by the sons of Alf Garnett, for the old East End had been abandoned to the Pakis and the Afros. Only the aged were white and they, as readers of the tabloid press, were afraid to leave their council flats. Their sons had swapped the docks for Ford's of Dagenham, and most of them had taken advantage of Mrs Thatcher's right to buy and purchased their council houses. They were the bow window brigade, the upwardly mobile, made famous by Tebbit's autobiography of that name. Devotees of dished-telly, robust patriots to a man, strong believers in 'law 'n' order', they had no time whatever for 'them blacks'. They were the New Tories, supporters of the 'new Conservatism' which 'Maggie' had once made her own. Dismayed by her overthrow, they had avenged themselves, when able to do so, on those Tory MPs who had voted for Heseltine on the first ballot. 'Traitors, they were, every man Jack of them.'

It had been said of Essex that 'even the newsagents were white'. But the fact would not prevent them from selling out the *Essex Bugle* were it ever to carry the story of Langford's lust. The girl was, if not black, then certainly Asian. 'More like milky Nescaff, but a real goer' had been Langford's description of her a year or so ago to his mates standing before the fruit machines at the local Conservative club. She had bought a motor from him. Small and pretty, she had, unusually for an unmarried Asian girl, lived on her own. Langford had taken her for a spin ('lovely runner') and been invited back for a curry. Made happy by three tins of Foster's lager, she had opened her legs to him. A week later, when Langford had called bringing flowers, he had been told she had gone back to London leaving no forwarding address. He had shrugged and put it down to experience.

A year or so later, after he had added the initials 'MP' to his name, he had received a letter at the Commons marked 'Strictly Private. To be opened by the Addressee only'. It was from a firm of solicitors asking for recognition of paternity and for money. Foolishly he had written back, offering £1,000, but had been told by her solicitor that his client could get ten times that amount from the *News of the World*. Langford, who could have sworn he had worn a condom, had done nothing more. He had been tipped off by a friend of the *Bugle* with whom he went boxing that the paper had got wind of the story. In desperation he had spoken to his area whip, an effete young man who sat for a Norfolk seat. He, in his turn, had told Langford to go and see the Chief. He had done so. 'Rich,' he had said, taking a seat, 'I'm up shit creek without a paddle.' Ryder groaned inwardly; the phrase had not been one in common use at the Treasury.

Joshua Morris sat in his regulation armchair watching the Channel 4 news at seven p.m. on his miniature, hand-held television set. Joshua had a passion for electronic gadgets of the sort advertised in booklets to be found inside Sunday colour supplements. The telly did not work too well, but neither had a pyramid clock. Joshua also had a passion for detective stories of all kinds. He had been allocated a room to himself on the Upper Committee corridor where he had spent much of the last ten years. It was the one mark of his undoubted seniority. On one desk was a BBC computer, on another a picture of Felicity taken in Venice, as well as two pieces of early Staffordshire pottery, a recumbent Cleopatra and a reclining Mark Antony. Over his desk were two framed prints by Eric Gill: to his regret neither was erotic. On the walls he had hung originals of cartoons, the originals of his book covers and a commissioned satirical painting of a Tory Summer Fayre by Sir John Verney. Joshua had used it one Christmas as his card, thereby offending the stuffier of his local party activists. Nigel Lawson was shown, bottle of champagne in hand, his foot on the head of an old age pensioner. The room, which was cold in winter and chilly in summer, was grubby but comfortable. High up on the wall was his monitor on the screen of which was carried the name of the MP speaking in the chamber, the time and the subject for debate. Mr Robert Maclennan was on his feet. He would speak a dozen times before morning. Joshua had bought a copy of the love poetry of Robert Graves which he was dipping into prior to sending it to Felicity: when separated they made love by the exchange of books. At twenty-five minutes past seven he went down to dinner.

The Members' dining room of the Commons practises segregation. The northern end is reserved for Tories, the southern for the Labour Party. In the middle is a large cold table ablaze with salad, and a smaller one where sit the Liberal Democrats. The Tories tend to demand a cut off the joint with two veg; the People's Party plaice and chips. As Mrs Thatcher had gone up in the world, so the Conservative Party had come down in it, and the days of eggs and aspic were long since gone. Nevertheless Joshua, who spent most of the week in his daughter's south London flat, was a regular customer. He was pleased to see that his favourite place at the top of a table for nine was still empty. He took his seat. Immediately Catherine was at his right hand, ready to take his order. The wine waiter stood at his left. Joshua had succumbed to adultery but not yet to alcohol, the two occupational hazards of life at Westminster. It had been Sir Tufton's view that the Lords held the cup for adultery. Be that as it may, Joshua was strictly a half-a-bottle man.

'Evening, Josh.' It was Dame Elaine Kellett-Bowman. She was a good-natured woman who held fierce views. She also carried a little black book in which she would enter the bets that she would encourage friends to make with her – such as £100 that Joshua Morris would receive a knighthood. That was one Joshua knew he would win. He had already told the whips that he did not want a handle to his name. Knighthoods were the mark of the failed politician, the equivalent of a pocket watch given to guards on the old Great Western after forty years of loyal and unbroken service to the company. Joshua had also bet Dame Elaine that the Tories would lose the next election, but that was before Mrs Thatcher had been done away with. It could still go either way.

To Joshua's irritation he saw Ralph Grunte take the seat to his immediate left. 'Should we congratulate you?' he asked. Joshua had not bothered to look into the whips' office for the result of the afternoon's election.

'You must,' said Grunte. 'Thirty-five to ten. The Party has spoken.' Sir Ralph was clearly in good humour. He summoned the waitress and gave his order. 'Three cutlets, pink, and French peas. Sauté potatoes.' He then ordered a bottle of Moët. 'Can't beat champagne,' he said confidently. 'You know my views on Europe, but I will admit that there are only three things the English do better than the French: strawberries, asparagus and men's trousers.'

'What about sausages?' said Elaine from the window seat. Next to her was Donald Thompson, the jolly Yorkshire master butcher with a taste for pickled walnuts. 'Our sausages are the best in the world.'

Grunte, who had crossed swords with the Dame on past occasions, grunted. He turned to David Lancaster, who was taking his place at his left hand. 'Evening, John.'

Dame Elaine gave out a hoot of delighted laughter. 'John?' she cried. 'He's no John. I know you don't come here often, Ralph, but you ought to know the names of your colleagues by now. Ralph Grunte, meet David Lancaster.'

'Slip of the tongue,' said Grunte. 'Of course I know who you are. You're never off the telly. You and that Beaumont-Dark fella, to say nothing of Marcus Fox. And silly old Raymond Gower.' Grunte paused and cut into his cutlet. 'Never liked him,' he added.

Gower, an aged Welsh Tory who was universally beloved, had died a year or so previously. Clearly, Grunte had not been told.

The dining room was beginning to fill up. The running three-line whip had imprisoned most MPs and the kitchens were girding themselves for a hard night.

Emma Kerr, clad beguilingly in a flowery blue silk dress, sat herself opposite David Lancaster. She had spent the last half hour writing to her husband, a difficult letter which was long overdue. Life at Westminster was hard on marriages, but she was in no doubt whatever that she had outgrown Barry. Thank God there had been no kids.

Next to arrive was Charles Harvey, who had been writing a letter to Emma. He had put it on the board in the Members' Lobby and she should have had it by now. In the dining room he hovered for a moment, uncertain whether to take the vacant place on Emma's right hand. Before he could be sensibly discreet it was taken by Michael Heseltine, leaving Harvey the seat on her left, next to Joshua. As Harvey grabbed the low calorie menu (Emma had remarked upon his incipient pot), the last remaining seat was taken by Edwina Currie, who had just faxed through her copy. 'A woman's work,' she had concluded, 'is never done.' For the next forty minutes at least there was a full house.

Michael Heseltine was a rare bird. He usually dined at home. Emma thought him sexy ('and at his age'). She had told Charles Harvey, and no doubt others, that she had voted for him as Party Leader. She had been careful not to tell her constituents. At the time Charles had said something about mace-waving and Westland. 'The fella's disloyal.' He was hopping around her bedroom as he said it, one foot caught in the crutch of his trousers.

Ralph Grunte had no time for 'Goldilocks', the term he invariably used when discussing Heseltine. He had voted for Margaret. However, flushed with his own electoral success, he shouted a greeting up the table. 'Not speaking at a constituency supper club, Michael?

Sick of rubber chicken?' The strange wine waiter, a thin young man with spots who looked no more than fifteen, opened the champagne with an unprofessionally loud report. Heseltine smiled ruefully but said nothing. He would be damned if he would ever speak for, or to, Grunte. In his half-spectacles he looked older than the television pictures of him might suggest. All those days on the road must have worn him out, thought Emma, to say nothing of wrestling with the problems of the poll tax. He turned to her. 'Suppose you wouldn't care to come and speak for me at a lunch in Henley?' he asked. Emma, pleased to indulge him, said she would come like a shot. Wasn't Michael in the market for a PPS?

Joshua asked Emma, who really had the prettiest eyes, whether she planned to stay on after ten. 'Unlike you, Josh, I have no pair. I shall be here until Robert Maclennan has a seizure or the cock crows, whichever is first.' Joshua was going to reply when he was suddenly struck by the expression on Dame Elaine's face. She was staring intently down the table at David Lancaster. He knew there was no love lost between them.

'What on earth do you think you are doing?' she said sharply. 'Stop it, you fool, stop it at once.' Her highly pitched voice had been made famous through television. The room, or at least the Tory end of it, fell silent. Joshua turned to Lancaster to see what was up.

The pubescent wine waiter was slowly and solemnly pouring a bottle of Blue Nun ('You would have thought he could have managed something better,' said Grunte, after the event) over the head and shoulders of the Hon. Member for Notts. South East. Lancaster's mouth had dropped open in surprise and a trickle of wine entered a corner of it. The faintly golden liquid poured steadily over his hair, down his collar and on to the sleeve of Grunte's £800 Stovel and Mason suit. Lancaster seemed rooted to his chair. Grunte leaped to his feet and knocked the bottle from the waiter's hand on to the floor, where it exploded into a mass of brown glass, spraying the occupants of the Chief Whip's corner table. Heseltine, possibly fearing another mace incident, quickly left the room.

'What a waste,' cried Edwina. Emma giggled nervously. Dame Elaine rose to her feet and to the occasion by tossing her napkin over Lancaster's dripping head. The wine waiter burst into tears and, sobbing loudly, allowed himself to be led from the room by the head waiter.

Grunte half filled Lancaster's still empty glass with champagne. 'Fella must be off his head,' he said. In the silence that followed, David Lancaster, the napkin still over his head, walked unsteadily from the dining room to the cheers of some caddish Labour MPs who were dining at the other end of the room in their shirt sleeves.

'What on earth got into him?' asked Dame Elaine of Catherine, the waitress, who, in her turn, unable to restrain her laughter, replied that perhaps he only wanted Mr Lancaster to taste it. At this sally she dropped a plate of poached eggs and spinach on the floor, and then followed Lancaster and the wine waiter out of the room. There were sounds of hysterical laughter from the corridor outside and then of a face being smacked. Emma got to her feet and began to clear up the mess. On Richard Ryder's table an obsequious young Tory humbly took a large piece of brown glass out of his steak and kidney.

'I should have stayed at home,' said Joshua. 'I only come here for the peace and quiet.'

Normality returned. No sooner had conversation been resumed than a messenger, splendid in tails and medallion, handed Mrs Kerr a pink telephone message slip. She opened it. 'Ring the *True Brit*. Ask for Ron Barton. Soonest.' The television monitor in the corner of the dining room struck a bell-like note. As in Orwell's *1984*, the unblinking screens followed MPs from office to library, to tea room, to restaurant. Only in the ubiquitous lavatories could they escape their message. The name 'Robert Maclennan' flashed up on the screen. 'That bugger,' said Grunte magisterially. 'He's never off his feet.' Joshua saw Emma pass the message slip to Harvey, who murmured something inaudible.

Grunte spotted Charles Irving, the Chairman of the Kitchen Committee and MP for Cheltenham, beckoned him over as if he were the Maître d' and began a breathless account of the recent outrage. 'Get rid of the chap, whatever you do.' Irving clucked reassuringly. Grunte signed his bill and, grasping his three-quarters empty bottle of Moët by the neck like a Sabine woman, left the dining room.

Dame Elaine gave a mock shudder of dislike. 'What a dreadful man.'

Joshua pointed to a waiter who was on his knees with a dustpan and brush, searching under the Chief Whip's table for fragments of the Nun. 'Lovers' quarrel, do you think?' he asked. If Tom Driberg could make love to the Commons waiters on the premises, to say nothing of his colleagues, why not David Lancaster?

At half past eight the division bells rang throughout the Palace. A Labour amendment to the report stage of the bill had been moved and opposed. MPs, who must vote in person – no buttons to be pushed as in other, more rational parliaments – have eight minutes to walk into their chosen lobby and register their vote. As there are two lobbies, the Party whips stand ready to point the uncertain in the right direction and to persuade the undecided to do their duty. Grunte parked his bottle on the plinth of Lloyd George's statue in the Members' Lobby (it was swiftly removed by a policeman and placed in the government whips' office for collection) and fell in with Teddy Taylor.

'Glad you saw off Meyer,' said Taylor in his barely comprehensible West of Scotland voice. Ten years as Tory MP for Southend had hardened his anti-common market views but had done nothing for his accent. Teddy was the original North Briton. He did not smoke, drink or swear.

Grunte, who indulged in all three vices, cried cheerfully, 'Keep the buggers out.' The Moët had worked its magic. Sir Ralph had even forgotten a letter from the Revenue which had arrived that morning in the post. Its message was as terse as its ink was red, and the sum of money demanded could have purchased a brand new Roller. Let's hope Marjorie will turn up trumps, he reflected. Good old Marge. But Marjorie Grunte (*née* Grunt), who was at that moment dining with her lover at the Moat House Hotel, Stratford-upon-Avon, had other uses for her money.

The library corridor that leads into the Members' Lobby and thence to the Chamber was lined with lobby correspondents, ready to pounce. They had been driven, like so many moneychangers, from the Lobby itself by the calling of a division. Joshua, who had not yet finished his half-bottle of Chénas, hurried into the 'no' lobby, determined to vote quickly and to return to the comfort of his table, glass and cheese. On a three-line running whip in June the lobbies resemble a

packed train on the Central line. Air conditioning in
the Commons Chamber, which has persuaded many an
MP to listen to a colleague on a hot summer's evening,
does not extend into the adjacent lobbies. There was
a strong smell, compounded of Old Spice, sweat and
toasted flannel.

Grunte, fielding congratulations upon his election,
took refuge in the lavatory. He found he was standing
next to the Prime Minister. 'Been a long time since I
stood in the company of the Queen's First Minister,'
he said cheerfully. Major took refuge behind his
spectacles.

Emma endured the badinage of two tipsy colleagues,
both of whom wanted her to speak in their constituencies. Harvey was buttonholed by a Midlands MP
with motorway problems. There was no sign of David
Lancaster.

On the return journey along the library corridor
which leads either to bed, books or booze, the lobby
correspondents closed in for the kill. Eleanor Goodman of Channel 4 News took Edwina Currie to one
side. 'Will you be given office by John Major?'

Michael Heseltine moved slowly like a ship under
escort. Roy Hattersley talked to John Cole. Michael
White of the *Guardian* stopped Joshua Morris. They
had been on friendly terms for years. 'What's this I
hear about the public baptism of David Lancaster in
the dining room? Has he been born again?' God,
thought Joshua, that's quick. There was no point in
asking White how he knew: lobby men were scrupulous
when it came to protecting their sources. Joshua
recounted the story. No doubt a charitable version
would appear in the diary column of the following day's
paper. It did, under the headline 'Dry Tory gets wet'.
A temporary wine waiter had been overworking – such

was the consumption of wine among MPs – and had become 'tired and emotional'. He would not be returning to the Palace of Westminster. The story might have died there had it not been for Ron Barton whose nose was as long as his breath was bad. He would dig more deeply.

David Lancaster went to have a word with Sam Langford in his room in Norman Shaw, the Old Scotland Yard building on the Embankment. Langford had picked up his briefcase in error earlier in the day. Smelling like a wine festival, Lancaster made his way from the Palace under the tube tunnel and down a hundred yards of main road. Langford was busily stuffing unopened constituency letters into his briefcase. 'That Ryder's a sod,' he said. 'I told him about my bit of trouble and all he said was that I had dug myself a hole and it was up to me to dig myself out of it. Stuff him.'

Lancaster scarcely heard a word. He was dialling the Commons catering department. Wayne Ellis, he was told, was unavailable. He had had a nasty turn and gone home. Lancaster ran outside and waved down a cab. The Government's majority would be one less at the ten o'clock vote, but the whips could go hang themselves. Lancaster knew he had to get to Wayne before the press did – before the stupid fool went and burnt both their boats. He climbed into the cab and quickly told the driver where he wanted to go. The taxi swung round in the road and headed for Sherwood Road, Battersea, where Wayne lived with two other young men.

'You an MP?' asked the taxi driver, eager to share his world view.

'No, I bloody well am not,' shouted his passenger.

Lancaster sat, racked by anxiety. How could he ever have been such a fool as to befriend that particular bit of rough trade? What in God's name would they make of it in Nottingham if it got out? They were a prudish lot. As it was, the chairman of his women's party still refused even to mention D. H. Lawrence. He had once asked the old cow at a tea party held in her terraced cottage whether her parents had ever met the author. 'We don't talk about that dreadful man in Nottingham,' had been her answer. You bet your sweet life they'll talk about Wayne and me. What a couple of poofters.

3

Emma sat at her desk in a room under the eaves that she once shared with Anne Widdecombe. Her head was in her hands as she stared at the pink slip of paper. What could Barton want? Dinner for two, or information? She was too terrified to try to find out. What should she say if the voice at the other end of the line asked her, point blank, 'Are you and Harvey lovers?' She could lie and say 'no', but that would make it worse. Or would it? They could prove nothing. She knew that she could not get away with 'no comment'. Were she to say that her private life was none of their business, that would cut no ice. The *True Brit* had made it its business. The rag thrived on the sexual misfortunes of the great and the good. A pretty married woman Tory MP and a married, Catholic junior minister . . . The tabloids would shine even more brightly.

Her telephone rang. She lifted the receiver and held it away from her. The voice was that of Charles Harvey. 'Couldn't say much at dinner. Have you got

39

my letter?' Emma said she had, but she had yet to read it. 'Don't,' warned Harvey. 'Tear the bloody thing up. I must see you. In the Members' Lobby after the ten o'clock vote, and then in my ministerial room. All right?'

Ralph Grunte felt that he deserved a celebration. It was, when all was said and done, no mean feat to have been elected chairman of an important Party committee. The chairmanship would open the doors of the London embassies: lunch with the Spanish ambassador in Belgrave Square (always a bottle of Torres Black Label at least fifteen years old); even a *dîner intime* at the French. Douglas Hurd would canvass his opinion. John Rogers had always boasted that, when he dined at an embassy in his role as leader of the British delegation to the Council of Europe, he had been served a magnum of Cheval Blanc '47. 'No dark horse in that bottle,' he used to say. Dear old John, whatever happened to him? Should have gone to the Lords. And, what was more, as Chairman of the Europe Committee, he, Grunte, would be telephoned by the BBC and asked for his opinion. The 'World at One', 'PM' and 'The World Tonight' – they would all be his oysters. 'We must not lose sovereignty to foreigners.' And Marge would surely do her bit to keep the taxman at bay. Good old Marge.

Grunte ('Chairman Grunte') made his way unsteadily towards the smoking room.

In the hour before the ten o'clock vote, the smoking room comes into its own. Large, with a high ceiling, its walls plastered with second-rate portraits of second-class Victorian statesmen, the smoking room remains the preserve of the Tory Party. There is a bar in the corner with a telephone which is used only by the stewards to order up more champagne. Jeffrey Archer had once used it to have a row with his publisher, but what more could one expect of Jeffrey? There was usually a group of Tories standing at the bar: the rest of the room is occupied by brown leather armchairs and sofas. After lunch the *Standard* replaces the morning papers. Labour MPs do enter, but generally sit at the far end, as if on sufferance, proof of the tolerance that is to be found at the heart of British politics. Women MPs enter only rarely, and then, like Piccadilly policemen, in pairs.

On the night of Monday 7 June the grim fact that the House would continue 'until a late hour' did not seem to have dampened the hilarity. A Scots Tory, clad in a suit of his own design (Joshua commented that he looked like a Royal Park keeper), was noisily recounting stories of past triumphs. A Welsh Tory, well into his cups, was declaiming the poetry of Dylan Thomas. Another, who had been challenged within his constituency party, was recounting the story of his triumph over those home counties Tories rash enough to have wanted him to stand down. Sir Ralph Grunte ('the "b" is silent as in bugger,' whispered one MP to his friend) called loudly for a bottle of the widow. It ought not to be too hard to find someone to share it with him, he reflected. He was Chairman Grunte (all he lacked was his little red book), and the night threatened to be long.

'How about making a speech in the Chamber, Grunte?' asked Budgen.

'You know I just might,' was the reply.

Joshua Morris's half-bottle of beaujolais was only enough to carry him effortlessly as far as ten o'clock, the magic hour of release for MPs belonging to third parties, the very old and the particularly infirm. A small amount of drink boosted him quickly, but the drop was equally severe. He took the lift to his room and, sitting in his armchair, reread Felicity's letters. The correspondence had begun five years ago after they had met by accident in the Central Lobby. As if by magic, they had recaptured the enchantment of their first affair, over thirty years ago. He still could not believe his good fortune.

Joshua found it almost impossible to work in the evening. When he had a piece to write he did so in the early morning. If he had a speech to make he preferred to perform at lunch. When he spoke in the House, which was rarely, he tried to be called early in the day. His late wife had once said that he lacked stamina; he certainly did so now. He was getting old, and all night sittings were to be avoided at almost any cost. He felt the next day as if he had sat up all night in a third-class carriage on a slow train travelling from Calais to Nice. He would usually stay in the House until eleven or so, then sneak off to his flat. It would take something unexpectedly interesting to keep him out of his bed. And, as far as he was concerned, the whips had no carrots and no sticks. He was beyond promotion. He was just expected to 'do the decent thing' for his Party. Damn the decent thing, thought Joshua. He took a Raymond Chandler from his shelves and set out down those mean streets. Murder in the Palace of Westminster? There were motives enough, although hatreds were kept within parties rather than across them. Murder in the Commons smacked of catch-penny novels in which houses of cards piled melodrama upon melodrama, and chief whips killed in order to reach No. 10. It was nine forty-five. Good though it was, Chandler failed to hold him.

Westminster is a strange place, he thought. At one level it is a refuge from the outside world, a monstrous womb guarded by a hand-picked force of the Metropolitan Police. The building was centrally heated, the telephones free; the stationery never-ending, the envelopes already stamped. Even the food in the five restaurants was passable enough. The company, with some exceptions, could be good. Even the old fools were fun, or some of them. And even a Government backbencher, who was undoubtedly the lowest form of political life, has the luxury of a ringside seat. Joshua knew all 'the great ones' by their Christian names. He had grown up with most of them. The Prime Minister was thirteen years younger than he.

On the other hand, the Palace, at first glance so imposing, was like a colander, full of holes. The press had stormed the gates, and the cameras lurked within the Chamber itself. You could not vote without being accosted, and what you believed to be your private life could become, all too swiftly, 'a matter of public interest'. Even constituents occasionally arrived at the Palace, bearing petitions or demanding food and drink; but not very often. At least elections only took place every four years or so. When the telephone rang, which it did frequently, it was from the media. Would he care to perform? To write? Had he a view? . . .

The division bell interrupted his melancholia. He pulled himself to his feet and began the long walk to the Members' Lobby. As he joined his Party in the 'aye' lobby he noticed Harvey talking to the Chief Whip. Ralph Grunte, supported by a whip at each elbow, made his way noisily towards the desks on which sat the recording clerks. Would St Peter be as obliging? He caught sight of Emma and smiled. She did not smile back. She seemed to be under strain.

After four minutes, Joshua sang out his name and
passed into the Members' Lobby. A handful of the
blessed made their way hurriedly towards the exit.
Lucky sods. By the time Joshua had taken the lift and
walked the corridors as far as his room, the monitor
showed that since the last vote at eight-thirty the
Government's comfortable majority had dropped by
two. A small bell tolled and the debate continued on
into the night. Mr Robert Maclennan was, once more,
on his feet.

4

Mrs Thatcher, as she insisted on being called, despite the baronetcy especially created for her husband Denis, would occasionally take her place high on the Government backbenches below the gangway from which she could keep her eye on 'dear John'. He had been, after all, her candidate. She had been removed from office by the events of November 1990, declaring at the time that it was a 'funny old world'. Her fall had delighted her enemies and shocked her friends. It was as if a dynasty, long in power, had finally fallen. Spectators in the gallery and beyond would watch for her arrival in the Chamber, an event which would still be greeted by the muted cheers of the unreconciled. When that happened, the more mischievous hoped that one day Margaret Thatcher and Ted Heath would time their entries together, walking, as it were, side by side into the Chamber, bride and groom united in mutual loathing.

When the division bell rang for the ten o'clock vote on the evening of Monday 7 June, Peter Worthington

Evans was the whip on duty on the bench. In the 'aye' lobby, while the vote was in progress, he tried, and failed, to make contact with Emma, the crush being too great; but he did notice Mrs Thatcher encircled by members of the No Turning Back Group of Tory MPs, a body of which she had become the President. They had been dining together, so he had been told, in a private room at Green's, a restaurant favoured by MPs. What mischief had they been making?

Worthy Evans had been informed when he joined the whips' office that the whips prided themselves on the fact that no meeting of Tory MPs, however informal, however small in number, went unnoticed. If this were true it was because MPs were notoriously incapable of keeping secrets; the more obsequious making it their duty to pass on such information to their area whip. The No Turning Back Group were unreconstructed Thatcherites and included several ministers within their ranks. The group's task was, according to Norman Tebbit, one of their number, to keep alight the sacred flame. Whom had they singed while toying with their Soles Véroniques?

Worthy Evans thrust Emma from his mind and went in search of Richard Ryder. He was conscious of the pleasure that is distilled by the bearing of bad news. The Major Government was already in trouble. Mrs Thatcher's public disapproval of its European policies in particular could prove a severe embarrassment. 'That bloody woman' was dead, but she would not lie down.

Peter Worthington Evans resumed his seat at the end of the government front bench. It is the custom for there always to be a whip 'on the bench' who can report back to the Chief, or summon the Leader of the

House if needs be. Dull debates can come suddenly to life. It is also the whip's task to make notes on a clipboard about the speeches made. These are generally brief and to the point – 'very satisfactory' or 'sound' – but they constitute, nevertheless, another part of the record which is continuously kept on the performance of Members of Parliament.

The House was nearly empty. The assiduous had returned to their rooms to read and write; the convivial had retired to the bars; the faint-hearted had pushed off home. Ministers of the Crown, conscious of the need to do their red boxes, that is, to scrutinise the papers which their private offices had given them for attention overnight, had taken refuge in their rooms beneath the Commons Chamber.

Charles Harvey shuffled his papers and waited for Emma. The Major Government's suggestion in a Green Paper that motor cars pay an additional annual fee to enter city centres had resulted in an enormous and hostile public response. Harvey was faced with the task of signing 250 letters from his department to other MPs' aggrieved constituents. He was also responsible for the content of the letter (which had been drafted by his office). Each letter that was sent might later have to be defended on the floor of the House. His private secretary had gone home at eight o'clock to his house in Canonbury; civil servants, however civil, are in bed by ten-thirty. Save, hopefully, for Emma, who had promised to come before midnight, 'to talk things through'. Harvey was confident of being undisturbed – undisturbed, that is, by anything more sinister than the sudden ringing of the division bell. There could be a whole series of votes at indeterminate intervals. Were Emma in the mood, when the bell rang he would have eight minutes to get dressed.

Twenty feet above his head, Peter Worthington Evans,
the whip on duty, shifted uncomfortably under the
television cameras which moved automatically in the
direction of whomsoever happened to be on his feet.
Worthy Evans resisted the urge to pick his nose; he
might not be watched but he could be recorded. On
the Labour side of a thin House were the shadow
spokesman and three backbenchers, one of whom was
Tam Dalyell. He would be good for thirty minutes.
Robert Maclennan of the Liberal Democrats was
already droning on; he would be good for forty. On
the Government side sat the Minister of State, Peter
Lloyd, who was responsible for the passage of the
Bill, and his deputy. There were only two Government
backbenchers, however, one of whom had already
spoken in the debate, while the other showed no sign
of rising in his place once the previous speaker had sat
down. He would be mute and inglorious. It was Worthy
Evans's task to find a Tory backbencher to make a
speech to 'keep the debate going'. It would be
unseemly were a series of Opposition speakers to take
the floor.

At that moment Ralph Grunte entered the Chamber
and took his place behind the Minister. Grunte was as
pissed as a newt. It was clear, too, that it was his
intention to address the House. Evans went over to
Grunte and congratulated him on his election as Chairman of the Europe Committee. 'The Chief Whip is
delighted.' In politics, all lies are white. Evans went
on to ask him whether he was in a fit state.

'Fuck off,' said Grunte, an instruction which the
Hansard writers, crouched in the gallery above the
clock, studiously ignored. The whip then went over to

the Speaker and whispered something in the great man's ear. For as long as there was another Tory rising in his place, the Speaker could turn a blind eye; but were Grunte to be the sole Tory he could not be ignored indefinitely. Oh Christ, thought Worthington Evans, what a bloody night. He had wanted to speak to Emma but could not find her, his head ached and he would doubtless be up all night. Bowing to the Speaker he left the Chamber in search of the Chief Whip.

David Lancaster's taxi deposited him outside No. 7 Sherwood Road. Every artisan's cottage had been painted a different colour and small Volvos stood attendance at each front door. Gentrification had, despite the proximity of the main line from Waterloo to Clapham Junction, and the Latchmere Sports Centre, transformed the mid-nineteenth century railwaymen's cottages into bijoux residences.

The door of No. 7 was opened to him by a young man with straw-coloured hair. It was Greg, Wayne's flatmate, an interior decorator. 'Oh, it's you. Wayne is still attending to the nation's business. Thought you would be, too. But come in, do.' David Lancaster did as he was told. On the table of the living room (two small rooms knocked together) was a ham from which a slice or two had been cut. There were also three bottles of 'House of Commons Claret'. Greg waved him towards a glass and settled down to watch the television, a documentary about the life of Gloria Swanson.

'I hear you two had a tiff. Time to kiss and make up is my motto.'

I'll kiss the little bugger when I catch up with him, thought Lancaster. Making a fool of me and an exhibition of himself.

49

'Wayne hasn't been himself for days,' observed Greg, tearing himself away from *Sunset Boulevard*. 'I expect he's hard up. You lot don't pay him very much at the House of Commons. No tips and not many perks.'

Lancaster could smell the ham. His views on the dignity of labour were less than sympathetic, scroungers all of them, but he gestured towards the purloined ham. 'Pity he's not Jewish,' he observed.

'What's one more or less in the House of Commons?' said Greg. 'My mum says you're all there only for what you get out of it.'

The 'News at Ten' came and went. 'Mrs Thatcher rebukes Major – soft on Europe.' Lancaster thought of his missed vote. In a day or two he would get a note from Peter Worthington Evans – if he could stop himself mooning over Emma Kerr – asking for an explanation. His absence would be noted, and his chances of promotion blighted. At ten-thirty Melvyn Bragg interviewed the two Amises, Martin and Kingsley, then gave a reading from one of his own novels, something about a blacksmith in Cumbria; there was still no sign of Wayne Ellis.

'Perhaps he's gone home to his mum,' suggested Greg. 'I'm going to climb the wooden hill to Bedfordshire. Last one up's a pansy.'

Joshua Morris sat in his office thinking about his mistress. He was sixty, and love, in the shape of Felicity, was an experience they shared every few weeks on her visits to London. Joshua had first fallen in love with Felicity when they were both students in the 1950s at Heidelberg. Well brought up in the homes of the professional middle class, they had not actually made love; they had been in love.

They had even been in bed together in small German hotels where motherly-looking Fraus had scrutinised their incompatible passports, only to wave them upstairs with a smile and a blessing. Felicity, who had been to a girls' public school, slept with the window open and in her regulation knickers; Joshua did not remove them. He dared not risk his great good fortune. In those days one was protected by love. Blissfully happy, they necked until exhaustion overtook them. Joshua's ears still rang with his mother's injunction delivered whenever he left the Hampstead house for meetings of the local Young Conservatives, 'Don't you get that girl in the family way.' In those days to be on the pill was to take two aspirin.

Felicity had been a tall, dark girl with long legs. Years later, in their second incarnation, he had measured them; 43 inches from waist to toe. She had a heart-shaped face, a taste for T. S. Eliot and a loving disposition. Joshua had fallen hard, but the romance had foundered on their return home. Felicity went her way under the auspices of a mutual girlfriend of stronger will, while Joshua went up to Oxford. Twenty-five years later in a flat in London he told her, 'You broke my heart.' Felicity, seated on her narrow bed, begged him not to do likewise. He vowed he would not.

The reunion began when he had run into Felicity's husband at the Hurlingham Club. As they spoke Felicity arrived, festooned with Harrods bags. To Joshua's astonishment she had barely changed. Her face was thinner; at her temples there was a touch of grey, left by her hairdresser. But she was as slim as a wand and as elegant as a dancer. It was the same Felicity for whom he had pined a generation or more ago. His breath, which age had made shorter, was taken away. He could not believe his luck. He had decided there

51

and then that come what may, and at what price payable, Felicity would at long last be his. In his early fifties, he embarked on an adventure of love; his arrows letters, books and exquisite light lunches. For a year or so the fortress held out, but eventually she struck her colours. What time had set asunder, love rejoined. They were like two children in a sweet shop. And she was due in London that Thursday.

Joshua opened his book and tried to read. Someone once said that it was impossible to work in the House of Commons and there was much truth in the saying. Joshua was at his best in the early morning, the afternoons were more difficult, the evenings impossible. In truth he liked to be in bed just after ten and wake next morning at the crack of dawn. Imprisonment in the Palace of Westminster was purgatory. It was almost impossible to sleep; the level of his blood sugar, depressed by his half-bottle of beaujolais, fell steadily, only to rise again in the middle hours of the night. How often had he hung around until two in the morning only to be released, and then to find, having driven back to his daughter's flat in Lewisham, that he could not sleep there either? Late-night sittings, he had come to believe, were the responsibility of the newly elected Thatcherite MPs whose inevitable promotion to junior office would be their proper reward. He was past ambition but he had taken part in the debates on the Broadcasting Bill, and he wanted to vote against the Government on a clause that would come up sometime later in the night. Joshua put his Chandler to one side and went down into the tea room in search of black coffee and congenial company.

Peter Worthington Evans had first met Emma Kerr when he spoke for her at the general election. He had

travelled by car across country from Birmingham to
Corve Dale, only too happy to escape from his own
constituency campaign. The West Midlands 'area'
office of the Party had suggested that he speak for
Emma, as she was fighting a Labour-held marginal
seat. Evans's own seat, all lace curtains, bow windows
and Trust Houses, was reckoned to be a safe one,
having polled more than fifty per cent of the vote at
the previous election. MPs, he reflected ruefully, hated
elections; candidates, on the other hand, loved them.
MPs who had been through the hoops before had
everything to lose, candidates stood to gain everything.

Worthington Evans, a chartered accountant in his
early thirties, had slipped uncomfortably into the rou-
tine of fighting elections. The early morning press conference, attended by a bored reporter from the *Birmingham Post* who would have been happier in pursuit
of suburban adultery, was followed by the morning's
tour of prosperous residential streets, standing, berib-
boned like a bullock on the back of a borrowed Land
Rover, and an 'executive ploughman's lunch' in an
ornate pub-cum-road house where his blue rosette
attracted unflattering attention. ('We only see you at
election time.') To Peter an election tasted of Branston
pickle.

Then there was the afternoon spent canvassing,
accosting bewildered housewives, shoving mendacious
leaflets into the hands of the unwilling. He would
return to his hotel at five and sleep for an hour. At
seven, after a meagre dinner, he would be driven by
his chairman to a draughty church hall were he would
'address' a handful of his elderly – mainly female –
supporters. The tradition of the public meeting died
hard in Chamberlain country. The public stayed away;
if it was politics it wanted, the telly provided a surfeit

of the political first elevens. However, the party agents, middle-aged men with hairy tweeds and bad teeth, who read nothing save for the *Daily Mail*, always insisted on holding public meetings. How else could you meet the people? they asked. Peter Worthington Evans was not altogether certain that he wanted to. But if Paris was worth a mass, four years or more at Westminster was worth three weeks of tedium.

When Peter arrived at the village hall on the eastern slopes of the Brown Clee, Emma Kerr was already speaking. A voluptuous, startlingly pretty girl with dark red hair cut à la Quant, she was wearing a bottle-green trouser suit and talking intensely about the enterprise culture. Had not a nude picture of her appeared in the local paper? Evans, who had planned to sit quietly at the back of the hall until recognised, came forward and sat in the front row. Emma was certainly a dish, better looking than Nicholas Ridley and not quite as noisy as Tony Beaumont-Dark. Peter felt his spirits rise. Were her eyes as green as her trouser-suit pants? She had a wide mouth and there was a touch of ruthlessness about her chin. He had heard about her, but they had not met. She was married, or so he had been told, to a Barry whom she led something of a dance. Her accent was high-school Birmingham refined, more Solihull than Sparkbrook. She would be a catch, he thought. As she turned to make a gesture by pointing out of the window in the general direction of Bromsgrove, Peter could see the line of her underpants beneath her trouser suit. Tory women MPs were, with a few honourable exceptions, plain and worthy women, the sort who favoured lisle stockings and pork-pie hats and sat astride their wooden chairs like so many masters of foxhounds. Emma Kerr would be a welcome ornament to the 1922 Committee.

Emma was getting into her stride. She had moved on from the need for enterprise and was embarking on a defence of the Government's record. She had picked up from somewhere the common and irritating habit of punctuating her speech with continual references to 'Mr Chairman'. When she did so the beefy figure in the brown suit and shit-coloured shoes at her side nodded frantically in approval. A voice from the back of the hall, thick with Mitchell and Butler's best, suddenly yelled, 'Kiss me,' and made a sucking noise. There was loud laughter in which Peter happily joined. Emma stopped and blushed.

'I'll vote for you, my love,' said another voice in a Brummy accent. 'Take 'em off,' cried someone, ever hopeful. A tired-looking woman in the front stood and yelled, 'Sexist!' to Bronx cheers. Things were looking up. The chairman rose heavily to his feet. He probably owned the local Nissan franchise.

'This is not a public house, it is a public meeting.'

This feeble sally, of which he was proud, gave rise to more applause and to cries of 'Time, Gentlemen, please.' Emma, confused, said she had spoken long enough but would now answer questions. At this the claque at the back set up a chorus of 'What are you doing tonight?' and 'Where did you get them pyjamas?' Peter had wondered as much himself. The bottle-green trouser suit was a little on the tight side but very fetching. It did wonders for her heaving bosom. But Emma was near tears and in danger of losing control of the meeting.

Peter got to his feet and shouted to attract the chairman's attention. 'Mr Chairman, I have a question for the candidate.' The noise dropped. 'We can all see Mrs Kerr is prettier than the Labour candidate, but she is cleverer as well. Will she tell us how the Conservatives will reduce unemployment?'

Emma was happy to oblige, and gave, fluently enough, the stock central office answer.

When it was all over and Peter Worthington Evans had explained how he had spent the last twenty years fighting against socialism, called for the return of the rope and praised Mrs Thatcher's sixteen years of leadership to the skies, the platform party went back to the chairman's house for a drink. It was a large, detached 1960s dwelling of the kind known as 'Edgbaston Executive'. The chairs were of black leather, the lamps were in brackets and the carpet was suitably Axminster. The pictures were of Southern Spain. The space above the mantelshelf was decorated by a large coloured photograph of the front of a Bridgnorth garage. Across the front was a banner reading 'Queen's Award for Industry'. Peter sat himself down next to Emma. 'You were wonderful. Let's get out of here as soon as we decently can, and I'll drive you home.'

That had been four years or more ago. Worthington Evans had been lucky enough to remove the bottle-green suit, and much else besides. Emma, who had 'come up through the Young Conservatives', took a small flat in Dolphin Square, a corridor's width from Peter's. Her husband, Barry, seemed to play little part in her life. 'He's a boring old fart,' she had said, lighting her Consulate after making love. Peter could not bring himself to disagree. Whenever he did turn up he seemed to talk about nothing save vintage cars. Barry, to the convenience of the lovers, stayed put in Edgbaston, leaving his wife to represent the electors of Corve Dale at Westminster and comfort her lover in her spare time.

They had celebrated her maiden speech in Peter's bed with a bottle of Lanson (Emma loved that romantic television commercial of the two lovers on the beach) and several coarse and predictable jokes. When Peter had been promoted within the whip's office they had celebrated in hers. Taking a leaf out of John Gummer's book (as reported in the press), Peter bought her two pillows, on one side of which was the legend 'Not tonight Josephine' and on the other 'Yes, please'.

Unlike some other star-crossed Commons lovers they did not sit together in the Commons Chamber holding hands. Evans was more discreet than that. But there are few secrets within Westminster, and certainly none within the whips' office. To Peter, Tim Renton, a former Chief Whip, had made a joke about Emma's 'universal' appeal; they had laughed but the implication was plain. Lay off. In the meantime, the sight of Emma in a Cardin suit had strangely disturbed the older members of the 1922 Committee.

Charles Harvey had not yet a handle to his name, but he was better looking and more fun than Peter. And he was a junior minister. Taking advantage of Peter's momentary discouragement, Emma had deftly transferred her allegiance, and she now passed Peter's door in Dolphin Square without coming in. She bought new pillow cases from Liberty's and took out a subscription to the *Spectator*. *House and Garden* replaced *Ideal Home*. Her coffee was no longer instant. She even attempted a joke or two at Mrs Thatcher's expense, offering up the old one about the then Prime Minister expiring in a Jerusalem Hotel. Denis was presented with a bill for £20,000 by a local undertaker. 'What, for only three days?' It had seemed funny at the time.

Harvey was far more sophisticated than Peter Worthy Evans – Emma had taken to calling him 'Worthy' – and better in bed. He was no Euro-fanatic but his practices were continental. Peter had more in common with Speedy Gonzales. Emma had come close to wondering whether the strain of his daily 600-word missive to the Palace was not proving too much for him. He kept banging on about lights at the end of tunnels. Did the Sovereign really read his daily offering? Emma thought not. Their affair had fizzled out without recrimination, 'not so much a bang, more a whimper' had been Charles's unkind description of its end. Peter, on the other hand, was deeply hurt. He watched Emma blossom under Charles's practised hand with feelings of jealousy, an emotion that he had, until then, never experienced. He could not bear the sight of them together. Charles's name had come up at a Wednesday meeting of the whips. Sydney Chapman had sung his praises. Tom Sackville opined that he was a coming man. Even David Lightbown had nothing but good to say of him. Outraged, Peter bit back a general condemnation. Charles was a shit, shallow, pretentious and vain.

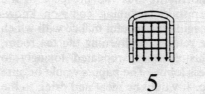

5

I wonder if he's gone to his mum's? David Lancaster
waited in Sherwood Road, the peace of his mind riven
by fear of exposure. Wayne's mother lived somewhere
in Forest Gate in a terraced house. He had once called
there en route for Epping Forest and Wayne had asked
him in for a cuppa. They had sat in the tiny living room
making polite conversation. The house had the sour
smell of poverty. A large, coloured print of the Queen
on horseback decorated the wall above the sideboard
while he thought he had spotted, in a glass-fronted
cupboard, a Clarice Cliffe teapot. He had meant to
take a closer look. Were it to be the real thing he
would make the old bat an offer. It was a bit like Alf
Garnett's house in 'Till Death'. He had not noticed a
telephone. There were two pages of Ellises in the book
but none lived in Forest Gate. Where else could the
little sod have gone?

Wayne Ellis, who was twenty and looked much
younger, had been taken on by the Commons refreshment department six months previously. Usually he

washed dishes but he had recently been pressed into acting as understudy to Michael, the wine waiter. Wine waiter, thought Lancaster bitterly. Some bloody wine waiter. He didn't know his Blue Nun from his Frascati. His hair still felt sticky; his shoulders smelt of cheap hock. What was horrifying was the prospect of the whole miserable episode becoming common knowledge. He could imagine the gleeful malice with which the story would be retailed, enlivening the tea room, embroidered by his enemies, repeated lovingly to members of the press lobby. The papers would be sure to pick the story up. It would be meat and drink to the tabloids.

But where was Wayne? He might have gone to that club in Dean Street in search of consolation. He could be pouring his heart out to some mock-solicitous girl from the *People*. He might at that very moment be folding a cheque made out in four figures. He could be dropping David Lancaster in the shit.

At that moment the bell rang. He got to his feet but then froze. It could be the press. The bell rang again, noisily, insistently. Greg put his head round the top of the stairs, only to be waved furiously away. The bell rang for a third time, to be followed by a gloved hand rattling the letter box. Lancaster did not move. Then there was a sound of receding steps and, after a moment, the slam of a car door. Lancaster pulled back the curtain an inch. A Maestro was moving away from the curb. The driver was out of sight, but the rear window of the car carried the legend 'I am a *Sun* lover'. Jesus Christ, thought the Member for Notts. I've had it.

Sir Ralph Redvers Grunte had once been described by Matthew Parris in his *Times* column as 'seedy, hearty,

with ruined teeth and wearing an expensive watch'. He
was not so much seedy as disreputable. His suits were
expensive, as were his ties; both were splattered with
grease. He had the meal-time habit of raising his fork
to his mouth and holding it poised before him long
enough to permit the food impaled upon it to drop
back splashily upon his plate. He was certainly hearty.
He was not the sort of man by whom one should be
painlessly congratulated. His teeth, or rather the bat-
tered appearance of those that remained, gave proof
of his Scottish ancestry, while his watch, a gift from
the Prime Minister of Japan, no less, did everything
but tell the time. Besides being a menace to all those
who used the lifts in the Palace of Westminster and,
given the height of the ceilings, there were few, save
perhaps for the Minister of Sport, who did not, his
least amiable characteristic was the persistence with
which he blew his nose. His trumpetings had even
earned a rebuke from the Speaker; his habit of gazing
interestedly into his handkerchief once the performance was over had been tactfully ignored. Nicholas
Soames, Churchill's grandson, whose mimicry
delighted his less stuffy colleagues, was capable of a
splendid imitation of 'Old Grunt': it could not be
embarked upon without loud raspberry noises and the
use of an enormous red bandanna handkerchief.

Grunte thought that Alastair Goodlad, the Deputy
Chief Whip, had been remarkably civil. (Ryder had
funked the interview.) He had been properly pleased
by his election as Chairman of the backbench Europe
Committee. The observation he had made that he had
'kept that swine Meyer out' was received without comment. 'At least we know that your local party would
never de-select you, Ralph,' was Goodlad's equivocal
response.

Goodlad, who had once been mistaken for an English butler, the sort that is to be found in the lovelier homes of Sacramento, California, called upon a junior whip to fetch a pot of black coffee. On its arrival he poured two large cups. It would be wise to keep the swine talking for some time to come. Sober him up.

'John was very happy to learn of your election,' said Goodlad unconvincingly. John Major had as little time for Grunte as he did. 'And you know he has no patience with the Euro-fanatics in our party. All this talk of a single currency would rob us of our power to take decisions in the national interest. We would be ruled by bureaucrats from Brussels.' He winced as he said it. It was balls but Grunte would know no better.

The word 'bureaucrats from Brussels' seemed to revive his guest, who had been showing the first signs of somnolence. 'We must keep the buggers out,' Grunte cried and, fumbling in his back pocket, brought out a silver flask, redolent of the hunting field. He unscrewed it and, having poured half his cup of coffee back into the pot, refilled it with brandy. He did not offer the Deputy as much as a drop. 'Got to keep yourself going during an all-night sitting,' he observed. 'Want to make a contribution to the debate.'

Joshua Morris set out on the long walk from his office under the eaves to the tea room downstairs. Fifty yards of narrow, dimly lit corridor past a regiment of doors, each named after an MP, a slow lift ride down to the Members' dining room, then into the lobby and along yet another passageway past the door of that holy of holies, the smoking room itself. The Scots Tory who had been dancing an hour or so ago was asleep in an armchair. Leaving the library to his right, Joshua turned into the tea room. What better way was there for a politician to keep physically fit? There was the gymnasium, tucked away in Norman Shaw south. Joshua had meant to attend, but had never summoned up the will. He was too old to be jumping up and down to the command of a female instructor. The gym was sponsored by Jim Spicer, a genial one-time Para who spent much of his time doing physical jerks. Spicer, who sat for a Dorset seat in the Conservative interest, had told him that Emma Kerr had joined and could be glimpsed by the fortunate (Charles Harvey's name was mentioned) standing on her head or climbing up ropes. Joshua was tempted, but not enough to join.

The Commons tea room is, in fact, three large rooms in one. At the north end is a serving area where black and Irish girls sell tea, coffee and salad suppers. Around them, as if warmed by the urn, cluster Labour MPs reading the *Guardian*. The second room is traditionally the preserve of the Tories; the third stocks newspapers and magazines and is shared by clerks of the House, clever girls with good degrees who pick at their meagre lunches and read the *Independent*.

Joshua stood in line for a cup of stewed black coffee. The television monitor showed that Tam Dalyell was once more on his feet, addressing what passed for a house. He had been in that familiar position for twenty minutes and the time was eleven fifteen. I shall push off at two, thought Joshua, in an attempt to keep up his spirits. He knew escape to be unlikely.

All-night sittings were hell. The debates, which ostensibly were the cause of their incarceration, were never of much interest. Labour MPs filibustered in an attempt to keep the other side out of bed; nobody who lacks the wit of a Ustinov should attempt to waste other people's time, Joshua reflected. He personally was a ten-minute man.

Government ministers and a whip were obliged to hold the fort while the footsoldiers of the backbench slept fitfully in armchairs, caroused with an air of desperation, or tried to do some work. Charles Harvey was signing his name to his 200th letter. Where the blazes was Emma? David Lancaster was keeping a vigil of his own. Peter Worthy Evans was rereading his missives to the Queen and thinking bitterly about Emma. Under an Essex moon, Sam Langford was in bed with his wife. Richard Ryder was ensconced with the Prime Minister.

'She's very bitter, you know. She'll make trouble for us all. Why don't you have a private word with her? Invite her to Chequers for the weekend.'

'Not Chequers,' sighed John Major, 'she'll start rearranging the furniture, to say nothing of the pictures.'

Edwina Currie was dreaming of fame and fortune. She had been asked to become the 'little Lion', her face upon every egg. Nicholas Ridley opened his third pack of Park Drive and stuck another pin into a wax model of Herr Kohl. In the middle of the three tea rooms, Joshua joined a table of fairly cheerful Tories. Nick Budgen was reading out loud a piece that he had written for the following day's *Express*. It was a plea for Enoch Powell to be sent to the Lords. Budgen read his copy in a fake Black Country accent. Teddy Taylor, the incomprehensible Scot, nodded in agreement. Nicholas Baker, another Government whip, was wearing his bookmaker's suit, a sure sign that the House was in for a long night.

'How much longer?' asked Joshua.

'God knows,' said Baker. 'We can't get agreement with the other side, and I fear it will go very late. There will be several more votes. We know we can rely on you, Josh?'

Joshua sighed in reply.

'Solved any murders, recently?' The questioner was a young man with a mane of hair, of whose name Joshua was not altogether certain. Was he the one who wrote books under an assumed name? He had presumably won a seat at the last election; he spoke with a faint Brookside accent. He was wearing a dark blue bomber jacket and a pair of red leather carpet slippers with what looked like his initials on the toe caps. Would that be a clue? Joshua felt that he could not scrutinise his companion's footwear too closely. He was clearly dressed for the night. Joshua ignored the opening gambit and told of Mrs Sally Oppenheim, a pretty woman once a dancer who, in the Heath years, had turned up in the 'aye' lobby wearing her negligée. It had been too much for the Tory party of twenty years ago; she had been rebuked by the Chief Whip. Francis Pym had told her to dress properly.

'Would they call you in if Neil Kinnock was bumped off?'

The Liver Bird was nothing if not persistent. Morris replied that he would certainly refuse the case. 'There would be far too many suspects.' The joke was a feeble one but it would have to do.

'Did you really solve a murder when you were at university?'

Joshua reluctantly told the tale. 'The chaplain at Queen's was found dead in the Fellows' garden early one morning. Not that he didn't deserve a violent end. His sermons were long and more than usually dull. He had a thing about purity. So did we all, but he was in favour of it. Dead he was, and not a mark on him. The plod were baffled. In Oxford in the early fifties there was no crime save for the odd fight on Saturday evenings between Town and Gown. Or an undergraduate

driving his motor car after dark without showing a
green light on his front bumper. My aunt's brother
was the Chief Superintendent. I used to visit him in
Abingdon and play tennis with his daughters. Anyway,
to cut a long story short, the old boy was poisoned by
his wife. She was a fungi buff. She fried a death cap
for his supper with a slice of back bacon, the one
which takes exactly twelve hours for the symptoms
to manifest themselves. Leaves no trace. But it was
October, the mushroom season, and his good lady had
written books on fungi. I showed the Super my copy.
She confessed when she saw the game was up.'

At this point Grunte walked through the tea room
singing softly to himself. The brandy was taking effect.
'I wish someone would bump off old Grunt,' observed
Budgen. Two Scots Tories went past, deep in con-
spiracy; they were among the last friends of Michael
Forsyth. Tam Dalyell was still on his feet. Baker asked
Joshua who were his favourite writers of detective
fiction.

'Conan Doyle, but I must declare an interest. I'm
the President of the Sherlock Holmes Society.'
Joshua's voice took on a mock pomposity. 'We dine
once a month in the upstairs room of an Italian restaurant in Baker Street. Sinister waiters brandishing
gigantic phallic pepper mills. Holmes would not have
approved. The best writer would have been "Agatha
Sayers": if only someone could have combined Christ-
ie's plots with Dorothy Sayers's narrative intelligence.
I like Chandler very much. He writes so well. All those
mean streets in Los Angeles in the early forties. And
Marlow, of course, Marlowe with his "e". Chandler
writes so entertainingly that it doesn't much matter
that his plots defeated him – as well as his readers.
Edmund Crispin is good. Did you ever read *The*

Moving Toyshop? Real name was Bruce Montgomery. He taught me English at Shrewsbury. He used to read to us out loud the ghost stories of Monty James.'

The monitor pinged; it read 'Sir R. Grunte'.

'What about P. D. James?' asked Liverpool.

'A very nice woman,' said Morris. 'I once interviewed her for a glossy. She collects Staffordshire pots. She's the best writing today. But she suffers from literary snobbery. Her novels do not find favour with the corps of Booker judges. Crime novels are not considered to be literature, but they can pay. Phyllis James has a very pretty house in Notting Hill Gate. The English,' said Joshua, warming to his theme, 'only write stories in which gifted amateurs become detectives. Holmes, Sexton Blake, Poirot, Lord Peter Wimsey, Fell. Even James's policeman hero is posh, a poet called Adam Dalgliesh. How many policemen have you met called Adam, let alone Dalgliesh? Every other nation writes *romans policiers*. The cop as hero: Maigret. It's yet more evidence of the English cult of the amateur.'

'What about Marlowe?' said someone. 'He was a private eye.'

Morris was not fazed. 'Chandler,' he replied magisterially, 'went to Dulwich College.'

A colleague passing the table shouted, 'Don't sit there gossiping, you're missing the fun.' He pointed to the television monitor. Grunte's name had disappeared to be replaced by the ominous words, 'Points of Order'.

Uproar in the House is relatively rare but never unwelcome. The huffing and puffing, outrage and umbrage which so shocks the genteel viewer is translated by the Orwellian and ubiquitous monitor as 'Points of Order', or – and this is very serious indeed – 'Sitting Suspended'. To Joshua Morris's cry of 'What fun?' the answer was 'Grunte. He's pissed. Still thinks Margaret's at Number Ten.'

Members of Parliament do not run. When they are obliged by circumstances to do so, to beat a colleague to a cab or to arrive at the division lobby before the doors are locked against them, they break into a dignified trot like so many Suffolk Punches. But now the corridor leading to the Members' Lobby and the Chamber became a race-track over which MPs, grave and gay, but mostly merry, hastened to see the fun. Despite all that is written about life in the Palace of Varieties, MPs lead dullish and frustrating lives, obliged as they are to listen to ministerial speeches and bounded as they are by ambitious rivals, resentful wives and curmudgeonly constituents. So Grunte's last stand was definitely not to be missed.

Speaking from the backbenches is not as easy as it looks. Ministers who sit on the front bench can lean forward on the dispatch box and read from a draft written for them by a Wykehamist in their private office. Backbenchers have to write their own scripts. The back of the bench in front of them reaches only as high as the mid shin; lean too far back in pursuit of some rhetorical point and there is the risk of sitting down abruptly; lean too far forward for dia'. ·ical effect and the speaker could topple forward o to a somnolent colleague. Notes have to be held i. one hand, spectacles in the other. It is as well to be thin, essential to be sober and to have some idea of what it is you want to say. The House may not be listening but the world is watching. A lifetime of self-indulgence had made Grunte stout, he was clearly drunk, but he knew only too well what it was he wanted to say. He pushed his spectacles up on to the bridge of his nose, adjusted his trousers, took a deep breath and began.

'Madam Deputy Speaker.' Sir Paul Dean, neat, dapper, silver-haired and patrician, bore no resemblance whatsoever to Betty Boothroyd, who had once been a Bluebell Girl.

Dean stared frostily at Grunte. 'Sir Ralph Grunte,' he repeated.

Bob Cryer on the Labour benches came to life. He whispered to Mark Fisher to send for the Labour whip on duty who was in Annie's Bar. 'This could be fun.'

The rules of order should compel Hon. Members to keep, more or less, to the subject under discussion. The rules were elastic, but not so elastic as to accommodate what it was Grunte wished to say.

The Hansard Report gives the substance but not the flavour of Grunte's midnight performance. Over the years Hansard writers and editors have acquired the qualities enshrined in the three brass monkeys. 'Madam Deputy Speaker' became simply 'Mr Speaker'.

'I have been a Member of this House for nearly twenty years,' began Grunte. The Hansard Report then reads 'interruption', a polite translation of the cry from a tie-less Labour MP of 'far too bloody long'. Grunte, swaying slightly as if standing at the top of Beachy Head, took no heed. 'If I might be allowed to say so, I have been a loyal member of my Party. Can I say that we have in my Right Honourable Friend the Member for Finchley – Mrs Thatcher, no less – the most distinguished Leader of our great Party, certainly in my lifetime.' This opinion, which was predictable enough, was delivered in a challenging tone. Peter Lloyd, who had swung round in his place on the Government front bench, found himself nodding in approval and murmuring 'Hear, hear.'

Tories are expected to show piety whenever the name of the leader is mentioned, especially when 'addressing' their local parties; but what had Grunte in mind? Had not Mrs Thatcher been done away with? The Hon. Member for South Warwickshire warmed to his theme. 'She has given this great country of ours what it has long craved: leadership. She has never spared herself.' At this Sir George Gardiner, the first of Mrs Thatcher's many biographers, wiped away a manly tear. 'May she live for ever!' cried Grunte, tossing his spectacles away in a dramatic gesture.

Mr Mark Fisher, a bald, middle-aged Labour MP who was Shadow Spokesman for the Arts, was on his feet. 'Will the Honourable Member give way?' Grunte sat down and began to blow his nose. Fisher raised his voice. 'Am I to take it that the Honourable Member still thinks his Right Honourable Friend the Member of Finchley is still the Leader of his Party? Where has he been these past months? Or is his tribute a subtle attack upon his Right Honourable Friend the Prime Minister himself?'

Ralph Grunte had never spoken to Mark Fisher, an Old Etonian, but he believed him to have changed sides – to have crossed the floor of the House. Grunte shoved his bandanna into his sleeve, a custom that he had picked up from Sir Charles Mott Radclyffe in the days when it was Tories who had been to Eton. He would crush the apostate. 'The Honourable Member is a traitor to his class.' (At this juncture Hansard records 'Interruption'.) 'All I will say is that we, on this side, are well rid of him. Let him hob-nob with his trade union friends. I for one will have no truck with traitors and turncoats.' At this Sir Paul looked decidedly pained. Several Labour MPs were on their feet shouting, 'Points of order.' Dean, who could pick and choose, called Mr Bob Cryer.

'May I make it clear to the Honourable Member for South Warwickshire that he is still confused. My Honourable Friend has never been a member of the Tory Party. Could it be that he is confusing Mark with Nigel Fisher, father with son?'

Peter Worthington Evans, who had forgotten all about Emma while Grunte had been on his feet, moved in front of him and whispered that he had got it all wrong: Fisher *père* had most certainly been a Tory MP, Fisher *fils* was most certainly not. Grunte looked taken aback, then said, *sotto voce*, 'I'm damned if I'll apologise to that bald bugger. He must have broken his father's heart.' His response was clearly audible. Pandemonium broke out. Tories who had arrived breathless in the Chamber cheerfully yelled 'Hear, hear' and 'Filial ingratitude'. Others, wishing to keep the Grunte show on the road, roared their encouragement. At least twenty Labour MPs were on their feet. Mr Robert Maclennan looked stunned, Mr Robert Rhodes James, the patrician Member for Cambridge, suitably shocked. Mr Patrick Cormack, a Tory MP who was wearing morning dress – for he had either come from or was en route to a colleague's memorial service – climbed to his feet. He was a self-appointed guardian of what was regarded by some as good form.

'Mr Deputy Speaker,' he yelled. It was at this point that Worthington Evans left to find the Chief Whip; a messenger was sent to awaken the Leader of the House whose suite of rooms was but a step away. Things were beginning to get lively.

Sir Paul Dean, too, was now on his feet. Grunte sat down. It was then that the Deputy Speaker made an unusual mistake. He could have asked Grunte that he put the record straight, that he admit to having

muddled up the two Fishers. He ought perhaps to have
turned a deaf ear to the vulgar and common abuse.
Instead, he called upon Grunte to withdraw his 'grossly
unparliamentary remarks'.

'He *is* bald,' said Grunte truculently. 'Bald as the
proverbial egg. As for his sex life, I don't give a toss
what he does in his spare time.' At this there was
further uproar. Mr Andrew Faulds, a bearded actor
from the Labour benches, rose and asked whether it
was in order for one Honourable Member to call
another a bugger.

'We can all see, Mr Deputy Speaker,' continued the
hirsute Faulds, 'that he is bald.' (This was greeted by
what Hansard called 'laughter'.) Ms Clare Short, a
short, dark and formidably feminist Labour MP, was
on her feet. This was going to be fun.

John MacGregor, the leader of the House, now
entered the Chamber. He had been reading *First
Among Equals* in bed. He had just reached the point
where a leading Labour MP was about to be black-
mailed for consorting with a prostitute. He was wearing
his pyjama jacket under a black coat and silver tie. Sir
Paul, who had been in anxious consultation with the
clerks on the table, called upon Ms Clare Short to
make her point of order.

'Mr Deputy Speaker, is it not a disgracefully sexist
thing for an Honourable Member, who is in no condition to be on his feet, to be permitted to make
remarks about the private life and sexual preferences
of my Right Honourable Friend? He is using the word
"bugger" simply as a term of abuse.' This sally was
greeted with kissing noises from those Tories below
the gangway who had abandoned the pleasures of the
smoking room for the Chamber.

Joshua Morris got to his feet. 'Since when, Mr

Deputy Speaker, has the word "bugger" been a term of abuse? In England it is surely a term of affection.' There was much laughter.

Sir Paul Dean, once more rising, shouted for order. 'I call upon the Honourable Member for South War-wickshire to withdraw his disgraceful remarks.' Grunte, who had paled, got unsteadily to his feet. 'If he does not,' said Dean, 'I shall name him and ask him to leave the Chamber.' The Chief Whip had moved to Grunte's side while the Leader of the House had turned towards him, urging apology. Grunte dug his hand into his back trouser pocket, pulled out his flask, unscrewed it and took a swig. A full House resounded to cries of 'Cheers'.

'Mr Deputy Speaker,' said Grunte. This time there was no mistake about gender. The House shushed itself into silence. 'If I have mistaken son for father – or is it father for son – I most certainly apologise to you, and through you, sir, to the whole House. It is no joke to be bald.' Grunte began to laugh. 'I, for one, lost much of my hair as a result of Hitler's war, when a bomb fell close to my father's caravan. But what more can you expect from the Hun?'

His ingratiation did not succeed. 'I hereby name the Honourable Member,' cried Sir Paul, white at the gills. 'And I hereby suspend the House for ten minutes in order to permit decorum to be regained.' He got to his feet and left the Chamber. A clerk removed the mace. Grunte left his place and staggered across the floor of the House, his hand outstretched in the direction of Fisher: upon arrival on the Opposition front bench he changed his mind and planted a kiss on the top of Fisher's bald pate. He was bundled from the Chamber by a posse of whips. Later Worthy Evans put him in a cab and sent him home. The lobby correspondent of the Press Association urgently filed his copy. It would be too late for the mornings, but not for Breakfast Television and the first edition of the London *Standard*.

6

After the incident in the dining room the head waiter had told a distraught Wayne Ellis to come into his office and 'lie down'. He had no great opinion of Parliamentarians. They were greedy eaters and poor tippers. Every Christmas a letter was sent to MPs reminding them of their obligations towards the staff. The response was ungenerous. Most people made a payment of ten pounds. Had they tipped each day in the normal manner the annual take would have been much higher. Nevertheless, work at the Palace was a nice little earner. Wages were paid for twelve months even though the place was open for less than nine.

The head waiter was sitting on a stool in his tiny office. 'What got into you, you silly bugger? It's back to washing up for you, that is if Uncle Charlie will keep you on.' Peeing into the soup was the waiter's traditional revenge; or at least it was when George Orwell was down and out in London and Paris. Pouring a bottle of wine over a customer's head was eccentric and noticeable. It could get into the public prints. The head waiter took a long look at the snivelling Ellis. 'Have you been at the bottle? There are some fine wines that have gone walkabout. Anything to do with you?'

Wayne, whose tears were running down his pale face, sobbed, 'I'm not saying nothing, save that David Lancaster is a filthy swine.' That was no way to talk about a tribune of the people.

The door of the office opened and Sir Charles Irving entered. Irving, a large-faced man with cuffs, was the MP for Cheltenham and the long-serving Chairman of the Kitchen Committee. He had turned a deficit into a gold mine. This was due less to the modest profit on the grub and more to the excess profits on a stall which sold souvenirs to the visitors – cuff links with the Westminster portcullis, House of Commons aftershave and bottles of monogrammed spirits which were given by MPs to their deserving constituents. His knighthood, which was a gift from Mrs Thatcher, was – or so it was said by the wags – an award for enterprise rather than gastronomy. He could occasionally be glimpsed at the door of the Members' dining room, rubbing his hands in greeting.

Like most MPs Irving had a bedside manner. He told Ellis to clear off home and to keep his mouth shut. 'I don't want a word of this in the papers.' To the head waiter he counselled caution. He, too, was to keep his silence. 'If the reptiles get wind of what happened tell them it was an accident. New to the job. Tell them we like our wine too much to waste it.' The head waiter left to spread the word, leaving Sir Charles free to look for David Lancaster.

Ellis, who had already collected his mac and a chicken sandwich, went down the corridor to the basement, intending to leave for home by the 'factory' entrance, but then he changed his mind and took the lift marked 'Members Only' three floors up to the Upper Committee corridor. It was forbidden territory. He would wait for Lancaster in his room. He had, when all was said and done, spent some time there in the past. He should, he thought, make his peace.

It was rash of Harvey to have entertained as publicly so nubile a colleague. Emma was not as famous as Edwina Currie nor as assiduous as Emma Nicholson, but not for nothing had she been christened by a malicious woman Labour MP 'the Tory Party's tit and bum'. According to the *Brit*'s Midlands stringer, Emma Kerr's marriage was on the rocks. Barry Kerr, or so it seemed, had been excluded from Emma's private as well as her public life. He had been spotted several times in a Happy Eater on the Coventry Road in the company of a hairdresser called Marlene, and Emma was never at home.

There was also the friendship between Emma and Peter Worthington Evans. Here Barton had less to go on. While it was easy enough to persuade MPs of all parties to gossip on matters of people and politics, they clammed up swiftly when it came to responding to questions about the private lives of other MPs. One Tory might remark upon the voting record or the attendance of another Tory whose politics he disliked – for what hatreds there are in Westminster are to be found within, rather than across the parties – but to gossip about a rival's love life to a reptile would have been universally regarded as a shit's trick. Chaps did not drop other chaps in it, and most certainly not to the tabloids. And, pondered Barton, Worthington Evans – why the 'Worthington'? Was he related to the brewers? He was a member of the Government whips' office, a part of the *broederbond*, the brotherhood of the self-selected that guarded its secrets jealously, and from whose premises and operations the press was excluded . . . Still, whips must eat lunch like everyone else, although Barton had yet to see Evans and Emma breaking bread together. He had, however, got wind of something. He would, when convenient, speak to the Midlands' stringer. In the meantime he would invite Emma to lunch with him.

As for Lancaster, the newspaper's 'library' had quite a bit on the Boy David. Once Barton learned of the episode of the wine he scented a scoop. He would catch up with the waiter later that day and get his story. After he had done so, Lancaster would be asked to comment on what Ellis would have said. Bum boys like Ellis rarely bit their tongues; they were usually only too happy to do the dirty on former lovers. If it were a little matter of money the sum would be small: the amount that the paper paid an MP for occasional contribution. There was one snag. Lancaster was known to be friendly with the Minister of Posts and Telegraphs. They had once shared a flat in Lambeth. There was some evidence that they shared the same predatory tastes. 'The backbencher and the wine waiter' wasn't a bad story; but nothing like as good as 'Tory bigwigs hunt in tandem. Vice in high places.' Wouldn't the running of the first preclude the second? Would it not be wise to wait – to keep Lancaster and Ellis on ice? And it was rumoured that Lancaster was in line for promotion, and Ellis could be paid to lead him to other fish. The bigger they were . . .

Ronald Barton had been born in Motherwell, the son of a publican and a sinner. His mother was a tart. At the comp. he had always been good at English. His early ambition was to play centre back for United, but he was not quick enough off the ball. Instead, he had wangled a job on the *Glasgow Herald* but he was not to that decent paper's taste. Like many Scottish scribblers he moved south to London and found employment eventually with the *Sun*. He had written to Kelvin Mackenzie, its editor, congratulating him on the paper's headline at the time of the sinking of the *Belgrano*. From then on it had all been downhill. It had been Ron who had unmasked the transvestite Privy Councillor. It had been Ron who introduced Ruby Wax into the House of Lords, and – a third battle honour – it had been Ron who revealed to the world the story of the Labour MP, the dolphin and the chorus girl. Now, at two o'clock in the morning of Tuesday 8 June, he felt weary. Sitting in front of his monitor he pushed 'escape', then chose to 'save' all that he had tapped into his word processor. The division bell was ringing. He at least could go back home to Dulwich. He felt pleased with himself. He had loaded both barrels of his gun: if he did not get Lancaster then he had Harvey and Emma Kerr in his sights. The editor would be pleased with him, and his salary would rise in appreciation of his talent. And the exploits of Ralph Grunte were always good for a laugh.

MPs left the Chamber in high spirits after the Deputy Speaker suspended the House. The levels of the blood sugar of the elected had been hugely raised by the excitement. The 'midnight sag' so commonly experienced by legislators separated from the warmth of their beds by the call of the Party had been banished, at least for a time. The smoking room filled with cheerful Tories taking a far from charitable pleasure from Grunte's downfall. 'Never liked him,' was the verdict of Cranley Onslow, the chairman of the '22. The steward was obliged to use his telephone to order up more champagne.

Labour MPs, with their passion for Newcastle Brown, made either for the Kremlin or Annie's Bar where they relived the events of the previous twenty minutes. Mark Fisher (who secretly preferred the smoking room) was greeted with cries of 'Where's the bald bugger?' and many mugs of brown ale.

As for the Liberal Democrats, Alan Beith had been working in the library throughout the fracas, while Paddy Ashdown, who had slept throughout the excitement, slumbered on uneasily on his divan, tormented by dreams of electoral success and reliving past martial triumphs off the coast of Borneo. Had he not killed a man with his bare hands? Liberal ladies in the West Country certainly believed so. Ashdown's face broke into a silent smile.

Mrs Currie had little time for such nonsense. She had remained in her office throughout the affair, writing up her diary for publication. A publisher had paid her a handsome advance on royalties: £55,000 for 60,000 words. No kiss but lots of tell: those had been her instructions.

Peter Worthy Evans, his stint on the bench over until five a.m., sat in the whips' common room, drinking Richard Ryder's whisky. The driver of Grunte's taxi had been disobliging. He did not want his passenger to be sick all over his cab, thank you very much indeed. A ten pound note had done the trick. His 'fare', he had been assured, lived only round the corner and was simply tired and emotional. 'Just like George Brown,' had been the cabby's reply. Grunte had been borne away into the night singing a rude song, saluted by respectful policemen; to be awakened no doubt by early-morning calls from disrespectful journalists. Christ, what a pain in the arse that man is, thought Peter. No sooner had he closed his eyes than he began to think about Emma. How could she have behaved so badly to him?

'What are we going to do about Margaret?' Ryder had called to collect his bottle. Peter came to, banishing from his thoughts Charles Harvey and sweet prospects of revenge. 'She's told the press that John is betraying what she calls the legacy of Thatcherism, has sold out to the Germans and is remarkably "grey". She even adapted the old Churchill joke about Clem Attlee – you know the one: "an empty taxi drew up at the House of Commons and Attlee stepped out" – in her speech to the Don't Turn Your Back Group.' Ryder's inflexion put capital letters to the popular rendering of 'No Turning Back'. 'Most of them are so thick they'd never heard it before.' The Chief Whip, who was a mild man, was clearly very angry indeed.

'Any chance of persuading her to take a seat in the Lords?' asked Peter. 'She would then be Waddington's headache.'

Ryder shook his head. 'The trouble is, of course, her following in the constituency parties, many of whom believe she was bundled out of office as the result of a conspiracy. They don't see that she destroyed herself. And she wants to give the Conservative Political Centre lecture at the Party Conference, which means more aggro. I suppose if she wants it she must have it. I understand Chris Patten had asked Herr Kohl to give it, which might not have been altogether wise.'

'Why not a job at the UN?' asked Peter.

'Too big a fish.' Ryder promptly changed the subject. 'Did you get Grunte off to bed safely? What a performance. I gather Fisher is to raise the matter with the Speaker tomorrow.' He looked at his watch. 'Tomorrow? I mean at three-thirty.'

* * *

81

Before joining the *True Brit*, Ronnie Barton had been the lobby correspondent of the *Sun* for five years. He believed that there was a skeleton in every man's cupboard if only one bothered to look. The *Brit*, like all tabloids, had a taste for patriotism, populism and scandal; especially scandal. The discovery of an event which would combine all three ingredients, and keep running indefinitely, was the ambition of every hack in his dirty raincoat.

Ron had been brought up on the Profumo affair, and had sat through the film *Scandal*, which was based loosely upon the goings-on of 1963, three times. After his conversation with Emma in the Lobby earlier that evening, he had returned to his flat in Lordship Lane, Dulwich. The paper paid a Commons' attendant, who was obliged anyway to stay up with the House, a retainer: in return, he was expected to rouse Barton from his bed if things turned lively. He had telephoned before midnight while Grunte was still on his feet. 'We've got a bit of fun here,' he had reported. Barton had cursed, dressed, but not arrived in time. He was obliged to pick up what he could from MPs in the Lobby as the PA man was keeping his counsel.

The *Brit*'s first edition had gone to bed but he was able to fax a paragraph through to the night editor: it would make the later editions. 'Tired Tory named by Speaker. Calls Labourite a very rude word indeed. Fun and Games at the Fun Factory' and more besides. No doubt the paper's redoubtable team of leader writers, headed by a Ron Spark lookalike (he, too, wore a beret and dark glasses, as did his opposite number at the *Sun*) would concoct an editorial that would combine piety, prurience, shock and outrage. He could see the opening sentence now: 'Bugger me if it isn't the Mother of Parliaments.'

Wide awake, despite the smallness of the hour, Barton sat in front of his word processor and sketched in the outlines of two other stories on which he had been working. Grunte was comedy. He did not matter a toss, save that his antics served the newspaper's purpose, which was to ridicule and thus undermine the institutions of the state and the people who manned them. Politicians in the *Brit* were, more often than not, venial, just as civil servants were idle, judges out of touch and footballers randy. Grunte had served his purpose. Ron was much more interested in Emma Kerr and David Lancaster. Not together, of course; that, in the words of the old Jewish joke, would be a very mixed marriage. Plenty of Hon. Members had the hots for Emma, while Lancaster's baptism could only be the consequence of unrequited, or disappointed, homosexual love.

Barton had watched Emma and Charles Harvey together at Bibendum. They were clearly very, very good friends. Harvey, who was a well-known Catholic who reviewed books for the *Tablet* (he had invented the slogan 'Protestants take the pill; Catholics the *Tablet*'), was married with three small daughters. He was also a junior minister and a coming man.

Charles Witherspoon Harvey, thirty-nine years old, married to Miriam Joseph and with two Montessori children, had been described by *The Times* on his promotion to the post of Parliamentary Secretary to the Minister of Transport as 'the rising hope of the fierce, unbending Tories' – proof, as if it were needed, of that once great newspaper's fall from grace. Harvey had little in common with the young Gladstone. He was not particularly stern, and his night-time expeditions into the West End of London were in search, not of fallen women, but of great restaurants. He had, for a

time, written a column for the *Telegraph* called 'Dinner
with Harvey'.

He had run into Emma Kerr at Simply Nico's. She
was with Peter Worthington Evans and the two couples
had made up a foursome. On the way home Miriam
said she thought Emma common and Peter boring. She
was right, of course, but her opinions did not bother
Charles. Peter did have all the charm of a Midlands
Young Conservative with views; but Emma, common
or no, was uncommonly pretty. She told the table that
she had never had an avocado pear until she had been
elected to Parliament. Charles thought her red hair
very fetching; after they had shared two bottles of
Californian chardonnay he wanted to make love to her.
Later Miriam was scathing about the avocado (she was
to refer to Emma as 'the dud avocado' thereafter),
rude about Peter ('the kind of Tory who would spend
his holidays at Alton Towers') and very tight-lipped
towards her husband. 'You made a fool of me, making
up to that ginger tart.' They had slept silently apart in
what had been Miriam's parents' double bed and, next
morning, there was no breakfast.

For some time Charles had been finding Miriam tire-
some. She had become silent, which is always a bad
sign in women. When Charles had telephoned her from
the House, and later from the Ministry, there had been
long pauses which he, Charles, felt obliged to fill. She
would answer his questions but seemed reluctant to
offer any information of her own. She had given up
cooking; or rather she increasingly used made-up
supermarket meals, poppable in the oven. She had
even stopped talking about her money, hitherto a
favourite topic.

Miriam was rich, not Heseltine rich, but reasonably
well off even so. An only child, she had inherited more

than two million on the death of her parents, together with a town house in Norwich. During their courtship she had once boasted that, leaving inheritance aside, she would never starve, 'I'm too pretty.' There was a second reason. 'All I need to make my living is a pencil and a copy of the F.T.'

In the first five years of their marriage Miriam had been as good as her word. She *was* very pretty, and she had a passion for moving her money around, telephoning her squad of brokers, sitting in front of the television marking her stocks and shares. In the mid–1980s, during the Lawson boom, she threatened to make Charles seriously rich. There had been setbacks since then, but as far as Charles could tell there was still a lot of water in her well. Their love-making had become infrequent. The last time Charles had tried to make love to her he had been asked what day of the week it was. He replied, through a mouthful of her hair, that it was Saturday. Miriam had abruptly broken off her embrace. 'If it's come to Saturday nights only, then you had better find someone else.' Perhaps she had a lover? It might well be one of her five stockbrokers. At least she never complained of brokers' pomposity, an affliction which she increasingly attributed to politicians. He was not aware of having 'made up to Emma', although he had found her fun. She had tiny, brilliantly white teeth, set in a mouth like a letter box, a feature which Charles had always found sexy. She had asked his views of people and politics and had laughed at his jokes. Nico Ladenis himself had come over to their table and Emma had asked whether he would teach her to make a soufflé. When she stood up to go, Charles noticed that she was wearing stockings with seams; very 1940s. He had been unwise enough to mention this observation later to

Miriam. It was probably the genesis of the 'ginger tart' remark.

Miriam's spitefulness gave Charles just the little extra encouragement he needed. At least Emma did not think him an economic illiterate. She thought M4 to be a motorway; Charles knew it was a financial measurement but of what he was not too sure. Miriam, on the other hand, read Sam Brittan first while disapproving of the hostility of his brother, Leon, towards Margaret. At breakfast in Tite Street, Charles turned quickly to the Westminster 'scene', to Matthew Parris or Simon Heffer; Miriam read the city pages. Emma, he was soon to discover, turned always to the fashion.

A few days after dinner *chez* Nico, Charles offered to share his taxi with Emma. They had been waiting under the canopy in New Palace Yard after the seven o'clock vote. Emma had asked him back to Dolphin Square to supper. Charles was not expected home until ten; after an almost imperceptible hesitation he accepted Emma's invitation. He stopped the cab at an off-licence and bought a bottle of Krug, remembering as he did so the avocado. I bet she never tasted Krug before she was elected to Parliament. That will be one 'first' to my credit.

Music is not so much the food of love as food itself. The restaurant trade is founded upon seduction. The beloved must first be fed if she is later to be made love to. Emma changed into her trouser suit, donned an apron and cooked a fry-up: eggs, back bacon, black pudding, tomatoes and fried bread. As she broke the eggs into the pan, she cried, 'That's one in the eye for Edwina.' They were not friends.

Charles, standing at the door of the kitchen, opened the champagne and admired Emma's backside. As she stood away from the stove to avoid the flying fat she bent forward to watch the progress of her dish. Was she wearing knickers? Charles, who was a Kennedy Catholic, felt the tug of lust. Confession was for constituents. He did not know that among Midlands' Tory MPs Emma's sin-green trouser suit was a totem, a prize that had been shared by seats as far apart as Dudley, Wolverhampton and Solihull. Romantic Tories likened it to the King's standard at Edge Hill; the more prosaic, as one more banner to be waved. 'Like my suit?' asked Emma, bearing a platter fit for two long-distance lorry drivers. 'Eat up your eggs.'

Six months later, it seemed to Charles that the affair was getting out of hand. His promotion to junior office had cast a shadow of apprehension over their coupling. The hoarding, 'Minister in Thames-side Love Nest', would bring his career to a halt. Cecil Parkinson had got away with it, but not without great difficulty. Public humiliation, resignation and exile: he owed his comeback to his role as courtier. 'Queen' Margaret, strangely enough, had not been a censorious woman when it came to matters of sex, and she had certainly been loyal to her favourites. But Cecil had been in the cabinet, and a former Party Chairman. Charles Harvey was a newly appointed junior minister of whom only the political correspondents had heard. He would sink, as he had risen, without trace. Although he would barely admit it to himself, Emma was, if truth were told, a pain. Not in bed; there she excelled. They made love every day after lunch in her flat. It was the only convenient time in a minister's life. His mornings, his afternoons (from two-thirty) and his evenings were packed with appointments. After ten o'clock, assuming there were no more votes or that Harvey could find a 'pair' from the other side, there were his boxes, and Miriam. He had let it be understood at the Department of Transport that he wished to lunch each day in the Members' dining room as a way of keeping in touch.

Emma's tiny flat in Dolphin Square was proximate, warm and soundproofed. It was as well that the walls were thick, for Emma was a noisy lover, much given to loud laughter, shouts of ecstasy and cries of encouragement. She came, thought Charles, rather like a tube train out of its tunnel. He remembered the injunction posted in a hotel bedroom in Paris – '*Défense d'émettre des cris de joie.*' However, the flat was not ideal for their purposes. Dolphin Square, with its swimming pool and pool-side restaurant, was a weekday 'home' for at least twelve other MPs, three of whom, including Petei Worthington Evans, lived in Beatty block. What was worse, the front door to Evans's flat was at the end of Emma's corridor, between her flat and the lift. She and Charles were often obliged to climb five flights of stairs in order to arrive undetected. Even then there was always the chance of Peter's knock upon the door. Charles had no wish to bump into Peter as he was buttoning up his flies.

Charles marvelled at Emma's sexual prowess. Her practices, picked up on the Midlands circuit, were catholic in their diversity. Charles was reminded of the Victorian judge in the Dilke case who had pointed out that the defendant had taught the woman in question 'all the French practices'. The bedrooms of Belfort had nothing on those of Brum. Would he dare to try one or the other on Miriam? He had a mental picture of a pale Miriam, sitting up in bed, wearing a pink bed jacket and doing her nails with tight-lipped concentration. She would be in for a surprise. He could always say he had picked up the idea from a Booker prize winner.

With her clothes back on, however, Emma was a bit

of a bore. She was entirely lacking in political cynicism,
a trait which Charles found attractive both in himself
and in others, and she was inclined to think in slogans.
He thought he could recognise Peter Worthington
Evans's prejudices, regurgitated in a slightly different
form. She would also call him 'Chas', which he hated;
her mother, who was often on the 'phone, called her
'Em', and she had the irritating habit of running her
hand through his thinning hair. It sometimes seemed
to Charles, as he struggled through receiving a delegation of road builders at the Ministry at three o'clock
in the afternoon, that Emma was altogether too much
of a good thing. And that bloody frying pan: Charles,
who had managed to keep his figure, now felt it to be
in danger. The pan was rarely out of her hands, but
then neither was he. Emma might taste of bacon, egg
and Heinz tomato ketchup, but she had the body of a
Diana. My cock has got me by the throat, he confessed
amiably to himself.

On the other hand, she would talk about Barry. It
would be difficult to imagine anyone much more boring
than Mr Kerr. 'I've grown out of Barry,' Emma would
proclaim, as they caught their breath. At the beginning
Charles felt that common politeness required him to
ask tentatively about her husband. 'What does he do?'
It appeared he sold caravans. He had also a taste for
Carling Black Label. He admired Norman Tebbit. He
would wake up in the middle of the night and eat a
Mars Bar which he had, earlier that evening, cut into
slices and put on a plate beside their bed. His favourite
dish was gammon steak and pineapple. He had wanted
to go into the 'RAFF', but his eyesight was not good
enough for the Royal Air Force. And he had spots all
down his back. There were times when Charles felt he
would scream if he heard that litany repeated once

again. Who bloody well cared how many caravans Barry Kerr sold in Droitwich last year? There was only one certain way to shut Emma up, and Charles took advantage of it. But how much longer should it all be allowed to go on?

It was Charles's brother Andrew who convinced him that he should break with Emma. He was a solicitor and a devout Catholic. He told Charles over a drink together one evening that he was not being fair to Miriam, who had given him three daughters. As a fellow Catholic she would never give him a divorce, even were he to seek one. His political career was about to take off. Norman Lamont had told Andrew at the Carlton that Charles had a future. As for Emma, who knew about her past? Pretty as a picture she might be, but she had – or so he had heard – slept around. Also, Miriam was stinking. Did Charles really want his source of funds to dry up.

Charles was told to pull himself together, confess his sins and stop behaving like a pubescent schoolboy. Chastened, he had returned home. Miriam nodded a greeting. She was sitting up in bed, reading a copy of *Country Life*; she adored its correspondence columns. 'Great Bustard seen on the Longmynd.' Charles was not so daft as to confess anything to Miriam. Instead, he kissed her. 'You're pissed,' was her reply. Later, in bed, he made up his mind to break with Emma. He would write her a letter tactfully telling her that it was in both their interests to bring their affair to an end. He knew she was politically ambitious. He would point out the dangers to both their careers. There was no need to become enemies; on the contrary, they should remain firm friends and allies.

It was this letter that Charles had put on the board in the Members' Lobby earlier in the evening. Now he regretted ever having written it. He had later warned her not to read it. He had been expecting Emma to arrive at his office beneath the Chamber for ten minutes or more. The room was empty, his boxes done. Charles poured himself a whisky and summoned up his strength for what might well be a *mauvais quart d'heure*. Anyone can begin the Beguine, he remembered. Give me the man who can end it.

7

After midnight is a good time for cabals. A division was not expected until around three a.m. MPs, their batteries only temporarily recharged by Grunte's speech, soon reverted to a state of post-alcoholic depression. The lucky ones slept in the deep leather chairs of the library, an array of trousered legs with heads covered with opened newspapers, a lull peppered by the noise of corporal explosions. The more robust sat at desks attending to constituency correspondence. The library staff, fellow prisoners, kept themselves busy attending to arcane tasks. They were for ever climbing ladders. Sometimes there would be a burst of chat, followed inevitably by sounds of 'shush'. The Commons library, four large interconnected rooms, *en enfilade*, came to resemble a war-time tube station in central London. All it lacked was Vera Lynn or a WVS trolley bringing hot milk in paper cups.

The smoking room was almost empty. A group of Tories for whom alcohol had become the great comforter sipped their scotches more slowly and amused themselves with bouts of malicious gossip. Asked with which great figure from the past he would choose to take lunch, Alan Clark replied 'Geoffrey Howe', and the resultant hilarity briefly lit up the room.

Clark, the son of 'Civilisation' Clark, lived in a castle in Kent and had a notable collection of motor cars, two of which were permanently stabled in the Members' underground park: a Rolls – AC1 – and a gangster's chevrolet. He was retelling a story that he had heard earlier from Joshua Morris. Joshua had asked a French general ('the sort that wears corsets') at a party in Strasbourg what he most liked about the British Army. The general had replied, '*Son courage, surtout en retraite.*' When asked what it was he disliked he had replied, diffidently and in English, 'All that Indian food they serve whenever I am invited for lunch.'

At the top of the Palace, in the battery of offices where the majority of the incarcerated had taken refuge, Joshua removed the three large, hard cushions that made up his regulation armchair and put them on the floor. He should have brought a camp bed, he reflected. Philip Goodhart had been seen earlier lugging his into the lift. Like all old soldiers he knew how to live off the land.

The three cushions were not long enough to accommodate both Joshua's head and his feet. He turned the light off, covered himself with his overcoat and tried to sleep. It was after one and the next vote should take place within two hours; too short a time for half a sleeping pill, even of the mild sort favoured by Felicity. The room was not properly dark; the all-seeing monitor screen with the words 'Mr Peter Lloyd' cast a milk-blue light over the room. Nor was there silence. Next door someone was having a row with his wife on the telephone. Joshua lay back, closed his eyes and bravely attempted a Molly Bloom-like inner soliloquy. An image of Felicity was conjured up, her face radiant with a smile of loving welcome.

'*Western wind, when wilt thou blow. The small rain down can rain, Christ, if my love were in my arms, And I in my bed again.*' *I wonder who the sixteenth-century Anon poet was*?

Felicity faded, to be replaced by the image of a provincial antique shop, dusty and incompetently run. Joshua collected early Staffordshire pottery, especially the square-base figures of gods and goddesses, made in response to the Classical revival of the 1780s and 1790s. On a shelf he would catch sight of a hitherto unrecorded figure of Mercury in the pale enamel colours of the potters Lakin and Poole. He lifted it gently and examined the base: it carried the potter's mark, a great rarity. Mercury, in green and mauve, seemed in perfect condition. The price, written on an adhesive label? £275. The vision faded. As it did so the monitor pinged, and Robert Cryer replaced Lloyd. Joshua deliberately spun the disc of memory. He had read somewhere that one's mind, with frustrating capriciousness, retained every experience, stored away as if on film, lacking only the index necessary for total recall. He had once, years ago at a London theatre, seen Ralph Slater hypnotise volunteers from the audience, permitting them total recall, even of natal experience. Joshua spun his disc . . . Very occasionally, some long-forgotten place, person or incident came on screen: a visit during the War to see Alfred, the gorilla, at Bristol Zoo, the theft of his Parker pen when at school, a forgotten stretch of road . . . Sometimes he would parade the dead members of his family, uncles, cousins, mother and aunts, all now buried in Shropshire churchyards, and try to remember their voices.

The thought of death conjured up an image which he had been determined to shut out. The man in the mansized cell, the entry to which was through a hole in the floor. He had read about it in Sybille Bedford's *As it Was*, a description of the trial of concentration camp guards held in Frankfurt in the 1970s. People had been forced into these boxes, where they stood, sightless, for the fifteen days in which they took to die. Joshua shut out the image of horror. Like many of his age, he could never forget the newsreel films of the liberation of the camps in 1945. He turned on to his side, pulled the coat around his shoulders and began to climb the Longmynd in Shropshire, a child with a picnic basket and a summer's wind in his hair. He would make a point of sending Felicity a copy of Hemingway's *A Moveable Feast*.

David Lancaster, tense with the fear of public humiliation, decided at long last that Wayne Ellis was not coming home to Sherwood Road. The unsufferable Greg had got out of his bed to tell him so. He had in all probability gone home to mum in Forest Gate. 'If he turns up I'll tell him you waited. You never can tell with Wayne. A sweet boy but with a nasty side to him. When crossed. Don't do anything I wouldn't do.' Lancaster cursed him and walked up to Lavender Hill in search of a taxi.

The streets were still mean but now empty. The *Sun* had left long ago; the reptile was tucked up at home in East Sheen, sleeping the sleep of the just. Lancaster debated whether to return home to his flat in Quex Road, West Hampstead, or to drive to the east of London, to Forest Gate, in search of Wayne. He could always go down to the House. He was away unpaired, and there must have been several votes since ten o'clock. He dismissed the idea of Forest Gate. Important though it was to placate his lover, he could not face the prospect of a rudely awakened mum and her recriminations. Nor could he face the House either, but his car was in the Members' car park. He suddenly caught the smell of stale wine. He had not washed his hair. He would return home to Quex Road and take the phone off the hook, clean his hair and get some sleep. As soon as he was up in the morning he would track Wayne down and, if necessary, buy his silence.

Wayne Ellis, who was patiently waiting for him in his Commons' office, listlessly reread his lover's constituency correspondence. At a knock on the door, he cried, 'Come in.' But it was not Lancaster; it was a small man in a double-breasted suit.

'Name's Barton,' he said. 'I work for the *Brit*.'

The third division of the night took place at nine minutes past two. The incessant bells roused 300 MPs from an uneasy sleep. They gathered silently in the two voting lobbies, as if returning from a wake, hair adrift, ties relaxed to show a hundred collar buttons. Compared to the vote at midnight there was no hilarity. It was the time of night when blood sugar levels had dropped to zero. Grunte, who was sleeping fitfully in his bed between silken sheets, a gift of the Motor Traders' Association, was never mentioned. He had been sucked clean of fun.

Slowly the voters shuffled forward to give their names to the two lady clerks sitting primly on their desks. They bowed automatically as they passed through the narrow doors where a Tory and Labour whip loudly counted them like so many sheep. 'Don't go home,' they were told. 'Another vote in an hour.' Some, despairing of sleep, went to the tea room where they revived themselves with large cups of bitter, stewed coffee; others returned to their offices or to the library in order to try to sleep. Charles Harvey, who had been waiting in his room for Emma since after eleven, sought her out.

'You've not read my letter?' The question was more *num* than *nonne*.

'Yes, I bloody well have,' replied Emma, who even at that hour of the night managed a bedtime bloom.

Harvey took her by the arm and steered her into the ministerial lift. 'Let's go to my room, as we arranged.' They travelled down in silence, each preoccupied with their own thoughts.

Emma was not a 'nice' girl, not in the sense that the elderly widows of Cheltenham colonels living quietly in private hotels would have recognised; but she could be excused. In the course of the previous day she had written one letter and received another: as the lift descended her mind turned to them both. The first had been to Barry, Barry of the caravans, of prawn cocktails and overdone steak on oval plates. Barry of the white wedding held in a brick-red Victorian suburban church, Barry of the blue suit and pink carnation. Boring Barry whom she had clearly outgrown. She had suggested that a divorce by mutual agreement should follow upon what already amounted to their separation. She had thanked God there were no kids. She had told him that he would be happier with another girl who had no objections to holidays spent in Bridport caravan parks, or watching motor racing. In short, she kissed him goodbye. Bloody Barry, what a terrible mistake it had all been. Her mother had told her she was far too young. She should have listened.

She had picked up the second letter from the board in the Members' Lobby some time before dinner. It was marked 'private' in Charles's big, bold hand. It was short, and she read it twice before the penny dropped. God, he wants out. The letter was affectionate (as well it bloody well might be, thought Emma, a picture of what the courts in this country call 'intimacy' springing unbidden to her mind). But it was sensible; that is, it took a worldly line, as between adults each of whom had as much to lose as the other. The affair had been a marvellous one; he did not want to bring it to an end – he loved her too much for that – but would it not be wise to cool it? He had been made a minister; she, too, would be made one in her turn. And he didn't trust Peter Worthington Evans ('Worthy-Evans', he had called him) who was fond still of her and jealous of Harvey. In conclusion, he had suggested a meeting later that night, and said something about the back-burner. She interpreted it, accurately enough, as the end.

Charles's ruminating was of a more philosophical kind. A minister's life is a dog's life, he reflected, but there were advantages. The office looked good in *Who's Who*. 'Parliamentary Secretary to the Ministry of Transport. 1990 – ' There was a car provided with a driver whose duty it was to wait for his master at all hours. There was the fleeting pleasure of introduction; 'Pray silence for the . . .', and of confession at cocktails; 'What do you do?' 'Actually' – Charles would wince when he heard the 'actually' – 'I am a junior minister.' The hours were hell and the pay poor, but at least he was on his way up the ladder of promotion. And there was a large and comfortable room, one of many such offices clustered beneath the Chamber itself. It contained an executive desk, two telephones, a drinks cupboard, two armchairs, and, best of all, a sofa, government issue, for the use of. For the use

of delegations, of supplicants, of fellow Members of
Parliament in search of favours; that is, not for copu-
lation, even between consenting Members.

The couple reached Charles's room and went in.
Charles locked the door and poured Emma a glass of
gin, but she waved it away. He took one for himself.
'I wish I hadn't written as I did,' he began. 'I don't
want to end the affair. I was afraid it was getting out
of hand. There's so much at stake. My brother read
me the riot act. He's so bloody devout. I do love you.'
He reached out to touch her.

Emma stepped back. 'The fuck you do,' she replied.

Emma felt her temper rising. It was after two in the
morning, she was tired and she felt no better than
anyone else did. And, after what she had been through,
first Barry and now Charles, a scene would more than
just clear the air. She came at him with her fists, shouting 'Shit'.

In the next-door room Mr Michael Portillo opened
an eye. He had always held the same opinion about
Charles Harvey. 'You're a sanctimonious shit,' cried
Emma, who, finding her wrists pinioned, had started
to knee Charles in the balls.

'Quite right, whoever you are,' murmured Portillo.
Charles let Emma go and fell to the floor, clutching
his groin. Emma, suddenly contrite, burst into tears
and, falling to her knees, attempted to rub the afflicted
parts. There was a tap at the door. Who in hell could
it be? There was another tap, deferential but nevertheless insistent.

'Busy,' cried Harvey through gritted teeth. 'Come
back later.'

'All right, it can wait. See you in the office at ten.
Don't forget the Chairman of British Rail.' It was Harvey's private secretary from the Ministry of Transport.

Why the hell wasn't he in bed?

Charles Harvey climbed to his feet and waited for a long moment before propelling the sobbing Emma towards the door. 'Get out, you bitch, you'll destroy us both.'

As he fumbled with the lock, Emma, her arm twisted behind her back, whispered, 'I'll crucify you for this. Or rather the papers will.' Harvey slammed his door shut and turned the key. Emma kicked loudly on the lower panels.

'Shit!' she yelled again. Mr John Gummer, who had been asleep in another room on the corridor, opened his door, only to close it quickly. Michael Portillo, sleep banished, broke into a wolf-like smile. How very unlike the home life of our dear Queen, he reflected. He was keeping a diary. How better to ensure a prosperous old age?

Harvey took a long drink of gin, and sat hunched for some minutes in his chair. The pain was beginning to slacken slightly. *I've got to stop her before she does anything stupid. It's no good sitting here. Christ, what a mess*. Harvey limped to the door and went looking for Emma. The corridor was empty, the rooms silent. It was half past two in the morning.

At ten past three, Joshua Morris had voted his Party's ticket for the fourth time. The debate on the Report and Third Reading of the Broadcasting Bill had begun eleven hours ago, at four o'clock the previous afternoon. Politicians and broadcasters did not usually get on. Eager party politicians who ran on zeal suspected the broadcasters of bias against them, while senior ministers distrusted broadcasters but had to keep their 'friendships' with certain prominent television people in good repair. It would never do for an ambitious young cabinet minister to quarrel with the Dimblebys, for instance.

Joshua, who was definitely not a partisan and suffered from an ability to see another person's point of view, had many friends among broadcasters. He had, in fact, become something of a broadcaster himself. Over the years the amateur detective had become the political observer, writing a good deal, speaking not often but sometimes rather well, watching with amusement the antics of his fellows. Long ago he had written a short book about the beauties of Shropshire which had, sadly, ended its days on Waterloo station. Peregrine Worsthorne, however, had praised his biography of Cecil Parkinson. 'A splendid life in only one volume; how much longer have we to wait for the other two?' he had asked. Joshua had been pleased by the comment, which had been printed on the back of the paperback edition. What were friends and enemies for, if one could not derive pleasure from their fads and fancies?

The Government lobby at the three o'clock vote smelt even more strongly of old scotch, old sweat and Old Spice. As the brave 200 waited for the doors to open upon their release, and shuffled slowly in their direction, Joshua noticed Richard Ryder deep in conversation with Chris Patten, the Party Chairman. Ryder looked too young to be an MP, let alone Chief Whip. Patten was looking even more lived-in than usual. Norman Tebbit, skeletal and touchy, disturbingly like Lon Chaney, seemed agitated. He had probably found a Tory moderate under his bed, reflected Joshua. At any rate, he was talking to Peter Worthington Evans. Joshua thought of joining them but before he could do so he felt a soft pull on his arm. It was Edwina Currie. She smiled pleasantly and asked whether he would come to Derbyshire and speak for her; a supper club. 'Choose your subject, Joshua. Cold ham and bakewell tart, no eggs.'

He was both flattered and dismayed. He had no wish to travel to Derbyshire and back in order to endure ninety minutes of chat followed by having to listen to his own speech. But, were he to go, Edwina would be obliged to come to Shropshire West, and the return match would please the ladies of Clee and Clun. It was important to please the ladies of Clun and Clee. 'Drop me a note, suggest a couple of dates, and I'll see what I can do.' Edwina smiled again and turned to go. Over her shoulder Graham Bright, John Major's PPS, who looked like Billy Bunter, was talking earnestly to Cranley Onslow. Bright was the Prime Minister's eyes and ears, his 'early-warning'. His master was presumably tucked up in bed, but Graham never slept. He was devoted to Major.

As the two men passed the clerks on their high stools Joshua saw Emma Kerr standing in front of him. She looked as if she had been dragged through a hedge. It was the custom for the most famous to sing out their names. Even Winston Churchill had done so. Emma was certainly pretty enough. Who could blame Charles Harvey, Peter Worthington Evans, Patrick Barratt and Uncle Tom Cobley and all? Joshua thought of Felicity asleep in her chilly Herefordshire house. She expected to be in London on Thursday. They would spend twenty-four hours together. Charles Harvey and Emma went their separate ways, Charles bruised, to his red boxes; Emma, to her room.

The Members' Lobby was more crowded than he might have expected from the ungodly nature of the hour. Joshua pushed past a group of noisy Labour MPs. People were getting their second wind. Leaning against the statue of Lloyd George was the lobby correspondent of the Press Association, but then he never went home. He had already done for Ralph Grunte. It was surprising, however, to see Robin Oakley of *The Times* and George Jones of the *Telegraph*. Ron Barton of the *True Brit* was sucking the stub of his pencil. Barton had once suggested to Joshua that he cover a murder trial for the paper. Joshua had refused. He might have done so for the *Observer* but not for a tabloid. His copy would have been cut and his conclusions distorted. A little further on, directly behind Barton, he spotted the woman from TV-AM whose name he could never remember. She smiled as he approached.

'Would you like to come on the programme and talk about the Grunte business?'

'No, thanks. Grunte was pissed. What more is there to be said?' He knew that, given the rules under which the lobby operated, his comment would be unattributed. He turned to the figure standing next to her.

'What's up, Mike? Why aren't you in bed?'

Mike White of the *Guardian* grinned. 'Couldn't stay in bed on St Crispin's Day. Haven't you heard? Kevin Catford is about to blow the gaff. He's decided that John Major has betrayed his inheritance – has abandoned Thatcherism. He's going to call foul in the Chamber at four a.m. Why the hell couldn't he wait until morning? He'll miss the morning papers. But I'm here to see the fun.'

The news that Kevin Catford was about to rock the boat spread down the corridors of Westminster and along the queue of the dispirited waiting for yet another cup of coffee. It acted like an electric current. It was as if a tonic restorative of near miraculous potency had been slipped into every cup. Once more fatigue was banished. Eyes were kept on the monitors which once more that night bore the words 'Mr Robert Maclennan'. Was it the sixth speech he had made during the debate? No one much cared. Joshua felt in need of coffee. He saw Peter Worthington Evans walking briskly through the tea room, fending off the cries of 'What's up?' He looked suitably grim, borne down with the responsibility of minor office. He was unshaven, and his grey suit unpressed. Only his Rotary Club badge twinkled in anticipation. It did not much matter what Tory MPs thought about Margaret Thatcher, they had no intention of missing the fun. Labour MPs, only too happy to witness their opponents in disarray, clustered round Tony Benn who was grasping his usual mug of milky tea. Joe Ashton was eating a toasted sandwich. 'Is it going to be Kev's Last Stand?' he asked as Joshua passed by.

Catford was no longer a Minister but he could not bear to be left out of things. Was he not the standard bearer of what had been called 'the back street Conservatives'? Well, let him wave it was the general view. How better to pass the long watches of the night? First the Grunte Show, now Kevin's boat-rocking exercise. He had never forgiven the Party for getting rid of Margaret. Joshua turned to Ashton. 'It's like having two Christmases. I don't think I can stand the excitement.'

Meanwhile Charles Harvey remained in pursuit of Emma Kerr. He waited in the Members' Lobby for five minutes or so, then rang her office. There was no reply. He went first to the whips' common room and asked if Emma had been permitted to go home. The pairing whip, somewhat distracted, said 'No.' David Lightbown was asleep in his chair. The room, which had the lived-in appearance of a rugby club's dressing room, was largely empty. So, too, were the glasses. Charles pressed on. Emma was not in the Members' Lobby, which seemed fuller than he expected. He walked through the Central Lobby, happily deserted, and looked into the families' room. A solitary Labour MP and his wife slumbered together on a sofa. They had not switched off the television, which buzzed quietly in the corner. Again, no Emma. Charles rang her office from a policeman's telephone nearby but there was no answer. In the smoking room the Scots Tory who had once danced the reel was reciting to glazed friends the poetry of Robert Burns. The library was full, but there was no sign of Emma. Charles glimpsed a despondent 'Worthy' Evans but he was damned if he was going to ask him, of all people. The tea rooms were crowded, and he caught sight of Edwina Curry. She was whispering in a whip's ear.

Finally, he took the lift opposite the Members' dining room and went up to her room. It was empty. She was probably in the ladies' loo. Charles sat in her armchair and waited. As he slumped, the monitor pinged, and the words 'Mr Catford' came on screen. Another rousing attack on the lefties in the BBC? Charles had no wish to find out.

By five to four the House had filled up. Mr Peter Lloyd, from the Government front bench, raised his voice an octave and gathered his strength. Could his colleagues really be that interested in the minutiae of his Bill? The Chief Whip trotted in and took his place. Kevin Catford was sitting on the front bench below the gangway in Churchill's old seat. Roy Hattersley, who had spent the hours writing the third volume of his lightly fictionalised account of his family's rise and fall, entered the Chamber. Kinnock was in Washington. Mr Robert Maclennan, who was on his feet, was interrupted by a Liberal Democrat whip who told him in an urgent whisper to sit down. 'Catford's going to blow the gaffe.' Maclennan, by now a little weary, wound up a speech to which no one was paying the slightest attention. The Deputy Speaker instead called 'Mr Catford'. The House, which by now had over 200 MPs present, fell silent. Catford got to his feet.

Kevin Catford was no Tebbit. And, if it came to that, he was no Parkinson either. He was not as savage as the one nor as smooth as the other. But few could match his devotion to Mrs Thatcher. In 1975, when Mrs Thatcher ousted Ted Heath as leader of the Party, Kev, as he was universally known in politics, had clambered aboard her wagon and had promptly published a biography of Mrs T. The wags called him the 'Hagiographer-Royal'. Mrs Thatcher herself had referred to him, after a temporary bout of electoral unpopularity, as 'the Captain of my Praetorian Guard'. A successful cabinet minister, clever, mordant and secretive, he had cultivated a deliberately proletarian image, even down to wearing a cloth cap. 'Pity no muffler,' had been Joshua's comment.

'Madam Speaker, may I crave your indulgence?' Sir Paul Dean was in his bed, his place taken by the other Deputy, Miss Betty Boothroyd. The south-west London vowels were undisguised. 'I usually have hard words for broadcasters. I have been known to disapprove of what I see as the left-wing bias of the BBC.' At this there was a murmur of approval from the Party's rottweiler wing. Catford ran a hand through his thinning hair. 'But tonight – or is it this morning? – I am about to do the meeja a favour. I am going to tell it that since Mrs Thatcher's resignation as our great

Leader' – at this Sir George Gardiner cried 'Hear, hear', and then looked sheepish. He was uncertain whether his approval would seem to relate to Mrs Thatcher or to her downfall – 'we have gone from bad to worse. The Prime Minister, and I have great affection for the Prime Minister' – at this there was a cry of 'pull the other one' from Tony Banks on the Labour benches – 'has changed course. He has been persuaded by others, less honourable than himself—'

At this there was a cry from the Labour backbenches. 'Where's Heseltine? He's the nigger in the woodpile.' It was Dennis Skinner, a man about whom it had been said that he would not hurt a fly unless it were stationary.

Catford continued, unabashed. 'The poll tax, once described by my Right Honourable Friend the Member for Finchley as the "flagship of the Thatcher fleet", has been abolished.'

At this there were cheers and Anthony Meyer was heard to say, 'And not before time.'

'Her tight rein upon public spending has been relaxed and, worst of all, her very proper stand against Europe has been abandoned. We have sold our birthright for a soft ecu. Those of us who voted for John Major in the leadership election did not expect to see our sovereignty abandoned and our economic policies, such as they are, put in the hands of a German-dominated central bank. This is not so much a Major Government, it is a Heseltine Government, and as the House knows I yield to no one in my admiration for the Right Honourable Gentleman, the Member for Henley.'

The word 'admiration' was played for what it was worth, and the absence of the word 'friend' did not go unnoticed.

'Mrs Thatcher was the victim of a squalid conspiracy.'

Joshua was tempted to intervene in order to make the point that whether or not there had been a conspiracy it was no worse than the one undertaken by Mrs Thatcher's friends in 1975 when she defeated Ted Heath for the Party leadership, but he thought better of it. The ladies of Clun and Clee still thought the world of Margaret. Catford continued his speech, turning round as if to draw support from those Tories who usually sit below the gangway.

'I conclude by saying, Madam Deputy Speaker,' – Betty Boothroyd had been looking anxiously towards the clerks on the table before her. Surely Catford was out of order? – 'that the Prime Minister's own position is no longer secure.'

At this there were gasps from the Government benches.

'May I ask him to guard his back? And to defend the Thatcher inheritance? If he does not then I will have to consider my own position.' Catford sat down abruptly.

At that moment the Leader of the House made an entrance, dressed in a kilt. Whistles of approval mingled with cries of 'Hear, hear'. Tony Banks offered to buy him an alarm clock.

The House emptied quickly enough; the Labour Party to gloat, the Tories to soothe their consternation with alcohol. Had not the Government troubles enough?

Once Catford had regained his seat Joshua spent some time chatting to the lobby correspondents who occupied most of the space in the Members' Lobby. He told them that he was surprised by the nature of Catford's charge. 'If there have been changes, they've all been for the good.' He was astounded by the fact that Catford had chosen to raise it in the way that he had. Margaret had had to go, and sooner rather than later. As for her successor, Joshua may have voted for Heseltine but he was perfectly happy with Major. Could Kev be suffering from the change of life?

The tea room was packed. In his earlier days the kitchen staff would have cooked bacon and eggs for those with strong stomachs. It was the classic end to an all-night sitting. Now the Labour Party ate beans on toast and the Tories toast and marmalade. Joshua went down to the bathrooms, on the ground floor of the building. He shaved in a large marble basin with brass taps. He felt hollow but curiously excited. He would return to his office and then, after the final vote, drive to his daughter's flat in Lewisham and spend the morning in bed.

As he walked towards the ground floor lifts he noticed that there was no sign of dawn breaking. He went out on to the terrace and stood by the parapet. He noticed that Emma Kerr was standing at the House of Lords end of the terrace talking earnestly to a man who had his back turned to him. After five minutes of fresh air and the contemplation of the flotsam that the Thames high tide threatened to wash on to the terrace itself, Joshua went inside and took a lift to his office.

It was getting on for four-thirty. He would write to Felicity and watch the early morning television. As he opened his office door he saw a red light burning on his special telephone. He dialled Members' Messages. Would he ring Independent Radio News? No, he would not. He turned on his set and switched it pointedly to the BBC.

* * *

The House finally rose at nine-thirty on the morning
of Tuesday 8 June. The vote on the Third Reading had
been held at seven-forty. The Government vote, which
had slipped down to the two hundreds in the dead of
night – the sick, aged, idle and infirm having been sent
home to bed – had risen to the low three hundreds.
The Prime Minister himself, wearing his grey suit, had
voted for the first time in the debate, accompanied by
a bleary-looking Graham Bright. He looked more than
usually grim. Richard Ryder, it later transpired, had
telephoned the flat at Number 10 at four-thirty with
the news of Catford's intervention. He had already
been on TV-AM and Breakfast Television. 'I have no
intention of ceasing to be the Queen's First Minister.
I have not betrayed my inheritance. We have work to
do.' Catford had been unavailable for comment.

The papers, free copies of which were distributed
around the Palace of Westminster every morning, carried no report of Kevin Catford's speech. The tabloids
led with Grunte, but it was not a story that would run.
The *Mirror* had a photograph of a younger, slimmer
Grunte pouring the contents of a bottle of champagne
over a red Jaguar. 'Cheers' ran the headline. 'Grunte
sinks in midnight champers.'

Sir Ralph himself had been roused not by hordes of
hacks (who had been originally primed to write the
story) but by his constituency agent. Jim O'Farrell had
once worked for Grunte's Garages. 'We are in trouble,
Sir Ralph,' he had told him. 'The telephone has not
stopped ringing.' To his secretary O'Farrell said, 'The
bugger's blown a gasket.' Grunte's recollection of the
proceedings of Monday night and Tuesday morning
were far from clear. They did not become so until he
had drunk three cups of coffee.

* * *

Peter Worthington Evans went home to bed in Dolphin
Square the moment the adjournment came up on the
monitors after the fifth vote. He felt exhausted; he was
due back in the Palace at two-thirty for the weekly
whips' meeting. He would snatch what sleep he could.

Charles Harvey was at his wits' end. His body ached
and he was near to panic. Try as he might he could
not find Emma. He had stayed in her room until the
division bells had rung for the vote on the Third Reading but she had not returned. Later he had told his
brother that he had written her a letter counselling
caution and begging her forgiveness, but he had torn
it up. He failed to catch sight of her at the seven-forty
vote; it was always hard to spot a particular person in
the crush, and he was chary of asking others as to her
whereabouts. He did ask Dame Elaine, but she had
not seen Emma for some hours. He noticed that Emma
had not taken a message waiting for her in the Members' Lobby. She must have gone home. The avuncular
policeman who had been on duty in the lobby had not
seen her. She had been glimpsed around midnight but
not since then. 'All tucked up, sir, I expect,' had been
his cheery opinion.

Charles summoned his ministerial motor car and
drove to Dolphin Square. He told his driver he was
going to have a word with Mr Worthington Evans
before going on to the Ministry. The Chairman of
British Rail was expected at ten o'clock, and he was
unprepared for the meeting.

Ron Barton lay in his bath in Dulwich collecting his
thoughts. His son's yellow duck had grounded on his
private parts. His deputy would cover the Catford/
Major story; he had bigger fish to fry. On regaining
consciousness (well before lunch) I should ring Emma

Kerr, he mused; we must continue our conversation. Then I'll put Jack on to finding Wayne Ellis, and ask Tracy to talk to David Lancaster. No shortage of hanky panky. People'd be surprised what they get up to in the fun factory. That Emma's hot stuff – she'd sell her grandmother for a bag of toffee. Or a roll in the hay . . .

Barton pulled the plug-chain with his toes and dried himself. Naked, he lay on the bed, staring up at his reflection in a mirror fixed to the ceiling. He was small but perfectly formed. Several years previously he had spent his bonus ('Vicar hangs himself in incest probe') on the very same mirror that Diana Dors had once had nailed to her ceiling in her house in the Thames Valley. 'Mirror, mirror on the wall, who's the fairest of us all?'

David Lancaster did not wake until eleven. He put his phone back on its hook and made himself some breakfast. He was fond of muesli with prunes. He hurried to read the papers. There was a bit about Grunte in the *Telegraph* but nothing about him. The *Mail* had a diary paragraph about Grunte, but nothing about the incident of the wine. Still, it was early days. The story of his humiliation would seep out into the gossip columns. If the reptiles got to Wayne Ellis before he did the story would move from the inside to the outside pages. He picked up the phone and rang Wayne in Sherwood Road.

The dreadful Greg was very solicitous. 'Yes, squire, I'll ask him to ring you the moment he arrives, but I expect he's gone down to the Employment. Looking for a job as a wine waiter. Will you give him a reference?'

Lancaster told him to fuck off. He went downstairs and got into his car. He would drive to Forest Gate.

As he moved slowly across London the car radio told him that Kevin Catford had accused the Prime Minister of selling out to the moderate wing of the Tory Party. Lancaster barely took in what he was saying. Mrs Ellis, a terrible woman whose sole comment on any subject ranging from the poll tax to the Prince of Wales was 'reely?', would know what had happened to her errant son.

The lift engineers did not arrive at the Palace of Westminster until after ten o'clock in the morning. A lorry had jackknifed at New Cross and the Old Kent Road had been at a standstill. They belonged to a small firm of south London contractors who had grown plump repairing the ancient lifts. They turned the power off, and one of them entered the shaft at the second floor in order to wind the lift down to the ground floor. The lift machinery was hot to the touch. His cries of alarm went unnoticed by the two other members of the team who waited for the lift to touch down. When it had finally done so, his instructions were only too audible. 'For Christ's sake, there's a woman hanging from a hook inside. I can see the top of her head. Get hold of a copper quick – and be careful how you open the lift door.' He was crouching on the roof of the lift, peering down into it through a gap in its roof. 'She's got red hair, and there's a nasty mess, blood or something, all over the floor.'

The cries of the workmen brought a policeman and a Commons attendant to the spot. They had been gossiping gently outside the door of the families' room. A group of waiters and waitresses who were reporting for duty turned and gawped, attracted by the fuss. The policeman put the blade of a clasp knife between the doors and forced them open. It had been ten years since he walked a beat. His arches had fallen, his sight was not what it used to be and a stately life had robbed him of breath. The doors resisted for a moment then broke open. A young woman with red hair was hanging by the neck from a hook at the back of the lift, suspended by a pair of green cotton trousers that had been tied tightly around her neck. She was still wearing her blue silk dress, and her knickers had been thrust into her mouth. Her feet swung to and fro an inch or so above the floor, on which was a pool of urine.

The policeman, his upper stomach seized as if by a giant hand, staggered back and and sat down on an adjacent bench. He was going to vomit. Before he did so he managed to cry out, 'Keep away and don't touch a thing.' A waitress, sobbing bitterly, held his head.

The head waiter, mindful of discipline, pushed through the crowd and peered into the lift. 'My God, it's Emma Kerr. It's an MP. Go somebody and fetch the Sergeant at Arms.' The attendant, who carefully avoided looking into the lift, ran off to do his bidding. The nursing sister whose task it was to minister to MPs when the need arose was not in her office, next to the families' room. She, too, had been up most of the night. The policeman got to his feet and went to a nearby telephone to call his inspector. Someone shut the lift doors and the waitresses wailed in unison.

After a few minutes the inspector and two more constables arrived, carrying a stretcher. Should he touch the body? Should he cut her down? Was she, in fact, dead? The inspector placed his hand over the heart. 'As mutton,' he said, as if to himself.

It is the custom, 'time-honoured' as the guidebooks say, that a Member of Parliament cannot die in the Palace of Westminster. Ministers have been known to drop dead at the dispatch box in mid-sentence, while backbenchers have expired on their feet, but the explanation has always been the same: 'The Hon. Member for so-and-so died on the way to St Thomas's Hospital.' Nobody had been murdered in the building since the then Premier, Spencer Perceval, was killed in 1812 by a lunatic. Airey Neave had been blown up by the Irish, but that had happened at the exit of the underground car park. The fiction would presumably have to be dropped in this case, for Mrs Emma Kerr, the MP for Corve Dale, had apparently been murdered and her body put on show.

The inspector had known nothing like it. 'Leave her until the CID get here.' He turned to the head waiter. 'Tell the catering manager to close the Members' and the Strangers' dining rooms until further notice.'

'Sir Charles will not like that one little bit,' the manager protested. 'And nor will the Members.'

'Sod Sir Charles,' replied the inspector.

He then told his constable to cordon off with coloured tape the corridors leading from the Lobby and the Lords in the direction of the lift and the dining rooms. The Sergeant at Arms would have to be summoned from his bed. The Commons attendant, who had only worn his uniform for a week, ran off to the Central Lobby to tell his mates what had happened.

'Edwina Currie,' he said, 'Edwina is hanging in the back of the lift with nothing on. They've done her in.'

He was told to pull the other one, but the sight of running policemen seemed to confirm his story. 'I don't know what the place is coming to.'

8

John MacGregor let himself down gently into his office chair. He had had a bad night and was feeling poorly. He called plaintively for a pot of coffee.

The Leader of the House enjoys a large room, furnished by what was once the Ministry of Works with furniture in the gothic taste: fumed oak, brass work and dull prints of forgotten politicians. He glanced at his agenda. It was ten-thirty a.m. The morning was thin enough, thank God: an appointment with the nursing sister who kept an eye on the health of MPs. She wanted to be given a supply of 'flu vaccine with which to guard against a fall in the Government's vote. She was cheerful but talkative, inclined to worry over the well-being of her flock. He would be happy to find the money for the vaccine. It would be spent in a good cause. The Leader of the House saw that he was lunching with the Speaker who, in his turn, was entertaining a parliamentary delegation from Bulgaria. Prawn cocktail, overdone lamb, and cabinet pudding followed by three speeches, one of which would be his. The Foreign and Commonwealth Office had supplied a draft.

He found himself gazing at a photograph on the wall opposite of John Biffen, one of his predecessors. Like Stanley Baldwin before him, Biffen was scratching the back of a large white pig penned in a Shropshire farmyard. Both pig and politician seemed hugely contented. I must give John back his picture, thought MacGregor. Why was there no picture of his immediate predecessor, Sir Geoffrey Howe? Had it been turned to the wall?

His secretary stuck his head around the door and interrupted, quite without ceremony, what had become an appealing train of thought. 'Edwina Currie,' he shouted. 'Someone's done her in. She's hanging in the lift. Dead as mutton.' The private secretary checked himself and continued more decorously, his Bristolian vowels properly subdued. 'She's hanging from a hook in the back of the lift. The maintenance men were called to stop the thing from going up and down' – he gestured with his arm, making a pumping motion – 'and one of them found her inside. Sister is with her, I gather, but she's beyond hope.'

John MacGregor shook his aching head. To gain time he asked his secretary to repeat what he had said. As he began to do so, MacGregor's mind turned to Mrs Currie's Derbyshire majority, for no MP can be called dead without the electoral consequences springing to the minds of friend and foe alike. Edwina's seat was safe enough even with the Government in its present mess. His private secretary had reached the point in his repetition where he began to pump his arm when a girl from the outer office put her head round the door.

'It's not Edwina Currie,' she said. 'It's Emma Kerr.' John gestured impatiently, his irritation getting the better of him. 'Make your bloody mind up,' he said quite softly, and then, rising to his feet, gestured to his private secretary to follow him in order to see for themselves. Fatigue, which had weighed so heavily a moment ago, was banished. His head no longer ached. Two attendants, who were gossiping in the corridor behind the Speaker's chair, were startled to see the Leader of the House trotting through the Chamber, scattering a party of visitors. Something was clearly up.

Sam Langford woke to an Essex sun. He felt rested. As he sat watching breakfast television in his kitchen/ lounge he was only dimly aware that the House of Commons, of which he was a member, had sat through- out the night. The newscaster, a West Indian girl, reported the fact that the House was still sitting with a faint show of surprise, as if to say, 'How daft can you get?' But she stayed with the text carried on her revolving autocue. At the end of the bulletin – riots in Birmingham, the murder of an Asian newsagent in Brentwood, the defeat by knockout of a British boxer – she repeated the headlines: 'Mr Kevin Catford, in a speech in the Commons late last night, has attacked John Major. He has accused him of selling out, of betraying the Party's Thatcher inheritance. He told him to "watch his back".'

Sam Langford put down his copy of the *Daily Mail*. 'Did you hear that, Dawn? Kev's come out against the toffs.' Dawn delicately cut the fat off her slice of bacon. She rather liked the toffs; they had such nice manners.

Sam Langford, the owner of a builders' merchant business in Dagenham had, immediately after his elec- tion to Parliament, swopped the *News of the World* for the *Sunday Telegraph*. The news of the screws was dead common, even though Woodrow Wyatt did write for it. His wife Dawn had said so. It might have been good enough for his dad and mum, but it was no longer good enough for him. A Conservative Member of Parliament at the age of fifty, with a flourishing business ('I will soon go public') whose accountant had told him that he was worth half a million, the driver of a 12-litre Jaguar and a turbo-charged Ford Escort, he was the first man in the avenue to install a jacuzzi. He was fond of telling his friends that until he got into Parliament he had always believed a jacuzzi to be a breed of dog. He had become a man of property, and the *Sunday Telegraph*, with its business news, sports coverage and Frank Johnson column, seemed just the job until, in the autumn of 1990, the paper carried an article entitled 'Essex Man', together with a drawing of a Tyson-necked brute in a shiny double-breasted suit holding a six-pack of Carling Black Label.

Essex Man was, or so the anonymous author of the piece had claimed, the 'new wave' of Mrs Thatcher's Conservative party. He was crude, uneducated, prejudiced and very patriotic. He had abandoned the Labour Party because it was soft on blacks and against hanging murderers. He had got a transfer to the Tory Party because he saw in Maggie the robust exemplar of this desire to get on. The father of 'Essex Man' had once been a docker at a time when there were still such people in the East End: union militancy had driven away the ships, and the Yuppies had taken the place of the dockers. Dad had moved in late middle age to the vast housing estates built on the bleak Essex Marshes. His son, 'Essex Man', had made money in motors, demolition and in the City.

Sam Langford had gone one better: he had persuaded the Tories of Ongar that he should carry their standard into battle. As an MP he had joined the 'No

Turning Back' group of Tory MPs and had amused himself by baying at Edward Heath whenever the former Premier made a speech.

The *Sunday Telegraph*'s article was, in Langford's words, 'a diabolical liberty', and he had instructed his local newsagent, who was called Jones, to send the *Mail on Sunday*, a journal in which Langford discovered Sir John Junor. They were, although they did not know it until it was almost too late, made for each other.

Langford had been a Member of Parliament for only three years but he had swiftly picked up the tricks of the trade. He had a flair for getting his name in the papers. He took his Thatcher mug of milky Nescafé into the sitting room and wrote out a statement for the Press Association. He then read it out at dictation speed over the telephone.

'Kevin Catford speaks for all real Conservatives when he backs Maggie. She was the victim of time-serving Tories. We must remain true to her inheritance. When I arrive in Westminster this morning I will carry with me the support of all my constituents and of all true Tories.'

The media, which had been striving to persuade Kevin Catford himself to appear on their lunchtime programmes, fell back on Langford as a worthy substitute. Kevin Catford spoke to the 'World at One' from the BBC's radio car; but Langford recorded two two-minute spots for commercial radio, as well as giving an interview to the *Sun*. Even better was the request from the *Daily Mail* to write a leader page article on the theme 'Essex Man speaks up for Maggie', 1,000 words at 50p a word. He promised to write the piece after lunch and fax it through to the paper by four o'clock.

Langford hurried to his garage, his grey shoes

perfectly matching the battleship tones of his Jag. His anxieties, which yesterday had been so strong, had faded beneath the excitement. He patted the flank of his car and murmured, 'Lovely motor,' and, after a second or so, 'to hell with Fatima.' With luck the girl would vanish back to the East End, or even to Pakiland itself, into the woodwork and out of his life. Sam Langford was a knight of sorts, riding to the defence of his liege lady.

The Sergeant at Arms placed his sword on the Leader of the House's table. 'This,' he said, sounding even to himself like Jack Hawkins, 'is a bad business.' He was, after all, a Rear Admiral. Better Jack Hawkins than Noël Coward, he thought, for the previous evening he had been watching *In Which We Serve* on BBC2.

'A damned bad show,' murmured John MacGregor.

The private secretary brought in cups of undrinkable coffee.

'The body,' said the Sergeant, scratching a silken calf with the tip of his Biro, 'has gone to the pathology lab at St Thomas's Hospital for examination. We await its report. The Chief Superintendent here suspects foul play.'

Christ, thought the super, who was in charge of the police in the Palace of Westminster, this is like the first act of a Priestley play.

'I shall have to make a statement to the House at three-thirty. Quite unprecedented. Not like poor Airey,' said MacGregor. He turned to his private secretary who was passing a plate of Nice biscuits around the company. There were no takers. 'Draft a statement for me with the help of the Clerk, the Sergeant and the Police Authorities. I must telephone the Chief Whip at Number Twelve.'

The Chief Superintendent shifted uncomfortably in a leather armchair that was far too low. Unless he sat upright he suffered from what Americans delicately call 'gas pains'. 'You will want me to take charge of the investigation, Leader?'

Leader? thought MacGregor. I'm not Hitler. 'I must consult,' was his reply. The situation was unprecedented. 'Could she have hanged herself?'

The Super thought it unlikely, but he conceded that it might be as well to await the lab's report. It would be on his desk by midday. In the meantime someone would have to prepare a statement for the press. The news of Emma's death was, no doubt, common knowledge throughout the Palace of Westminster already.

The Sergeant's secretary knocked and entered. She was a pale blonde with an Arlesford accent. 'The refreshment department has rung, sir. Shall I tell them business as usual?'

The answer was 'yes'. No MP should be allowed to go hungry.

MacGregor was already feeling the pressure of the day. He was pink in the face. He had been up most of the previous night and Catford's *démarche* had not made life any the easier: to that extent the Rt. Hon. Member for Arnos Grove had achieved his purpose. MacGregor's private office was keeping the media at bay, but for how much longer? What effect would the unwanted publicity have on the public? There was a message from Cranley Onslow, the chairman of the '22, wanting him to ring him back. Urgently. The Party would be restive. Catford goes ape, and now to cap everything a fellow Tory MP had been found dead, murdered, so it seemed. What if the killer were to turn out to be another MP? How could he (or she) be unmasked? What effect would such a scandal have upon the reputation of Parliament and Parliamentarians? There was already an element in the popular press that took a perverse delight in placing politicians in the pillory. David Montgomery's *Today* was a bad example. 'Killer in Westminster Love Nest. Our Masters and their Mistresses' by a correspondent. 'Watch this space.' Like hell he would, thought MacGregor.

The Leader of the House sat behind the expanse of his gothic desk, and pondered. Should he invite the Met. to undertake the investigation? Wouldn't the sound of coppers' feet treading the corridors of Westminster give rise to endless points of order in the Chamber, followed by actions for Breach of Privilege? What status did the police enjoy in what was, in fact, a Royal Palace? The first thing to do must be to alert Ryder. The Chief Whip should know all about Emma Kerr, her friends and admirers. Was he not the captain of John Major's football team, the man who was paid to know the best, and the worst, about his colleagues? Could he point the finger? Everyone knew that Emma Kerr was a fast woman, but she was heavily outnumbered by lubricious males. Was it not Disraeli who said that only married men were regular attenders at the House of Commons? *La belle* Emma had always been another reason to turn up and vote the ticket.

MacGregor, who was a cautious Scot of the sort that might have made a good ship's doctor, thought of Joshua Morris. Had he not discovered who killed the Grand Master of the Primrose League? Why not ask him to investigate? Better Morris, who was a Member of long standing, than an abrasive policeman like Taggart. Morris might not have been as grand as Adam Dalgliesh but he was not an aggressive tyke like Mark McManus. The Leader of the House watched more television than was perhaps good for him. He broached the idea of Morris to his private secretary.

'If he came up with something quickly, in a day or so, Leader, we might well keep the fuzz out of the precincts. It could be worth a go.'

'Don't call me Leader,' snapped MacGregor, whose mildness of manner could be deceptive. 'Am I wearing a brown shirt?'

Joshua was awakened by his daughter with the news that he was wanted on the telephone. Joshua, quite properly, spent his London allowance on the mortgage and upkeep of the small, first-floor flat in Lewisham. The street was silent, his neighbours respectable blacks whose children went to school and church wearing knee-length white stockings. His pretty daughter was unmarried and a commercial artist. Joshua had revised his Conservative Central Office 'biography' to end with the message that his last ambition was to have all four of his children in gainful employment; a *cri de cœur*. But the flat was convenient and he was glad to be of use.

It was John MacGregor's office on the telephone. Would Mr Morris come and see the Leader of the House on a matter of extreme urgency at five o'clock that afternoon? The secretary's voice held the flavour of Bristol; not of Clifton but of Redland and Hotwells. Joshua said he could do so, but what was up? 'Haven't you heard?' The private secretary's voice took on that accusatory tone so often adopted by those who have the advantage of prior information of value. 'Emma Kerr has been found dead. Hanging in the lift by her tights. Foul play obviously. The police are all over the Palace. I believe John will ask for your help.'

There was a pause in which Joshua resisted the temptation to say 'What?' There could be no misunderstanding the nature of the message, but the implications would take longer to digest. 'I'll do anything I can. Tell John I am at his service. Presumably he won't want me to say anything to anyone about our meeting?'

'That's the ideal,' was the reply, the intrusive 'l' attaching itself involuntarily to the final vowels; as is the custom in Bristol.

Joshua made himself a cup of coffee. The BBC news bulletin at midday led with the story of Emma's death. Kevin Catford's rebuke to John Major was pushed into second place. Joshua had had little to do with Mrs Kerr. He had admired her from afar, but who had not? Her gorgeous figure and flaming hair had brought her the attention usually reserved for the more brilliant parliamentary performer. She had been the butt of many a schoolboy joke, and the list of her admirers, which had doubtless been exaggerated to make a good story even better, was carnal knowledge; or common knowledge in the tea and smoking rooms at least.

He could only guess as to how much the press knew. Most of it, he supposed. But MPs do not get murdered. They get killed. Airey Neave, Tony Berry and Ian Gow had all died suddenly at the hands of the IRA. But not murdered by their colleagues on the precincts of the Palace of Westminster. Was Emma popular? he wondered. He thought so. She was friendly as well as pretty, and her giggles had lit up the tea room. Her politics had given no offence. Perhaps she was one of those persons about whom old friends would say that you had to know her very well indeed before you could dislike her. In which case it was vital to find out for certain who, among many, had known her very well indeed.

Joshua dressed quickly and was soon driving through Lewisham and up the Old Kent Road. The 'World at

One' would be interesting, but lunch in the Members' dining room ought to be more so. Why should Emma Kerr have been killed? Had she withdrawn her favours from a lover? Had she learned something to someone else's disadvantage? Was she killed in error? The last was surely not possible. If she had been killed by mistake for someone else she would not have been put obscenely on display.

At the Elephant the traffic stalled, and he bought a lunchtime *Standard* from an agile vendor. The front page carried a large photograph of Emma dancing with Peter Worthington Evans at the previous year's Blue Ball, the Tory Party's smart fund-raising event. 'Fun-loving Tory comes to Sticky End' was the headline. Fair enough, he supposed. The story was short on detail but long on Emma's political past. 'A prominent Midlands Young Conservative elected for the first time at the last election, married to a salesman . . . small majority in a seat where the by-election should prove difficult for the Government.' There was a small picture of Emma on her wedding day running a gauntlet of men holding car-jacks as if they were swords. The nude photo was also reproduced – 'Young Tory models for the motor trade.' The innuendo was plain. The late Member for Corve Dale had been fast.

As he crossed the Members' Lobby on the way to lunch, Joshua was handed a sheaf of pink message slips by an attendant, a former Royal Marine. 'You're in demand, sir,' he said pleasantly. Three of them were from newspapers asking Joshua to ring back. I'm damned if I'm going to write Emma's obit for the *Independent*, said Joshua to himself. If the Indy obit pages could tell how a Maharajah was a proud member of the 'Mile-High Club', thanks to the favours of a stewardess, what would he be expected to make of

Emma? BBC Radio 4 wanted him to return their call.
So, too, did Felicity. That was surprising. Felicity and
Joshua communicated at regular times and on regular
channels. I wonder what's up? he asked himself, still
in the Lobby. He was approached by a second attendant, a former member of the SAS. The attendant
handed over a letter. It was from Peter Worthington
Evans. Could they have words before the seven o'clock
vote? In Evans's room? Joshua was intrigued. Worthy
Evans was not in his area whip; why should he want
to talk to him? He had been, however, a good friend
of Emma's. Who knew? He stuffed the messages into
his pocket. They could be dealt with after lunch.

'The bird's back in the nest.' Greg's cheerful cockney
voice gave David Lancaster a feeling of relief. He
glanced at his Dunhill wristwatch: it was after eleven
in the morning.
   'Very seedy, he is. But contrite. I put him to bed
with a hot milky drink laced with rum. Sleeping like a
baby. Come round to Dunroamin' later in the morning
and I'll cook you lunch.' Lancaster said he would be
there before twelve. He replaced the receiver. Contrite, was he? the little swine. I must bring the whole
nonsense to an end, even if it does mean giving Wayne
and his dreadful mum two tickets for a Mediterranean
cruise in the *Orpheus*. They would soon get bored with
the lectures on the ancient world. The stakes were too
high. He couldn't afford to run the risk of exposure,
and Ellis's escapade with the wine would not be easily
forgotten. He had learned some time ago that a taste
for rough trade means turning a blind eye to the vap-
idity and treachery of teenage 'bum boys'. They may
look like the Young Apollo (Lancaster winced at the
thought of Wayne's spots) but they were usually as

thick as planks, and deceitful with it. His and Wayne's lovemaking had been intense but short-lived. How reliable was he? Lancaster felt fear. Wayne could lose him his seat in Parliament, and with it his livelihood and reputation. It would mean more than two bloody tickets for a Mediterranean cruise, he thought bitterly. I shall be obliged to pay him alimony; so much a month as if he had been an abandoned wife. A meal ticket for life.

Lancaster rescued his car from a prowling black woman traffic warden and set off once more, this time to Battersea. He turned on the radio. Emma Kerr had been found dead in the Commons. A fuller report was promised for later. Lancaster shrugged. Emma meant nothing to him. He slipped a tape of Maria Callas into the machine. 'One Fine Day,' she trilled. For her it might well have been, he reflected. But not for poor bloody me (or Emma).

The way from West Hampstead to Battersea follows the path of the No. 31 bus. It cuts southwards through the social layer-cake of London's postal districts. West Hampstead shades into Irish Kilburn, shabby safe-houses in depressing streets lined by dusty and damaged trees.

Kilburn becomes the western end of Maida Vale as it climbs towards Neasden and the Wembley Heights, a rash of council housing, Chinese take-aways, launderettes and newsagents selling pornographic magazines, the pitted pavements a haunt of sharp black kids wearing trainers, and white OAPs shuffling homewards fending off stray dogs with half-filled carrier bags. The route then plunges under the elevated West Way, opened in the 1970s by the young Michael Heseltine, and wanders through the black slums of Ladbroke Grove, the muggers' paradise. It is in all likelihood the most disheartening five-mile journey in London. Yet after Notting Hill Gate the traveller enters a different world – Kensington Church Street, with its antique dealers and generals' widows, its restaurants that charge thirty pounds a head for lunch, a land where nearly everyone is a poll tax 'winner'. Good Old Maggie.

The 31 bus route finishes at World's End, the backside of Chelsea, under the council flat where Christine Keeler feasted on her memories. It is only another ten minutes across Battersea Bridge and past the Latchmere Centre with its fly-blown fight posters and a raft of railway bridges. David Lancaster, whose spirits were low enough in Quex Road, NW6, was even more depressed on arrival in Sherwood Road, SW11.

Greg was wearing a frilly apron. 'We'll let His Lordship sleep on a bit longer. I shall cook one of my omelettes and toss a green salad.' His high-pitched laugh grated on Lancaster's nerves. Lancaster picked up *The Times*. It carried a sententious leader, calling upon its readers to defend Thatcherism. There was a small report on the front page about Sir Ralph Grunte's 'midnight outburst'. The libel laws had discouraged the writer from mentioning drink; unbelievably, he had fallen back on the tired old formula of 'tired and emotional'. There must be a different code by now for 'pissed', thought Lancaster, turning to the arts page.

Greg, frying pan in hand, put his head around the door. 'Oh my, wasn't our wandering boy sorry for himself. But I expect he will want to tell you all about it. The course of true love and all that.' He brought a Japanese radio into the sitting room and turned it to Radio 4. The forced hilarity of the 'News Quiz' wrestled for Lancaster's attention with a report on the previous night's television. Richard Ingrams won. Lancaster did not know who he disliked the more: Ingrams or Robert Robinson. Greg rushed through the room, making for the front door. 'Whoops a daisy,' he cried. 'Out of eggs.'

Wayne Ellis's appearance coincided with the start of the weather forecast. He was wearing an old dressing gown of Lancaster's, a garment that looked as if it might have belonged to the young Noël Coward. Wayne looked sheepish, as well he might. Lancaster waited for him to break silence. A deep depression was expected over Rockall, Bailey and Fastnet. Where the hell is Fastnet? Lancaster's fuse spluttered into life. 'You've made me a laughing stock in the House, pouring a bottle of wine over my head like that. And for no good reason. I had no intention of cancelling your cruise.'

Wayne said he was sorry. He didn't know what had come over him. He had spent part of the previous night at the Captain's Cabin, a club in Seven Dials; later he had taken a mini-cab back to his mother's in Forest Gate. He thought he had lost his job in the Commons refreshment department – 'That Irving won't want me back.' What was worse, he was cleaned out, broke. Greg had a friend coming to stay, and he had nowhere to go except back to Forest Gate. 'You know what a cow my Mum can be.' Lancaster knew only too well. There was always the boxroom at Quex Road. As Wayne knew only too well.

James Naughtie's voice trailed the items to come on the 'World at One'. 'The murder of Emma Kerr, the MP for Corve Dale, has dismayed the Commons.' Naughtie's voice was Scottish in its disapproval. 'The body of the thirty-one-year-old Tory MP was found this morning hanging by her trousers in a lift opposite the entrance to the Members' dining room. Mr John MacGregor, the Leader of the House, is to make a statement to MPs this afternoon. In the meantime, Scotland Yard is making enquiries.'

Wayne's mouth fell open, revealing teeth made brilliant by the National Health Service. He shouted, 'Oh, my Gawd,' and burst into floods of tears. Lancaster looked at him coldly. 'What a lovely lady,' sobbed Ellis. 'I opened my heart to her last night. Told her what a beast you had been to me. She was so kind.' Wayne's bellowing redoubled its volume just as Greg kicked open the front door, a box of eggs in one hand and a bottle of hock grasped by its neck in the other.

'Come now,' he cried. 'Kiss and make up.'

Sir Ralph Grunte was forced awake again at eight o'clock by the incessant ringing of his electronic alarm clock. It had been a gift from the Birmingham Chamber of Commerce. The room revolved, but Grunte shut his eyes and started to collect his thoughts. How civil of the cab driver not to accept money on his return home after midnight. He said something about having been paid once already, but by whom? He had been one of those cabbies who, once they cotton on to the fact that they have an MP in the back, bombard their victim with a volley of prejudice. 'All them blacks . . .' He had been insufferably matey. Grunte knew that he had, as he would have put it, 'drink taken', but there is no excuse for such familiarity. Had he not been elected the Chairman of the Party's backbench Europe Committee, entrusted by his peers with the task of protecting Britain's sovereignty under threat from unscrupulous foreigners? He had a dim memory of standing to make a speech in the House, but his recollection did not stretch to its effect or to its conclusion. He had slept badly, troubled by dreams in which he had kissed the bald head of Mark Fisher, the Labour

Party's frontbench spokesman on the arts. Thank God it wasn't Clare Short's.

He staggered to the bathroom in his long night shirt, looking rather like a disreputable Arab. The noise of his evacuations and ablutions resounded with all the vigour of a tropical storm. It was not until he sat looking into a cup of black coffee that he remembered that at ten-thirty he was due to show a party of constituents around the House. Twenty-five snotty-nosed kids and two prissy schoolteachers, the fifth form of the Arden Hill Convent School. He felt far too ill. His secretary, Mrs Peters, would take his place.

At the other end of the telephone, his secretary's voice sounded far from enthusiastic. She was a major's widow, who 'did for' two other Tory MPs, and was doing her level best to swop Grunte for someone more congenial. In fact, she was looking forward to a free morning during which she would visit the Harrods food hall, but she told Grunte that she had an appointment at ten-thirty with another of her 'gentlemen'. Mrs Peters was efficient, although sickeningly coy. 'What have you been up to, Sir Ralph? According to TV-AM this morning you have been a naughty boy. I gather your speech made quite a stir.' Ann Peters's voice held a touch of malice. 'I expect you're all over the papers.'

Grunte put down the receiver without a word and quickly collected the *Daily Telegraph* from his letter-box. He could find no report of any speech, although he was pleased to read a paragraph in 'Peterborough' about his election. It was headed 'Speaks for England?' The bloody woman must have been drunk. Comforted by the lack of any mention of his speech (surely to God he couldn't have kissed that bugger Fisher on his bald head?), Grunte began to get dressed. What he

did not know was that the *Telegraph* had been put to
bed just after midnight; the London editions of the
tabloids stay up very much later.

The school party, which had left the Forest of Arden
in a charabanc at six-thirty without having breakfasted,
stood morosely in the Central Lobby, their unattractive
bottle-green blazers with a yellow stripe providing a
touch of bilious colour. The girls, who were fifteen
years old, wanted to go to the pictures or, at the very
least, to wander around the West End looking at boys.
The two schoolmistresses had a long day to which to
look forward. A sedate progress around the Lords and
Commons would be followed by a sandwich lunch in
Green Park, a visit to Westminster Abbey and the
Tower of London, then back to Warwickshire. The
girls had been promised fish and chips to eat on the
bus. Sir Ralph had agreed to address the party in a
committee room after his tour. To 'put 'em in the
picture', he had said.
  The school party was surprised to see the tiny figure
of Mr John MacGregor trotting manfully across the
lobby. He was puffing like Billy, and was closely followed by a youngish man. It turned to watch him
disappear down a corridor, only to return with what
appeared to be a stretcher party. Two uniformed men,
flanked by three policemen, carried a stretcher on
which was a person almost entirely covered by a table-
cloth. A woman, evidently, for her pretty, pink-
toenailed feet protruded from the soiled covering. The
Leader of the House was escorted by a tall man in knee
britches, silk stockings and carrying a short sword. A
nurse in uniform brought up the rear of the procession.
A policeman shouted, 'Make way', and the group
snaked round by the side of the attendants' desk and

disappeared. The startled girls were assured that someone had been taken ill. As the 'sick' woman's face had
been covered, this explanation cut no ice. It was ten
twenty-five, and there was no sign of Sir Ralph Grunte.

The senior form mistress took a copy of *Today* from
her bag and began to read it. On the front page of the
tabloid, alongside the lead story ('Maggie Digs In') was
a photograph of Sir Ralph, a bottle of champagne in
one hand and a brimmingly full glass in the other. The
headline read 'Brotherly Love', and the caption to
the picture (taken at the opening of the Birmingham
Exhibition Centre some years before) said simply
'Cheers'. The article that followed, which had been
cobbled together from Press Association reports, told
of a commons outrage in which Grunte, 'obviously the
worse for drink', had been rebuked by the Speaker,
and, having kissed Mr Mark Fisher, whom he had
previously insulted (here the papers' lawyers had hesitated), on the top of his head, had been bundled out
of the Chamber by his Party's whips.

The story, which was continued over on to page two,
was there illustrated by a photograph of Grunte on a
horse, stirrup cup in hand. 'Tally ho,' cried the subedi-
tor. The report ended on an ominous note. It was not
the first time Sir Ralph ('balding, fun-loving and sixty-
one, twice married with two children and a Staffordshire bull terrier') had been in trouble with his constituency party. A Mr Sam Hammersley, the Chairman of
the Arden Tories, was quoted as having said that last
night's episode was 'the giddy limit'. Nowhere in the
paper was there a mention of Grunte's election as
Chairman of the Party's Europe Committee.

As the senior form mistress was in the act of passing
the newspaper to her colleague, Sir Ralph Grunte
entered the Central Lobby from the St Stephen's end.

'Dear Ladies,' he bellowed. He moved towards his guests, right hand outstretched. He was dressed as if for the Warwickshire county show: check suit, red silk pocket handkerchief, highly polished brown brogues. The form prefect, who this time last year had had her bottom pinched by Grunte ('You are making it up, Fiona, take a stripe'), broke into a nervous grin. The bruise had taken six days to disappear.

The senior form mistress hurriedly pushed her copy of *Today* into the depths of her cavernous bag, displacing a Jilly Cooper novel; her junior accepted Grunte's hand, Sir Ralph, with the playfulness of an elderly bookmaker, turned it palm downwards and bowed over it, bringing her fingers to his lips, presenting a shiny expanse of backside to the fifth form. There was a wave of laughter, quickly stilled. 'Gather round me, girls,' Grunte commanded. 'I shall tell you all about the Mother of Parliaments.' The reek of stale brandy hung in the air. The girls watched him warily. The metal tip of his zippered fly protruded at half mast. Another three inches, thought the junior form mistress, and I'll have him arrested.

9

Charles Harvey had gone without sleep. Unable to find
Emma, he had gone home to bathe and put on clean
clothes. His ministerial Montego honked deferentially
outside his drawing room window at precisely nine
forty-five to take him to the Ministry. It was as black
as an undertaker's car. Miriam had been constantly on
the telephone, speaking either to her mother, who
lived near Nice, or to various girlfriends. Harvey's telephone bills were horrendously high: it was just as well
the Revenue was prepared to allow two thirds of the
cost to go against his Parliamentary expenses. He felt
hollow and light-headed. The effects of deprivation of
sleep would not hit him properly until after lunch, and
it was his bad luck that he would be obliged to sustain
his Secretary of State for Transport Questions at two
thirty-five that afternoon.

A ministerial stint fielding Parliamentary Questions
came round every month or so; three quarters of an
hour at the crease, facing the fast balls of all and
sundry. Lunch on such days was a sandwich affair (no

alcohol) held at the Ministry, during which the three ministers concerned tried out on the civil servants their answers to questions already submitted and set about anticipating the supplementaries. An MP was allowed to table a question, which was then answered; he was then permitted a supplementary, the contents of which he was careful to keep to himself. The 'game' of answering Parliamentary Questions demanded good footwork, good forecasting and an alert mind. A decent night's sleep was a prerequisite.

The business of the House would then continue with a debate on the Community Charge introduced by the Liberal Democrats. Harvey would play no part in it. But it did mean a vote at ten. He would get his office to ring his 'pair', a northern Labour MP, to see if he would accommodate him. Such an arrangement, however, was subject to the whips' veto, for they held the curious view that the Government's majority should not be permitted to fall below a healthy number. Victory was not enough. Harvey realised with a sinking heart that he could well be stuck at the House until at least twenty minutes past ten. Why the hell had he not stayed a merchant banker? He would have been a lot richer, and better rested.

Great ministries are functional, unattractive buildings that resemble hospitals but without the smell of patients or carbolic. The Transport Ministry shared a hideously ugly complex in Marsham Street, built in the late 1960s, and the 'home' of the Department of the Environment. Beneath the complex were deep shelters into which the anointed were invited to take up residence in the event of a nuclear attack; there was a bed reserved for his boss, but not for Charles Harvey. As a junior minister, with responsibility for railways among other things, Charles had an office on the twenty-second floor with a view across the rooftops of official London. The Secretary of State, however, occupied an office on the twenty-third, with a view that stretched as far as Hampstead Heath to the north and Crystal Palace to the south. Cynics feared that the sight of so much real estate, ripe for development, would prove bad for the characters of great men. And who could say they were wrong?

Harvey's office had none of the fake walnut and instant ancestor that typifies the lair of a successful banker, and it lacked the executive toys, abstract art and Eames's chairs so beloved of advertising agents who have gone public. It was simply furnished. On his desk was a coloured photo of Miriam, taken at Gleneagles – they had been guests of BR – and a chunk of marble, pinched from the Temple of Apollo at Delos. Pride of place went to a Basset Lowke model of a GWR Star class locomotive. Charles had long been a railway buff. On the wall were three prints, a Lowry, a Piper and a Ben Nicholson, all of which were the property of the Crown. Four armchairs of the regulation kind encircled a low table on which there lay an assortment of tired magazines ranging from the *Spectator* to the *Railway Gazette*. In an anteroom lived his private secretary and two typists. The coffee was instant, but the cups, made of heavy white earthenware, bore the insignia of the LMSR: he had found them in the Portobello Road.

Harvey sat himself down and began to read the brief with regard to the visit of the Chairman of British Rail. Reid wanted more money for investment; the Treasury and the Prime Minister's office had combined to stiffen Harvey's resolve not to pay the piper. It was their view that British Railways was not well managed.

Charles Harvey did his best to concentrate. The brief

should have been absorbed late last night, but Emma's
visit had prevented him from reading it. What an appalling scene she had made – a scene that could not have
gone unnoticed by his ministerial colleagues at work
on their boxes in adjoining rooms. She might just as
well have advertised their affair by taking space in
the *House Magazine*. And where the hell had she
disappeared to? It was vital that Harvey made contact with Emma as soon as possible, if only to reas-
sure himself that she did not contemplate doing anything that might be damaging to them both. The
column of figures on the page moved in and out of
focus. For the fifth time he read the two opening para-
graphs of the brief. His genitals hurt and his head
ached. He cursed Emma, only to ask his private secretary to try to get Mrs Kerr on her home number.
'There's no answer, Minister.'

At ten-thirty, Bob Reid, flanked by two of his execu-
tives, was ushered in. As can sometimes happen, the
meeting passed off more easily than Harvey had
feared. He drank cup after cup of noxious coffee and
let Reid and his party make the running. They had a
case to make and make it they most certainly did. They
explained the gross underfunding of the railways, the
inelasticity of continual fare increases and the general
lack of new rolling stock. They complained of ASLEF
and the National Union of Railwaymen. They hoped
that the new Prime Minister himself was not prejudiced
against the railways, as Mrs Thatcher appeared to have
been, and feared that 'unlimited' sums earmarked for
motorway construction would only make congestion
worse. Harvey secretly agreed, but set his face to show
no more than polite attention. He did not attempt to
question any of Reid's assumptions, or his figures. He
said only, after fifty minutes, that his guests had raised

important points of principle, and that he, Harvey, would like time before he could make a considered response. His private secretary intervened once in order to encourage Harvey to press a particular point, but Charles waved him away.

At half past eleven, the British Railwaymen were shown the door, and Harvey, awash with coffee, went down the corridor to the ministerial lavatory. When he returned to his office his PS was standing by his desk with a message in his hand. 'Sit down, Charles,' he said. They were of the same age and on good terms. 'I have some terrible news. Emma Kerr has killed herself. Her body has been found hanging in a Commons lift.'

Peter Worthington Evans was not informed of Emma Kerr's death until he woke at ten. He had returned to his flat after the last vote at seven-forty, before the adjournment of the House, and the traditional cry of 'Who goes home?' It was not his turn to put out the lights. He had closed his curtains, taken the telephone off the hook and fallen into bed. In the course of one long night he had put a drunken Grunte into a cab, alerted Ryder and others to Catford's intervention and spent three hours on the bench listening to what had been, with two remarkable exceptions, a very dull debate. He would be expected to return to the House for the weekly whips' meeting that would be held early that afternoon. Before then he would be obliged to telephone the thirty members of his flock, the Tory MPs for whom he acted as 'area whip', and for whose voting intentions and general attitudes and behaviour he was responsible. Ryder had asked for the temperature to be taken once more in the light of Kevin Catford's *démarche*. Would they back the new

Government? That was the question he had to put. He set his alarm for ten.

On awakening, Peter had to run the gauntlet of protective wives. No, Charles/Harry/Julian were not available. They were asleep, and their spouses had no intention of wakening them. The hours they were obliged to spend at the House of Commons were unforgivably long. What a way to run a railroad. One wife told him openly to get lost. Red-eyed Susan. She had the reputation of a termagant. Peter had sat next to her at an area Conservative dinner. She had worn an emerald-green evening dress and a brooch in the shape of the head of a fox with ruby eyes; she was a meteorologist. Lucky old Harry.

Eventually Peter made contact with Sam Langford in his office in Norman Shaw North. Langford's views came as no surprise. Kev was right. Mrs Thatcher had been treated very badly and Major & Co. were selling out. Peter waited patiently for him to finish the diatribe.

'You know my views, Peter. You must like 'em or lump 'em. By the way, have you heard about Emma?'

Evans asked guardedly, 'What about Emma?'

'Snuffed it,' was the reply. 'Hanging by her drawers in some lift. Naked and unashamed. What the hell's the place coming to, I'd like to know?'

Peter had often wondered himself. 'What the hell are you talking about?' Angrily he stressed the word 'hell'.

'What I said, Peter. Keep your shirt on, matey. I'm telling you she's dead. The body was discovered earlier this morning. Some say she did herself in, others that she was killed. John MacGregor's knickers are in a twist, I can tell you. There's to be a statement at three-thirty. Bloody pretty woman.'

Peter sat in his chair, his head held in his hands. He was shaking with shock. Poor Emma. Poor silly bitch. Poor beautiful silly bitch. Their affair had not lasted very long, and he had been shattered by her betrayal. He had fallen very hard for her. His thoughts turned to Charles Harvey, who had stolen her affections. That languid snob with his rich wife, his facetiousness and his studied manner. Harvey had once written a piece in *The Times* in which he had made fun of the Young Conservatives. It was all about red-brick universities, compulsory tennis and drawing the raffle. Peter had taken offence. He had no wish to be patronised by that bloody public schoolboy. He thought of Emma as she had been the afternoon they had walked across Hampstead Heath and had supper in a Polish restaurant in the village. They had returned to her flat and she had let him love her.

Peter went into the bathroom and was sick in the pan. As he cleaned his teeth another thought struck him, and fear overtook remorse. Christ, there would be an investigation into Emma's past. That is, unless she had killed herself, and that seemed most unlikely. She was not the suicidal sort. And even then the coroner might make inquiries as to her state of mind. The affair could become common knowledge. Could Charles have ditched her? Could that swine have broken her heart, as Emma had broken his? Setting his chin, he decided that if he could drop him into the shit he'd do it.

Peter drove down to the Commons and made his way to the whips' common room which let on to the Members' Lobby. As he crossed it he saw Grunte in the midst of a party of schoolgirls, holding forth like some Old Testament prophet. He had quite forgotten about old Grunte. He owed him the price of a taxi.

Lunch in the Members' dining room on Tuesday 8 June was a relatively subdued affair. Morale was not helped by the presence of policemen both in uniform and plain clothes examining the lift at the entrance to the dining room itself; an area had been cordoned off with tape around which MPs and guests, en route to the Strangers' dining room further down the corridor, were obliged to skirt.

Not everyone had heard the news of the discovery of Emma's body. Grunte most certainly had not, but he was already living in a fool's paradise. He had marched his 'gals' round the Lords and Commons and shown them the oak ceiling of Westminster Hall. He had marshalled them upstairs into a committee room where, for ten minutes, he had told them of the long hours of duty, the burdens of high office, the pressure of constituency correspondence and the obligations both of chastity and sobriety, all of which, when taken together, were but a small part of the price paid by the public-spirited men and women who put themselves forward for public office. At this the senior form mistress murmured 'Amen'.

When he finished his pep talk, he stood at the door of the committee room, handing out to each of the girls as they passed a sweet drawn from boxes of Cadbury's Roses chocolates. It was a habit in which he indulged during elections; a habit which a series of Party agents had tried unsuccessfully to discourage. Clutching Grunte's gift in hot hands, the giggling girls made for Green Park and school sandwiches; the two mistresses thanked Sir Ralph for his time and trouble. They would most certainly mention to the headmistress Sir Ralph's kind suggestion that he might one day give away the prizes at the school's speech day.

Grunte sat at the large table by the window. As was

his custom, he mustered the 'condiments' in a row before him. Grunte was as territorial as a cock robin. His head had cleared and the adrenalin was flowing. Booze did not affect him. 'Place is overrun with coppers,' he said cheerfully to Joshua, who tactfully agreed that that was indeed the case. He had rung Felicity who had told him that she had changed her plans and was on her way to London. They were to meet at six forty-five in the Central Lobby. This was the best of news, for they had not seen each other for three weeks. Felicity would be bringing a picnic of little delicacies: boned quail stuffed with prunes soaked in Armagnac, home-made pâté, French bread and brie: it was Joshua's task to provide a good bottle. He had, waiting in the larder (not the fridge) in Lewisham, a bottle of Corton Charlemagne, Laflaive '86. A *dîner intime*; but how soon could they decently get away? John MacGregor wanted to see him later that afternoon and there was a vote at ten. Perhaps he could find a pair?

Peter Worthington Evans sat down at the table without a word. He looked pale and distraught. He knows, thought Joshua. But by now most people would have heard of poor Emma's 'accident'. Those who had not heard it on the radio news bulletins would have learned of it from their secretaries, from whom there were no secrets. Others, who reserved dictation for later in the day, would have been informed upon arrival. In the Members' cloakroom downstairs was a ticker tape, the sheets from which were put on display by an attendant. Joshua had the habit of marking with a red pencil news that he considered to be important: the relegation of Huddersfield Town to the fourth division; the results of Wimbledon and the death of a much-loved Member of Parliament. The account of the discovery of Emma's body hanging in the lift that morning had been underlined twice, once in red, then in black. A gaggle of Members stood in front of the machine, appalled yet obviously excited. Ominously, the cause of death was not given. 'I hope to God she wasn't done in,' said Sir George Gardiner. There was a murmur of agreement.

'A bloody bad business.' It was Sam Langford. He was a stranger in the dining room. He dined occasionally but rarely lunched.

Joshua nodded in assent. 'Poor woman,' he said. 'And what a terrible end.'

Langford bridled. 'Had it coming to her, if you ask me. A prick-teaser if I ever saw one.'

Joshua fought to contain his temper, and there was a general intake of breath. The tone of Langford's rebuke was offensive: if Tories discussed serious matters (which they did rarely) they did so with a light touch; good manners serving to dampen the fires of controversy. But Langford was universally regarded as being beyond the pale. He was, as the 'old things' put it, 'a frightful fella'. His comments about Emma triggered an extraordinary response. Peter Worthington Evans, who was sitting opposite Langford, leaned across and punched him in the face.

Langford shouted out in pain and drew back his right arm, to strike. Joshua caught hold of it. Evans got to his feet and aimed another blow at Langford. It landed on his ear. He was shouting, 'Take it back, take it back, you bastard.' Nicholas Soames, an Hussar and all of sixteen stone, grabbed hold of Worthington Evans and pulled him away from the table. Langford dragged his arm away from Joshua's grasp and got to his feet.

'You fucker,' he yelled at Evans. 'You'll have to find another poke.'

Lord Hailsham, who had just made the journey from

the Lords on two sticks, stood aghast. He had never in fifty years in Westminster witnessed such a scene. A solicitous waiter helped him to a seat. Langford marched out of the dining room, scarlet in the face; Evans shakily resumed his seat. He was trembling with passion. Joshua filled Evans's glass with wine from Grunte's half-carafe. Evans, who had been pasty, had turned a nasty purplish colour. 'Drink it up, quickly,' Joshua commanded. It looked as if Evans was about to have a seizure. The head waiter and three of his staff were hovering over the table clucking like so many indignant fowl. What happened on Monday night, with wine being poured over a Member's head, was bad enough; fisticuffs was worse. Members sitting at other tables had got to their feet; slowly they subsided.

Hailsham took command. 'Bring two bottles of champagne,' he thundered, 'and get back to your post.' It was the voice of a Lord Chancellor.

The wine waiter brought glasses for the table, and the two bottles of House champagne. At Hailsham's bidding he filled every flute.

'Cheers,' said Grunte, raising his glass to Hailsham. 'Frightfully bad show, but then I always did think Langford to be *vin ordinaire*.' He turned to Joshua. 'What is the difference,' he asked loudly, 'between a woman suffering from pre-menstrual tension and an Islamic fundamentalist?' All waited. 'You can reason with an Islamic fundamentalist.' All smiled, faintly.

Joshua ate his mushroom omelette and tomato salad. Worthington Evans made his apologies. 'Can't think what got into me.' He was still trembling uncontrollably.

There was a stressful silence, broken by Grunte. He was inspecting the menu. 'Root vegetables. Can't abide roots. Give me the most appalling wind. All right for an hour or so then I'm blown up like a balloon. Nothing I take'll get rid of it.'

Three voices each began a separate conversation in an attempt to steer Grunte away from the state of his bowels. Loudly, Joshua asked Hailsham what dish he thought was eaten by Christ at the Last Supper. Was there anything in the New Testament which gave a clue? 'Fish,' cried Quintin. 'Courtesy of St Peter.' At this there was general laughter.

Peter Worthington Evans, his colour less imperial than before, spoke to Grunte. 'You owe me ten quid for that taxi.'

A shifty look came into Grunte's bloodshot eyes. 'What taxi?'

Worthy Evans's colour began to mount once more. 'You bloody well know what taxi. The one I shovelled you into last night after your so-called "speech".'

Grunte rose slowly to his feet, a picture of injured innocence and massive dignity. 'I have to say that I am not prepared to remain at table with a man who is as offensive as he is violent. I will take my complaint to the Chief Whip.' He turned to Lord Hailsham and bowed slightly. For a second he looked like a stage butler. 'My Lord, thank you for the bubbly.' Grunte moved slowly towards the door.

'*Nunc dimittis*,' intoned Joshua. 'Now let thy servant depart in peace.'

Worthington Evans made a tremendous effort. He told quietly but with some glee the story of Grunte and the taxi: 'Ten quid it cost me to get that sod home. Driver afraid he would be sick all over his cab. And that is not his only bit of luck. Catford's speech and now Emma Kerr's death have knocked Grunte out of the papers, although one or two of the tabloids carried the story this morning. The Chief spent most of the

morning arguing Mark Fisher out of making a formal
complaint to the Speaker after Questions this afternoon. It's about time the Labour whips did us a favour.
We had to say that we'd make public the affair of the
cockerel and the Labour MP in Baden Baden. That
brought them round.'

Joshua, who had been listening with half an ear to
the Worthy Evans recital, wondered what on earth the
affair of the cockerel in Baden Baden was all about.
He was tempted to ask but thought better of it. Life
was already full to overflowing.

Nicholas Soames joined the table. 'I'm told there is
free champers.' Hailsham filled his glass. 'Ian Gilmour
told me that the day he came into the House for the
first time an old buffer he didn't recognise came up to
him and said, "Are ye Jock's boy?" Gilmour said he
was. "Well done," he bellowed. 'What had Ian to do
with it?'

Nicholas Soames was a favourite of the waitresses
who, upon his arrival, all came running. 'Catherine,
my dear,' he boomed, 'bring me my usual.' The 'usual'
turned out to be a large plateful of smoked salmon. In
a Tory Party which had, in the words of an elderly
survivor from the days of Harold Macmillan, 'lost a
button off its cuff', Soames was alone in sporting five
buttons on his. 'The mark of my regiment' was his
explanation. He had not heard the news of Emma's
death. Joshua told him the details. Whether it was
murder or suicide was not yet officially established
although, as Morris pointed out, suicides do not usually
suspend their own corpses by their trousers from the
backs of lifts.

Peter Worthington Evans excused himself and
thanked Hailsham for the champagne. 'I must go and
see the Chief Whip,' he said.

As soon as he had gone, Quintin observed, 'And so I wouldn't wonder. Can't have colleagues assaulting each other in public, whatever the provocation. I don't know what the place is coming to.'

Joshua called for his bill and duly signed it. He would return to his office upstairs and deal with his correspondence. There would be a statement at three-thirty by MacGregor on Emma's death. At five Joshua would meet the Leader of the House as requested. At five forty-five he would meet Peter Worthington Evans. At six he would attend the meeting of the '22 Committee of all Tory MPs called to discuss the charges made by Kevin Catford and others about the leadership. He would then meet Felicity in the Central Lobby. Back to Lewisham, supper and early to bed.

10

Ron Barton left Britannia House with a flea in his ear. His editor had not been best pleased. 'Find out, and find out before the Bill who done her in.' Happily the the editor did not often put his pen to his paper. What were journalists for, for Christ's sake? Ron Barton had left Motherwell comp. with an 'O' level and a desire to be insincerely rich. He and others like him wrote the copy; the editor, as he would say, kept his finger on the pulse and pointed them in the right direction. 'That Emma Kerr had it coming. I want the story and I want it fast. There's a bonus in it for you. Next time the Yard sends a copper to Miami to bring home a villain, you can take a fortnight off.' The editor made it sound like a fortnight in Babylon. It was Ron Barton's ambition to live in Miami, the city with a better class of vice.

As the paper's motor drove him towards Westminster, he brought out his pocket dictaphone. 'Emma Kerr. Early thirties. Tory MP for Corve Dale since the last general election. A real goer. Married to a dull sort in the Midlands. Foot-loose and fancy free. Who did she once fancy? *Cherchez l'homme*.' Ron liked that. He could lead his story with '*Cherchez l'homme*', although he would have to have a word with the subs.

Emma had been active politically in and around Birmingham before her election to Parliament; the paper's Midlands stringers could feed him the necessary info. Once she had been elected she quickly surfaced in the gossip columns. She had been seen about with Marcus Kennedy, Paul Easterbrook, Peter Worthington Evans and Charles Harvey. Lunch here, dinner elsewhere, and a long evening spent at the Blue Ball. It was only ten days or so ago that he had spotted Harvey and Emma gazing into each other's eyes over the calves' liver and onions at Bibendum. Very friendly they were, and Harvey a minister. If it came to that, Evans was a whip. Had he not bumped into Emma last evening in the Lobby and suggested lunch?

As a member of the Press Lobby, Barton was permitted to let his car enter the gates of New Palace Yard. The policemen on duty noted his arrival but were careful not to salute. Barton entered the Palace by a back door known to the clerks as the 'tradesmen's entrance'; his secretary Avril was at her desk. 'A Mr Kerr from Sutton Coldfield has telephoned you. Emma's hubby. He's left his number.' Barton's spirits rose. Kerr might cost the paper a bit, but what a story: 'WE DRIFTED APART SAYS MURDERED MP'S HUBBY.'

'Get him, Avril, my love. We was made for each other.'

Barton rang, only to be told that Mr Kerr was on his way to London and would be staying at the Regent's Palace Hotel. Avril left a message with the desk for Kerr to ring Barton soonest.

After a ham salad and chips in the Press Lobby's

café, Ron took the lift down to the Members' Lobby where he took up position under the statue of Clement Attlee. His pager, stuck into the belt of his trousers like a gun, would alert him in case of developments upstairs. Acting on impulse, he had sent Avril to the hotel to await Kerr's arrival, so as to prevent any attempt by a rival paper to win an interview.

The Lobby was packed with journalists. John Cole of the BBC, Mark Lawson of the *Independent* and Robin Oakley of *The Times* were clearly more interested in John Major's future than in Emma's past. Barton's junior would take care of Catford and Co.; Barton was on to the story that really mattered.

John MacGregor found the autopsy report on his desk on his return to his office after lunch. The Bulgarians had been bloody: too many protestations of eternal friendship, too many toasts. (The Leader of the House had limited himself to one glass of Bulgarian plonk.) The senior Bulgar had survived the vicissitudes of his country's politics for more than twenty years. MacGregor had read his 'file', provided in advance by MI6. The man was a brigand. British politics were, in comparison, a piece of cake. The Party's opponents either won office in their turn, and made a mess of it, or, if the 'opponents' happened to be Tories, languished in a state of benign neglect. The Party whips simply withdrew their carrots. There might be something to be said, MacGregor reflected, for a Gulag of our own in the Isle of Man or some Godforsaken spot, where the Tebbits, Critchleys, Wintertons and Meyers of this world could build a railway. Might make life easier for everyone else, for a time.

The Leader of the House slumped into his armchair

and replaced his spectacles. He picked up the report and began to read:

> Emma Kerr had died from strangulation some time between five and seven-thirty that morning. It appeared that she had been throttled by the legs of her trouser suit, a garrotte that had been untied then used to suspend the body by the neck from a hook high up at the back of the lift. It was unlikely that she had been killed in the lift itself: the probability was that she had been murdered elsewhere, in a nearby office, either her own or someone else's, and the body carried into the lift. The garrotte had been tied from the nape of the neck and tightened with such force as to fracture the larynx, or voice box. Mrs Kerr was attacked from behind while sitting on a chair. She might not have seen her assailant.

MacGregor asked his office to fax the report through to the Inspector at New Scotland Yard, and his private secretary to use the text as the basis for a draft of the statement he would make in the House at three-thirty. As he gave instructions he waved his right hand in a curious, circular gesture. MacGregor had many of those little mannerisms which repel or please us in a public speaker according to whether or not we agree with him. His mind turned to other matters. What was to be done about Kevin? The answer was 'not much'. He was a law unto himself. Onslow had called a meeting of the '22 Committee for six o'clock, a meeting at which Kevin Catford would be called to account.

The statement at three-thirty was brief and received in a shocked silence. The Shadow Leader of the House echoed John MacGregor's sorrow and sense of outrage. He committed the Labour Party to give the police every cooperation. He murmured something about a promising career cut off in its prime. The Leader of the Liberal Democrats moved that the House adjourn as a mark of respect, a suggestion that was welcomed by the House as a whole. After a brief consultation with the Chief Whip, MacGregor accepted the motion, and at three-forty the House stood adjourned. The death of an MP was a commonplace occurrence; the killing of a Member by an act of terrorism was not unknown; but the murder of one MP, very possibly by another, was unprecedented.

As MPs, the bulk of whom were bone-tired from the effect of the all-night sitting, streamed out of the chamber into the Members' Lobby the Government whips did their best to alert their flock to the special meeting of the '22 later in the day. Some took no notice and made for home; others turned wearily towards the tea room or to their attic offices. Sam Langford, who was sporting a black eye, said to a neighbour that Emma Kerr had got what was coming to her.

Ralph Grunte, who felt like a man who had got up late and has been late all day, sat in his office reading the accounts of his midnight escapade in the tabloids. Earlier, Marjorie had rung him from a hotel in Stratford-on-Avon. 'You're an old fool,' she had told him. 'And what's more, you're not getting a penny of my money.' Grunte had also received a pink telephone message from his accountant marked 'Ring me, urgent.' On top of everything else, the Revenue was breathing down his neck.

At five o'clock Joshua was ushered into the Leader of the House's room. He sat in an armchair and refused a drink. The Great Ones in the Party went in for cocktail cabinets, not the sort favoured by Lancashire multi-millionaires which light up when attacked but discreetly wooden affairs in which sit bottles of malt whisky and Gordon's gin. The Leader poured himself two fingers of the hard stuff.

'Bad business about Emma Kerr.'

Joshua said nothing. The comment was a rhetorical one.

'There's no doubt that she was murdered. By whom we do not yet know. I don't want the police treading on too many sensitive toes, blundering into Members' rooms, upsetting the Skinners of this world. I know Bernard Braine is very unhappy at the prospect of a full-scale murder hunt taking place within the Palace. So, too, is the Sergeant.' Bernard Braine was the Father of the House, a nice old thing with a short fuse. 'Would you help me find who done it?'

The use of the word 'done' was nicely judged. It had all been too much for the Leader of the House. It was rather as if Brutus and Cassius had been obliged to attend to a domestic killing while on their way to the Capitol. 'You know the place and the people well; you've been in the House as long as I have' – longer, thought Joshua, but he let it pass – 'and you have a reputation as a sleuth. Were you willing to take it on I could give you twenty-four hours before bringing in the police. Will you give it a go?'

Joshua was tempted; but there could be snags. Were a public announcement to be made as to his task, the newspapers, broad and narrow, would give him no peace. And would 'the colleagues' be prepared to talk to him? He would also need to be given the full cooperation of the whips' office; access to the personal files which the members of the *broederbond* had long kept on other MPs. If Ryder were to talk to him freely, he was prepared to try his hand; but there would have to be nothing said about his 'appointment', if that was what it could be called. Perhaps the Chief Whip might give him a chit, a *laissez-passer* with which he could at least open his colleagues' doors? And could it be taken as read that he was looking for a Tory MP?

The Leader of the House drained his drink and patted his lips with a handkerchief that he took directly from his cuff. Years ago he had once seen Sir Fitzroy Maclean make a similar gesture. It was the custom of the grander sort of Scot. He had appropriated it, and it was now his own. 'I am afraid the chances are that the guilty man is one of us. Emma had several lovers in her short time here, but no one has ever suggested she spread her favours across the party divide.'

Joshua liked the use of the word 'divide'. Politicians talk a language of their own, swiftly adapting the clichés of one trade to suit another. To the outsider it sounded pompous, almost as grating as the habit adopted even by the most recently elected MP of referring to the Great Ones in public by their Christian names – 'John', 'Michael' and 'Douglas'. Even Mrs Thatcher herself had succumbed, referring in public to 'Winston', much to the irritation of the Churchill family. In truth she had never exchanged a word with the Old Warrior.

'Okay,' said Joshua, 'I'll give it a whirl. Incidentally, Peter Worthington Evans has already asked to see me "on a private matter". He was friendly with Emma for a time. He should be waiting for me now in my office.'

'I thought he might be able to help you,' said Mac-Gregor, who rose to his feet and escorted Joshua into the corridor. He was obviously relieved. 'Keep me in touch; any time of the day or night, and ring me tomorrow morning to report progress. Tread carefully: our colleagues have long toes. Good luck.'

Joshua walked through a darkened Chamber and into the Members' Lobby. Outside the government whips' office was a notice with the message: 'House Adjourned. 1922 Committee meeting due this evening postponed until Wednesday.' The attendants had switched off the lights on the letter and telephone message board. Ron Barton sat on a wall-seat, contrary to the rules. He caught Joshua's eye. 'Mr Morris,' he called, rising to his feet, but Joshua ignored him, walking swiftly down the corridor towards the Central Lobby. Barton made to pursue him but thought better of it. Was the President of the Sherlock Holmes Society of Great Britain on the same track? Had he, too, realised the connection between Harvey and Emma, and seen its importance? And was not Morris something of a sleuth? He would wait a moment or two, then telephone his office.

The lift opposite the door of the Members' dining room in which Emma's body had been found that morning was operating normally. Joshua entered with a feeling of distaste; there was still a smell of some chemical in the confined space. He pressed the button for the second floor and looked closely at the brass hook from which Emma had been suspended. He did not recall seeing a similar hook in any of the other lifts. The screws seemed bright, and one of them was of steel, the other of brass. They were not a pair.

Peter Worthington Evans was already seated in Joshua's room. He made an attempt to get to his feet, but was waved down. 'I can't offer you a drink. I don't keep any. But I'll lend you my ear.' Joshua's room was rarely visited by anyone save the cleaners. A visitor would have to be escorted upstairs, and only Felicity was granted the privilege. Her picture stood on Morris's desk. Constituents were entertained in dining room or bar; family were taken to the families' room, where abandoned wives bickered over which programme to watch and neglected small children punched each other with impunity. It was where Labour wives took their knitting and Tory wives dressed for dinner.

'Before you say anything, Peter, I should tell you that John MacGregor has asked me to make some discreet inquiries about Emma's death. Have you come to see me about her?'

Peter Worthington Evans lit a cigarette, an act which left Joshua hunting through desk drawers for a forgotten ashtray. 'I expect you know Emma and I were friends?'

Joshua savoured the word 'friends' and waited silently in the hope of more information. None came. 'Emma was married, of course,' Joshua commented. 'I met her husband at some reception downstairs. Dullish fella called Barry.'

Worthy Evans drew on his cigarette and rose to the bait. 'She was unhappy. The marriage had turned out not to be a success. I won't deny I saw a good deal of her for a time. More recently she had moved on to pastures new.'

Joshua could remember Emma sitting on Ralph Grunte's knee at a *vin d'honneur* in Strasbourg on the occasion of a visit by the Party's Europe Committee to the Council of Europe. He had been struck then by how attractive she was, bosomy, flame-haired and cheerful with a tuneful laugh. She had, he had been told, once worked for a time for old Grunte as his researcher before the electors of Corve Dale had given her a ticket to Westminster. There had been a smoking room rumour to the effect that she was the only 'centrefold girl' to have addressed the Party Conference. She had been a model, she had appeared in the *Sun*, she had been hung naked under the heading 'June' in a motor agents' calendar on sale in the Midlands. Speculation as to the identity of the other eleven prominent Tory women had given rise to much hilarity. Nick Budgen had ticked them off on his fingers. The *Corve Dale Bugle* had carried a picture of her soaked to the skin, having been tossed into the Avon after a YC ball. She was very fetching, but the large screen and small size of the reproduction had robbed the photo of much of its excitement. It had had no effect on the result.

Although she was very pretty, Joshua had paid Emma scant attention. He felt no need. It had been amusing, though, to watch her progress at Strasbourg. Over three days she had been lunched by a Frog, dined by a Kraut (the terminology was Grunte's) and rogered by a Wop – or so Grunte had insisted. 'Ran into the greasy sod coming out of her room at the Hotel Gutenberg. Looked as if he'd won the war.' She had moved around the European Parliament building like a four-masted sailing ship under escort by a fleet of multi-national frigates. Several of the girls of the corps of interpreters, whose other task was the provision of home comforts of all kinds, had had their noses put out of joint. Joshua had wondered at the time whether there was a literal translation of that phrase into the French. Emma Kerr's effect upon *les parlementaires de l'Europe* had more than made up for Mrs Thatcher's unremitting hostility towards them and all their works. Three Dutch Liberals had travelled with her to the airport to see her off. They had presented her with a box of little red cheeses.

Worthy Evans had not been in Strasbourg. He had

been sitting in the whips' common room biting his nails.
Joshua decided to take one bull by its horn. 'Did you
sleep with her?'

Evans nodded and then smiled. 'What a damned silly
question. What did you think I did with her? Sit up in
bed reading the *Reader's Digest* to her out loud? What
else was there to do with Emma, for Christ's sake?'

He lit another cigarette. Joshua resisted the temptation to open his window. This was no time for a
rebuke, however understated. Evans must be encouraged to tell all. 'I'm sorry, Peter, to ask you painful
and impertinent questions, but I'm still intrigued as to
why you are here, and what it is you want to tell
me. Can you throw any light on the circumstances
surrounding her death? When did you last see her?'

'I always knew you were a copper *manqué*,' replied
Evans. 'I'm here to do you a favour.' Joshua wondered
why. 'Did you hear what happened last night after the
two o'clock vote between Emma and that shit Charles
Harvey?'

Joshua said, 'Tell me.'

Peter Worthington Evans crossed his legs; the soles
of his shiny black shoes carried the word 'Bally'. They
must have been uncomfortably new. Joshua's telephone rang. He held it to his ear and listened. The
voice was that of a man. Joshua replaced the receiver
without speaking and pressed the 'out' button. Bound
to be the press. 'What happened between Emma and
Harvey?' he asked.

'Came to blows,' was the reply. 'He beat her up in
his ministerial room under the Chamber after the two
o'clock vote last night. Michael Portillo, who has the
room next door, says it was like Enfield High Street
on a Saturday night – she screaming at him, then burst-
ing into tears. There was the sound of blows and of

furniture being overturned. Portillo says he very nearly
intervened but thought better of it. There were, or so
he says, loud oohs and aahs, and the sound of furniture
being knocked over. In the end, just as Michael was
about to open his door to remonstrate – he was hard
at work on his boxes, you understand – he heard Harvey's door open and slam and then Emma begins kicking the door down. After three kicks and a cry of
"You shit" there was silence. A couple of minutes later
Portillo opened his door, only to catch sight of John
Gummer doing likewise. They didn't speak to each
other. Now – what do you think of that?'

'A lovers' tiff,' said Joshua flippantly. He set his
face. 'How come you know all about it? Was it Portillo
who told you?'

Peter came over 'whipish'. 'I am not at liberty to tell
you.'

Worthington Evans turned his cigarette pack upside
down, but it was all too empty. He looked at Joshua.

'Can't help you, don't smoke.' He leaned forward in
his chair. 'When did you last see Emma?'

'At the three o'clock vote last night, but we didn't
speak. I remember thinking at the time that she looked
flustered; her colour was high and she wasn't talking
to anyone.'

'When did you last see Harvey?'

'I can't remember. As you can guess I had no incentive to seek him out. He had been seeing Emma for a
month or more, and he had shut me out. I was in no
mood to pass the time of day. Thankfully I have no
cause to have any dealings with him. I'm not his area
whip, and I'm not responsible for the Party's Transport
Committee. But I do know this. Harvey is no bloody
good. He's one of those slimy swine who have more
than their fair share of natural advantages. I think

Emma thought so, too. I got the impression from something she said to me that their affair wouldn't last. And that is not sour grapes.' Worthington Evans got to his feet. 'I'm going home. It's been a hell of a day. If I can help you any more, get in touch.' He had the air of someone who has been through a severe physical ordeal. 'I loved that woman,' he said, and quietly closed the door behind him.

11

David Lancaster stood at the bar of the Commons Chamber to listen to the Leader of the House's statement about Emma Kerr's death. He had had few dealings with her, although he had once tried to persuade Emma to come down to his constituency to speak at a supper club. She had refused prettily enough.

As a boy, Lancaster had been interested in women, but that was twenty or more years ago: a humiliating failure to hold an erection with a girl called Dolly in a Paddington bedsit had been most discouraging. She had lost patience and consoled herself by taking bites out of a ham sandwich. She had munched while he had striven mightily, but sadly not mightily enough. And she had demanded her two quid. He found later that he never suffered from the same disability with boys. Wayne had once rattled a bag of crisps but Lancaster had soon put a stop to that. He could see that Emma was 'a jam pot' who had various pinstripe-suited 'wasps' drowning in her jar, but his interest was academic. Emma did not remind him of his mother.

He was not, however, beyond speculating as to
whom among 'the colleagues' might have killed her. 'I
wouldn't put it past that frightful Langford,' was the
opinion he gave to the Minister of Posts and Telegraphs
in John Major's first administration. They were sitting
in the window of a café in Cricklewood. David was
buoyed up by feelings of relief. Wayne, who had been
complaining of the onset of 'flu, was tucked up in bed
in the boxroom at Quex Road. He had assured his
lover on the way to West Hampstead that he had not
breathed a word to a soul. Had he done so, quipped
Lancaster, he would personally have taken a pair of
nail scissors to Wayne's balls. Wayne had giggled nervously and, after a pause, Lancaster had laughed too.
On arrival at the flat Lancaster had made Wayne a
milky drink. 'Don't wait up. I'm off to another wine
and cheese in the constituency.'

The Minister of Posts and Telegraphs ate a chocolate
éclair. He had been described by the *Guardian* as 'a
clever young man destined for great things'. He was
wearing slacks and a tartan anorak. On his head was
a woolly hat with a bobble on top. His private secretary, to say nothing of his area whip or his constituency party chairman, could have passed the lighted
window of the café and failed to recognise him. He
looked like a chorus boy dressed as a Canadian trap-
per's mate. Lancaster – tall, with George Brown-like
wings of hair and a golf-club tie – could have been his
father.

David Lancaster sipped his Lapsang Souchong tea
and ate a toasted teacake; the butter dripped down his
chin and on to his waistcoat. He felt the return of the
itch of desire. The impression of respectability he made
was enhanced by a gold chain worn across his belly,
on one end of which was a sovereign. It bore the

head of Bertie, Edward VII, *Rex Imperator*, and had belonged to his grandfather, a Hatcham Alderman.

Lancaster had his funny little ways but they were not obvious. He was, in fact, widely regarded as a dullard. Years ago he had narrowly escaped the pursuit of a censorious police constable who had been on duty in the gents at Piccadilly. It was in memory of that brush with the law that Lancaster wore dirty white running shoes. They sat incongruously beneath a length of blue serge trousers and a pair of burgundy-coloured socks. Lancaster was still capable of a turn of speed at the age of thirty-nine. Was he not a regular attender at Jim Spicer's Commons gym where he bounced up and down to music, and touched his toes at the word of a female instructor? He was not the sort of man to leave much to chance.

Father and son sat quietly in the front of Lancaster's blue Scorpio. Radio 4's 'PM' told of Emma Kerr's short-lived political career. Mrs Thatcher had asserted that she had been betrayed by her party. England was in trouble in the Test. However, rain was forecast. The sign 'Gents' shone beguilingly across the Cricklewood Broadway like a distant harbour light. It offered a flight of steps leading into a dingy, white-tiled, smelly paradise. The Minister of Posts and Telegraphs filed his nails; Lancaster wondered what it was that Wayne had got up to last night. Whom had he met at the club? Two pairs of unblinking eyes watched the Gents.

Cricklewood Broadway had the reputation among cottagers of attracting a good class of person; nice Jewish boys, Asian students, and out of work waiters. After twenty minutes, the hunters spotted two young men descending the stairs. Leaving the keys in the ignition, Lancaster and the Minister of the Crown abandoned their car and crossed the road in search of quarry. A shower of rain made patterns on the dust of parked cars and drove shoppers into convenient havens. From the distant heights of Harrow came the slow rumble of thunder. A Jack Russell terrier crossed the Broadway looking neither to its left nor right, oblivious to the cries of outrage and abuse. It was late afternoon on a summer's day in north-west London.

The sight of two men, one young, the other middle-aged, running for their lives along the Broadway pursued by two young men in blue blazers raised a shopper's eyebrow. An old lady of a charitable disposition wondered aloud to her companion whether or not the display was part of some sponsored event to raise money for a good cause; her friend, more attuned to the way of the world, suggested that the pursued were undoubtedly burglars. They watched as the two hunted men suddenly separated, the younger turning into a side street, the older leaping on to the platform of a Routemaster bus. One pursuer disappeared up the side street; the other, about to board the same bus as had his quarry, was tripped by an elderly gentleman who thrust his silver-headed cane smartly between the policeman's knees. His victim was brought heavily to the ground, cracking his head against the bus stop. The gent, who was a big noise in the neighbourhood watch, was only doing his duty: young men should not pursue the old with a view to doing them an injury. Several passers-by gathered around the prostrate policeman, while the bus drew away en route for Kilburn.

David Lancaster, who was not used to travelling on public transport, offered the black conductor a five pence piece. He was badly out of breath. The conductor wanted a good deal more. Lancaster, who denied he was joking, got off the bus opposite the Gaumont State cinema in the Kilburn High Road, crossed the road and bought himself a ticket. He sat inside the dark for more than an hour, trembling with exertion and crippled by anxiety. He watched, much to his displeasure, a skin-flick entitled *Las Vegas Nights*, the red-haired heroine of which reminded him of Emma Kerr.

The Minister for Posts and Telegraphs was luckier than he deserved. The road down which he turned divided almost immediately: he took the left fork, the policeman the right. As the *Guardian* political correspondent had asserted, the Minister was bright – bright enough to see that the curve of the road suggested a circle around which his pursuer, providing he did not break his stride, would soon appear. He stopped for a second or so to catch his breath, stuffing his conspicuous pink woolly hat into the back pocket of his jeans. Next time, if there were a next time, he would give Cricklewood Broadway a miss. He turned to retrace his steps in order to rejoin the main road, noticing as he did so two uniformed men standing at the base of the road.

With that flash of inspiration which his Oxford tutors had said would take him to the very top, he opened a front gate and walked boldly up the front door. The house was semi-detached 1930s art deco with a green tiled roof and metalled windows. In the front garden were three gnomes. The Minister banged on the door and set his face in a supplicatory grin. He could have been spending the early evening 'on the knocker' in his constituency of Cleobury West. To his relief there was the sound of a bolt being drawn back. The door opened to reveal an elderly man in dressing gown and slippers.

'Yes?' the man demanded. His tone was not encouraging.

The Minister beamed. 'May I introduce myself? I am your' – here there was a slight hesitation – 'Labour local government candidate. I am canvassing for your support against the poll tax.'

The Tory Party may have come down in the world but its candidates, local and national, do not canvass their electors wearing anoraks, jeans and trainers. The elector, who had thought his visitor to be a Mormon, invited the Minister of Posts and Telegraphs inside and gave him a cup of tea – and what would have been in other circumstances an earful. 'Well, at least that bloody woman has gone, but I don't think Major is up to much.'

The Minister solemnly agreed with him. He, too, was beginning to have his doubts. But then he had voted for Margaret. After twenty minutes listening to his host, he asked if he might buy a telephone call in order to summon a mini-cab. He left a further twenty minutes later with a five pound subscription for the local Labour Party in his pocket and the conviction that Labour Party activists were every bit as boring as his own.

As the cab turned into the Broadway, he saw Lancaster's Scorpio pulling out from the kerb. A young man was behind the wheel, and three others were in the car. It had been pinched. The cab driver was told to proceed slowly in the direction of Kilburn, but there was no sight of David Lancaster. It had been a narrow escape.

The adjournment of the House threatened to upset Ron Barton's plan of campaign. His birds would be scattered across the basement flats of Lambeth and

Westminster. Joshua was unusual in that his London pad was as far out as Lewisham. Some Tory MPs spend the week in their clubs, camping out in attic bedrooms but lounging in some of the more elegant of London's drawing rooms. The service, too, was suitably deferential. Labour MPs shared digs, Dennis Skinner and John Prescott being seen as the People's Party's answer to that other 'odd couple', Walter Matthau and Jack Lemmon. One Welsh Liberal MP even lived in the Regent's Palace Hotel.

Barton had collected MPs' London telephone numbers which he kept in a small black notebook on his person. He found Peter Worthington Evans's and Charles Harvey's. Sam Langford's he could not find. Joshua Morris's had been written in pencil then crossed out. He must put Avril, an idle girl with a sarff-London accent and big tits, to work compiling an accurate record of so many bolt holes. God knows what they all got up to away from their wives and kiddies. Power, he had read somewhere, was an aphrodisiac.

Ron's pager bleeped. He reached for it as if for a gun. The tiny screen bore the instruction 'Ring Avril'. Barry Kerr had arrived from Birmingham and was at Barton's disposal. He was, said Avril, a creep. Working first for the *Sun* and then for the *Brit* had given Barton a taste for high living. He felt like taking tea at the Ritz; but it would not be wise to give Barry the wrong idea. The sod believed he had something to sell, and there was no doubt that Ron would buy his story for the paper. MY LIFE WITH LOVELY EMMA – BEREAVED HUSBAND SPILLS THE BEANS. His editor, however, was not as generous as once he had been. 'Rupe tells me times is hard,' had been his sad comment. Better make it tea at the Swiss Centre; at four o'clock, prompt.

* * *

171

Barry Kerr was very large with a shock of black hair. He wore his Rotary Club badge as if it were the Military Cross. His shoes, however, would not have passed muster in Camberley. Despite the summer weather he carried a raincoat over his arm, together with an executive-type briefcase. Hairs protruded from his nostrils and out of his ears. 'Terrible business about Em,' were his first words.

Barton set his face in a mask of concern, an uncharacteristic expression which usually went with a foot in the door, and squeezed Barry's upper arm. 'Bear up squire,' he said. 'How can I be of help?'

Barry blew his nose on a dirty white handkerchief. 'I don't mind admitting I'm all cut up. She was a lovely girl, was Em. Of course, she hadn't much time for me once she got herself into Parliament. It all went to her head, as you would expect. But we had two lovely years together after we was first married.' The accent was road-house Brum, whining and genteel.

'China or Indian?' asked Ron. He had once seen Albert Finney ask as much of a guest on a play on the telly.

'English, of course,' replied Barry with a show of irritation.

Ron ordered a pot of Indian tea and a plate of cakes. 'Go on, Barry,' he said. 'Get it off your chest. What exactly went wrong?' He took out his notebook.

Barry needed no prompting. His story was humdrum enough, save for the names of Emma's friends and admirers. Emma, whom he had first met at a Solihull Young Conservatives dance, was a real 'goer' even then. She lived with her mum over a dry-cleaners, her father was dead, and she worked as a 'confidential secretary' to a property developer. She drove an MG Metro, and dressed very well. 'She was ginger, then,' sighed Barry. 'But she got steadily redder.' After she had been elected to the District Council she had begun to have parliamentary ambitions. Wasn't Edwina Currie a big noise for a time on the Birmingham Council before going on to make a national name for herself? Edwina was a tailor's daughter from Liverpool; if she could make good then so could Emma.

Barton listened politely. He encouraged Barry to tell him what had gone wrong with their marriage. Had it been roses, roses all the way?

'No, it bloody well wasn't,' was Barry's reply. Emma, once she had been adopted as Tory candidate in Corve Dale, got herself a job working as a researcher for Ralph Grunte, the MP for somewhere in Warwickshire. He was a randy fat slob who soon wanted more from Emma than she could give from nine to five. It was lunch here and dinner there, and weekends in London. Emma – or so she claimed at the time – was helping Grunte with his book, which was called *The Mother of Parliaments*; looking up references and typing Grunte's copy, that sort of thing. Grunte had even put her on the board of a company for a time, out of which she got a thousand a year.

Barry would tease Emma about Grunte – 'What can you see in that fat old git?' – but Emma wouldn't have a word said against him. She had said that he couldn't keep his hands to himself, but even so she had kept her knickers firmly on. 'I'm not that hard up, Barry,' she had boasted. Once Emma had been elected she had not seen so much of Grunte and had, of course, stopped working for him. In fact, she had a researcher of her own, a student from a poly.

'So you don't think Emma had it off with Grunte?' asked Ron. Barry said he didn't know. 'What happened once Emma got elected?'

173

Barry accepted a second cup and ate a slice of Battenburg cake. 'Then it was Peter Worthington Evans's turn. He's a prick. And violent with it. We had a punch-up years before Emma. We were at school together. He pinched my Vespa and when I tried to get it back off him he kicked me in the crutch. Bloody painful. The police got involved and he was bound over to keep the peace. Wouldn't like to be reminded of it today, he wouldn't. When he wasn't kicking his mates in the balls he was holding forth at the Young Conservatives. After he got to Parliament he had spoken for Emma at the last election and taken her under his wing. It was then that Emma took to staying in London at weekends in the flat paid for out of her Parliamentary London Allowance. She would come home two weekends a month and spend most of her time politicking: opening bazaars, attending fêtes. She used to say her life was spent drawing the raffle. She spent more of it with Peter, was what I heard. There are no secrets in the West Midlands. She even had her picture taken with Evans at some London ball – it appeared in the *Birmingham Echo*. It wasn't long before people in the Conservative Club stopped asking me how she was. The trouble was they knew only too well. All that guff in the papers about "the lovely Emma" and "the red-haired goddess" went to her head.'

'So Peter Worthington Evans and your wife were lovers. That's a fact?'

Barry fell silent and a cunning look came into his eyes. 'What's all this worth to your paper? You've got to come across if you want the whole story. There's lots more.'

'A couple of thousand,' said Ron. Barry remained silent. 'There might well be sales abroad to other papers, foreign rights and all that. Shall we say three and a half?'

Barry seemed to have taken grave offence. 'There are other names, you know. Emma was generous with it, you know. Three and a half is a bloody insult. There are other papers that would be very interested.'

It was Ron's turn to fall silent. He remembered his editor's injunction; extravagance was definitely out. But the story of Emma Kerr's unparliamentary end would run and run. He could scarcely imagine a better story. 'Of course we can do much better than three and a half,' he told Barry. 'Stay put while I phone my editor. Don't budge if you want to be sincerely rich.'

The editor had a wide vocabulary, few of the words of which exceeded four letters. Barry got the message. 'We can pay you ten grand for the exclusive rights.'

Barry took a jam tart with a blob of cream in its middle. He scrutinised it before popping it into his mouth. 'Make it twenty and I'm all yours,' he mumbled.

Ron said, 'Done.' It so happened that twenty grand had been the maximum he was authorised to offer.

12

It would be hard to find in all of England a more desolate spot than the Essex Marshes. Even in June a cold wind blows off the river sending a file of old copies of the *Sun*, cigarette packets and French letters blowing along broken pavements like an army in retreat. The great overspill-from-London housing estates built in the 1960s stand either side of dull arterial roads where garages and monstrous public houses play the part of oases, their lights and messages ('live music' and '5p off') a comfort to the unlucky traveller. It is a land where live, in Philip Larkin's words, 'a cut-price crowd, urban yet simple, dwelling where only salesmen and relations come'. They huddle together for protection against aliens from another world, the blacks, the bailiff and the man from the finance company, hellbent on repossession. Every road has its bow-window-fronted council house, Mrs Thatcher's mark, the sign of private and not public ownership.

Sam Langford drove his Jag slowly past chip shops, launderettes and tired greengrocers, stopping to ask shaven, surly youths the way to the British Legion Hall. 'I'm the MP,' he told them. They were unimpressed.

'Oh yeah? We thought you was Gazza,' was the reply. Langford, whose own hair had grown an inch a year since his election, recognised the rebuke for what it was; two fingers raised against the top dog. Yet he was their spokesman; his roots were theirs.

Forty people sat on hard chairs in the British Legion Hall. The meeting was one of several held locally on Tuesday evenings during the year where Langford had 'reported back' to his constituents. It was, however, a public and not a private meeting, although he recognised the bulk of the audience as Party members. They were nearly all women in their late fifties or beyond, drab in dress and tired of mind, poverty having robbed them of their looks and style. Poverty is relative; they were nowhere near as poor as their grandmothers had been, living in Bethnal Green; not as pinched as their pioneering mothers, many of whom lived out their last days in Essex County Council Sunset Homes, but poor nonetheless, poor enough to welcome the subventions of their children, poor enough not to want to pay the man to come and repair the washing machine, poor enough to have one good winter coat. But they were Conservative supporters. 'Essex Woman' is every bit as important as 'Essex Man', and, what is more to the point, there are many more of them. Langford knew that, in order to survive politically, he had to keep them on his side.

Langford was introduced from the platform by his party agent, a wizened dwarf of a man whose days were spent playing the machines at Conservative working men's clubs. He had spent his own working life putting the quality into Ford motor cars. 'Sam speaks for us,' he declaimed. 'He's one of us.'

'I knew his mum,' yelled a harridan sitting in the front row. She was well known as a woman of decided views who had, according to one of her victims, 'a mouth on her like the *Basildon News*'.

'Evening, Betty,' said Langford. 'Wouldn't be home without you.' There was much laughter.

'I'm keeping my eye on you, Sam,' she shouted.

Langford felt a twinge of fear. His report was humdrum. One oral question and two written in the House, and a speech on the Second Reading debate of the Pipelines Bill. 'We can't have 'em digging up half Essex.' He then launched into a strong defence of Mrs Thatcher, who, as Kev Catford had said a week or so ago, was being consigned to the 'dustbin of 'istory'. 'Maggie did us proud, and the country as well.' He suggested that the Party agent prepare a resolution of support which he, Langford, would later put to the meeting. There were growls of approval.

After ten minutes or so Langford invited questions. Two people stood up: one was a local district councillor whose newsagent's business had recently gone bust; the other was an Asian, whom Langord thought he recognised. He was the only 'Paki' in the hall.

The local councillor blamed the business rate for his collapse. 'It were the last straw.' But what was worse was the fact that he had been forced to sell out to a Paki who would lower the tone of the neighbourhood with his smells, stock the shop with pornography and sell groceries as well, he wouldn't wonder. 'We come out here from London to escape the wogs. Now we find 'em on our heels, breathing down our necks.'

There were shouts of support, and other people struggled to their feet, demanding to be heard. Langford, disinclined to hear what it was the Asian had to say (was he her brother?), pointed at another

questioner. 'We've got to send 'em back home where
they belong, Sam,' was the gist of his contribution.
Langford invited a woman in a green hat to have her
say. A dozen people were now on their feet, demanding to be heard. The Asian thought better of his question and left the hall. Langford passed his agent a cigar
and lit one of his own. He would keep this going for
half an hour or more and then buy a few drinks. We
can't have the blacks in Essex. He looked on top form;
but then, unlike the majority of his colleagues, Sam
had enjoyed a good night's sleep; or so was his agent's
opinion.

Joshua Morris spent the half hour after Worthy Evans's
departure attending to his constituency post, which
meant writing instructions in pencil on top of his constituents' letters and sending them on to his Shropshire-
based secretary. She was as skilled as he was. Letters
complaining about the poll tax were sent to the Department of the Environment, letters about dogs and their
dirt to the Home Office and letters urging that Maggie
should return on to the Prime Minister's Office.
Eventually replies would come, to which Joshua would
add his congratulations or commiseration. MPs were
post offices whose task it was to distribute complaints
among those who ostensibly, at least, had the power
to remedy injustice and right wrongs. It had long been
Joshua's view that the backbench Tory MP was the
lowest form of political life. Harold Macmillan had
once said that the only quality needed by an MP was
the ability to write a good letter.

At six o'clock he left his office on the Upper Committee corridor and walked the lonely passages to the
now sinister lift. There was not a soul about. In winter,
once the House was adjourned, only a few lights

remained burning, and the attendant staff disappeared, leaving an empty, echoing, half-lit Palace of a thousand rooms and half-a-hundred staircases. In summer, the place seemed abandoned, undiscovered. Joshua found the lift waiting at the second floor and took it down to the ground, a trip that the unlucky Emma had done twelve or so hours before. She had travelled up and then down and then up again on a futile last journey; a ceaseless Odyssey. Joshua quit the lift with relief and made his way to the Central Lobby. He sat in the marbled chill of the empty vaulted room with its ornate decoration and waited for Felicity to arrive.

Joshua positioned himself where he could command the corridor leading to the St Stephen's entrance. He felt a stirring of the blood; a mounting excitement. Love at sixty is no different from love at twenty. A very old man with silver hair and a limp walked painfully down the corridor from the Lords. Joshua studied his uncomfortable progress. Had he been in the Commons when Joshua had first been elected to Parliament? His aged face carried few clues as to what he would have looked like as a young man: winged chariots and all that jazz.

Joshua was deeply in love but he was not jealous. He had no need to be. Poor Worthy Evans was crippled by his hatred for Charles Harvey who had stolen Emma. Harvey was an elegant creature who seemed to have it all going for him. Clever, but not so clever that his colleagues might notice and take exception. Successful, but not ostentatiously so. He had not so far been the subject of an *Observer* profile. He had something of the arrogance of Edward Fox, whose upper-class cockney vowels had brought the Prince of Wales to life in the Thames Television series. Was Emma his Mrs Simpson? Joshua would have to speak

to Harvey on Wednesday in order to get to the bottom
of that late night row in the minister's room beneath
the Commons Chamber. What was the cause of it, and
what had happened after Emma's noisy departure?
Charles Harvey did not seem the sort of man to whom
fisticuffs came easily. Still, he had been around the
House for most of the night.

Was Worthy Evans jealous enough to kill Emma?
Joshua had always considered Peter to be a bore; alive
only, in the words of the wit Geoffrey Madan, 'in the
sense that he could not be legally buried'. He might
have taken to wearing Bally shoes but there was something very dull about Peter. He was a pullover man.
The powers-that-be had recruited him as a member of
the whips' office, but he was unlikely to progress
beyond membership of the Party's secret police to
junior office. He was a decent if dull Young Conservative, the sort that clambered into Parliament in a good
year when the Party's majority approached three figures. He would eventually be knighted. When it came
to Emma, Peter was boxing out of his class. He might
have held her hand during Emma's early days in the
House, but he clearly could not hold her affections
indefinitely. The competition would be too severe. But
would he kill her? Strangle her with a pair of her
trousers, then hang her body in a lift? Stuff her knickers in her mouth in a gesture of contempt? It seemed
unlikely, but worms had been known to turn. He had
certainly been in the House at the time of Emma's
death. He had not gone home until after the Adjournment had come up at eight o'clock. And he had not
taken his place on the bench after three a.m.

Felicity came up the steps wearing a navy-blue blazer
and white skirt and carrying a leather holdall full of
little delicacies. Indeed, she rarely travelled without

them. They were a love-offering, for she was not a greedy woman; Joshua had never known one who ate so little. Her motto was 'a very little bit of the very, very best', and the slimness of her figure was proof of her dedication. She was tall, dark, elegant, and the graceful way in which she moved belied her age. She was a little younger than Joshua but, when happy, looked ten years younger. She broke into a wide smile and they embraced, carefully pecking each other's cheek in case of censorious onlookers.

For two years they had been meeting every month or so, holidaying abroad discreetly; at home, staying in provincial hotels and in their children's empty flats. Their resurrected love had been slow building; for two years prior to her surrender, Joshua had taken Felicity out to lunch at a cross-section of London's better restaurants. She was writing a cookbook but had yet to find a publisher. The number of her recipes had grown steadily.

They walked swiftly through Westminster Hall under the great hammer-beam roof, then down the staircase into the Members' underground car park. In the lift, Joshua kissed Felicity lightly on the mouth. 'What a terrible thing to have happened to Emma Kerr,' she said.

Joshua took her by the hand. 'It's fallen to me to try and find out who did it. Get in the car and I'll tell you what I know.'

As they drove in the rush-hour traffic down through the Elephant and Castle and the Old Kent Road, the pilgrims' route to Canterbury, Joshua told Felicity what had happened. He had in his briefcase Emma's file from the whips' office. He had not yet read it. He knew of two lovers only, Harvey and Worthington Evans: there could well have been others. Felicity, who had been listening attentively, broke in to ask whether or not Ralph Grunte was a prime suspect.

'I've been reading all about his drunken speech in the small hours of the morning, when he kissed Mark Fisher on his bald head. It must have been hilarious.'

Joshua agreed that it had had its moments. 'Emma worked for Grunte before she was elected, as his researcher, but he didn't do it. The whips bundled him into a cab, pissed out of his mind. Emma died in the early hours; it seems at that time Grunte was out to the world.'

'It would take a lot to knock him out from what I've read about him,' said Felicity.

In Deptford Joshua swung the car across country, climbing a nameless hill covered with red-brick late Victorian villas, a short cut that avoided Lewisham High Street, and came out in Ladywell.

'You've been having a high old time,' Felicity observed. 'First Grunte disgraces himself, then the wine waiter pours a bottle of plonk over someone's head and then Catford rocks the boat.'

Joshua recounted the story of David Lancaster's discomfiture. 'Hell hath no fury.'

'Is Lancaster queer?'

'So gossip has it. I don't know him well, but I doubt if he will be dining in for some time.'

Felicity made a gesture as if putting a line through a name on a list. 'That knocks out Lancaster from your suspects.'

As the car turned into their road, Joshua told Felicity of his meeting with Evans. 'He's a shit,' was her stoutly expressed opinion. 'Murder, jealousy and lust, my God what a can of worms.'

There was nowhere to park outside his daughter's flat, so Joshua drove into an adjoining street.

'I hope Margaret makes a comeback,' said Felicity, 'but I know you don't.' Mrs Thatcher, her life and times, was the one subject on which the lovers disagreed.

Joshua laughed. 'I've always felt sorry for the Roberts family of Grantham – "It was not a swan that they had hatched, it was an eagle." '

Felicity recognised the quotation. She was better read than Joshua. 'Lytton Strachey on Florence Nightingale,' she cried triumphantly.

Joshua's daughter's flat was the converted upstairs of an artisan's terraced house, a row built on spec for the respectable poor at the turn of the century. The front bedroom had become the drawing room where there was a large, uncomfortable home-made sofa, an artist's desk and an assortment of pictures, most of which had once belonged to Joshua. The single bedroom had a depressing outlook (the curtain did not draw) but the bed was large and soft. The kitchen was of good size, but the hot-water tap over the sink did not work. Joshua arrived late and went early, and his daughter was rarely at home. In consequence, the patient plumber came and went. In summer, the flat was hot; in winter, cold, for there was no central heating.

Felicity and Joshua climbed the narrow and steep stairs and fell into each other's arms. In the early 1950s they had been two children in love: forty years on they were lovers only too aware of the passing of time. Joshua had once had a wife; Felicity had a husband; for one day out of every thirty-one they shut the world away and drowned in each other's arms. Joshua took the bottle of Corton out of the larder, opened it and left it to breathe. Felicity covered the tiny table with her quail. Then they took off most of their clothes and lay on the bed beneath the duvet, entwined together like two snakes, watching the light of the evening die, listening to the banished sounds of south London. 'I am the covers on the book of your life,' whispered Joshua, and fell gently asleep. Felicity held him and, as he dreamed of her, kissed his eyes.

13

On Wednesday morning, TV-AM continued the heavy news coverage of Emma's murder. A still was shown of her electioneering in a boat on the River Severn. This was followed by stock footage of her speaking at the Tory Party conference: urging Mrs Thatcher to 'index' child benefit. She had looked particularly lovely. The cameras then showed Sir Ralph Grunte being interviewed by the station's resident crumpet. Grunte was wearing so many checks that the television picture in Joshua Morris's daughter's flat could barely cope.

'Alas poor Emma, I knew her well,' intoned Grunte. It was almost as if he were holding her skull in his hand. 'I can say, without fear of contradiction, that we were, for a time, very close.'

The station crumpet perked up. A flash of intelligence came into her bright blue eyes. 'How close?' she asked. Could her editor have been prompting her, her instructions injected electronically into her shell-like ear?

Grunte gave her an old-fashioned look. He leaned forward and put a hairy hand on the interviewer's silken knee. 'Not that close, my dear. I was old enough to be her father.'

Marjorie, Grunte's wife, was watching him from her bed in the Shakespeare Suite of the Warwick Hilton Hotel. Her lover was trying to fold his *Times*; he was a great admirer of Woodrow Wyatt. 'What a lie,' cried Marge. 'I caught them both at it in her caravan.' Her lover grunted.

'How well then did you know her, Sir Ralph?' The 'Sir Ralph' came as a respectful afterthought.

'Emma Kerr was my researcher before she got into Parliament at the last election. She helped me with my speeches.'

This sally brought a snort from Joshua who was spreading Felicity's jam on a piece of Blackheath bread. 'Speeches,' cried Joshua, his mouth full. 'I bet she didn't have a hand in Grunte's effort on Monday night.'

Could Sir Ralph throw any light on the circumstances surrounding her murder? the interviewer continued. Would he be helping the police in their inquiries? The programme's editor must have screeched down the line connecting him to a tiny earpiece hidden beneath the interviewer's hair. She winced. 'Let me put it another way,' she said quickly. 'Can you help us to get to the bottom of this terrible business?'

'What I know I shall keep for the proper authorities. I will be speaking to the Chief Whip, a nice lad.' This was calculated to annoy Ryder who had, in fact, been mistaken for the Chairman of the Young Conservatives when he sat on the platform of John Major's 'coronation' immediately after his victory in the Party's leadership election. Ryder, however, did not watch breakfast television. He was reading about a forthcoming heavy-weight title fight in the *Telegraph*. The Chief Whip was a fight fan as well as an intellectual.

'I shall be able to put him fully into the picture,' continued Grunte. He paused for effect. 'Mrs Kerr had many good friends in the Conservative Parliamentary Party. I am perhaps in the best position of all to help the authorities. Although I am obviously a much older man, she was always happy to confide in me.'

'The old swine is going to make mischief,' shouted Marjorie, cutting across her lover's opinion that Wood-row Wyatt was the sort of man he would like to go tiger shootin' with. 'He was always going on about her being in love with Peter Worthington Evans, although how any half-way respectable girl could find anything to see in that creep I don't know. But then' – Marjorie hesitated – 'Emma was by no means half-way respectable. She probably got what she had coming to her.'

'There will be, of course, a memorial service at St Margaret's,' continued Grunte, wiping his brow with a red handkerchief.

'I hope to God he doesn't blow his nose,' whispered Joshua.

'A service at which it is my intention to give the address.'

That, thought Joshua, is one memorial service I won't miss.

The papers were full of poor Emma. The news of her death, put out over the PA at ten o'clock on Tuesday morning, had come too late for all save the evening papers. As expected, the Wednesday nationals had spread themselves. *The Times* devoted a page to pictures, and a pompous piece by Bernard Levin drawing attention to the hazards inherent in public life. His article was longer than usual with references to Jack

Profumo, Tony Lambton and Richard Wagner. The
Telegraph leader writer had used her death as an argu-
ment against having too many women MPs. Their
place, he argued magisterially, was in the home and
not the House: their presence clearly constituted a
grave distraction. The *Sun* carried the headline: TORY
BIMBO GETS HERS, while Barton's *True Brit* carried a long piece that purported to recount the 'high-
lights' of Emma's political career. There were pictures
of Emma with Peter Worthington Evans, Charles
Harvey and Sir Ralph Grunte ('The Party's Falstaff').
Trailed across the front page was the exclusive by
Emma's 'tragic' husband: 'Blind Barry tells all. Us men
are always the last to know.'

There was much more besides. Felicity promised to
keep out of Joshua's way, at least until the late afternoon, but she asked him to tell her briefly what he
already knew. He confessed that it was, as of nine-
thirty that Wednesday morning, not a great deal.
Emma had had a raft of lovers, one of whom was,
he supposed, the most likely to have killed her. The
important thing to establish was motive; if he knew
why exactly she had been killed it should not be too
difficult to name the culprit.

He told Felicity of Peter Worthy Evans's visit to his
room the afternoon before. It seemed that her current
beau was Charles Harvey, but Peter, whom Harvey
had succeeded, had told him of the row between
Harvey and Emma in Charles's ministerial room in the
small hours of Tuesday morning. After that, could
Charles have wanted to mend his fences, or to shut
her up? And why should Emma have volunteered any
information? What was in it for Peter? Both Peter
and Charles were ministers, for members of the whips'
office were members of Her Majesty's Government.

They would have every incentive to keep the reptiles away from their private lives. Peter was clearly both bitter and jealous. If he were as free with his opinions and his information as he had been with Joshua, he would be a perfect menace, upsetting the ordered ways of government.

'You don't believe Grunte could have done it?' Felicity's voice carried doubt. 'He's such a horror. I like the idea of the murderer giving the address at his victim's memorial service. That would be a first. Beat that, Lady James.'

Joshua thought for a moment. 'I don't believe so. He was pissed and in bed anyway. I don't think anybody actually likes Grunte but he does add colour to our proceedings. He is also a yardstick of sorts. There was criticism of me in the constituency a couple of years ago, the usual stuff – "we never see him", or "he's not one hundred per cent behind Margaret", or "spends his time writing for the newspapers". I soon put a stop to that. I suggested they invite Grunte to one of their supper clubs, you know the thing; quiche Lorraine, salad and cheese and a thirty-minute *tour d'horizon* by a visiting speaker. I can't tell you how awful Grunte was. He offended my chairman by something he said to her. Kept putting his hand on her knee. Upset the agent, and made a terrible speech, boastful and way over the top. And he kept "refreshing" his glass from a hip flask. After it was all over several of the local big-wigs came up to me and whispered, pointing discreetly in Grunte's direction – he was at the time trying to persuade one of my more religious local councillors to back a horse – "Are they all like that?" They meant at Westminster. "Most of 'em," I replied. "Some are even worse." That put a stop to the grumbles, I can tell you. The trouble is, Grunte wants me to pay a return visit to South Warwicks. Will put me up for the night.'

Felicity laughed. They drove up to the House along the Old Kent Road with its dilapidated Georgian and early Victorian houses, their 'gardens' taken up with used car lots and their front doors ablaze with the buzzers of multi-occupation. 'Dublin's a bit like that,' said Joshua. 'Faded beauty.'

'Was Emma at dinner when the wine waiter poured a bottle over the head of David Lancaster? I read about it in the paper,' Felicity asked.

'She was sitting between Heseltine and Harvey, and making up to Michael, as far as I can remember. Elaine Kellett-Bowman saved the day; Emma just giggled.'

'What made the waiter do it? Was he sloshed?'

'There's more in that little episode than meets the eye,' replied Joshua. 'As I told you, Lancaster has the reputation of being gay. It could be he's the kind that pursues waiters. I don't know. The gesture, and it was, in its way, rather a splendid one, was probably an act of revenge. A lovers' quarrel. But I don't see any connection with Emma's death. Lancaster wouldn't have looked at her twice. She wasn't his cup of tea.'

'What about Harvey? What's he like?'

'I'll tell you more when we meet again at four in the Central Lobby. He's due to see me at eleven in my room. John MacGregor fixed up the meeting.'

Felicity left, grasping a Harrods bag for a day spent shopping. She was to take her daughter out to lunch at Heal's in Tottenham Court Road, where Justin de Blanc's restaurant was cheap and cheerful.

Joshua permitted his car to be scrutinised by the security men at the Commons, who undertook the task with more than their usual thoroughness. Joshua had yet to collect his very own mirror attached to the end of a stick, a service, which, since Ian Gow's death by car bomb, had been provided for Members. He was obliged to open both his bonnet and the boot. He always found the exercise somewhat embarrassing; his engine was Japanese and proud of it, but his boot was a tip into which the detritus of two years' hard motoring had been pitched. A security man rummaged around within it, his face, as glimpsed in the inside mirror, taut with disapproval. Finally, declared safe (if not sound), Joshua was waved down into the garage, the floors of which descended like the circles of Dante's inferno. The bottom floor was reserved, not unreasonably, for Members' secretaries.

In the Members' Lobby Joshua, having first collected his post, fell in with Mike White of the *Guardian*. White was tall, bald and painstaking. 'What's this I hear about you playing detective? I'm told the Leader of the House has no wish to see the plod's heavy feet all over the carpets. Is he really leaving it to you?'

'I am not in a position to confirm nor deny the rumour,' replied Joshua. 'But I will keep you in hourly touch with my progress.'

'I bet it turns out to be Toby Jessel,' quipped White. Toby Jessel was a Tory MP of immense rectitude, famous for his battles against the noise of Heathrow Airport on behalf of his Twickenham constituents and for playing his grand piano in aid of Party funds. He was a most unlikely suspect.

'I have eliminated him from my inquiries,' said Joshua solemnly.

White changed tack. Mrs Thatcher, it turned out, was to speak to a press gallery lunch in that part of the Palace reserved for the lobby and known to MPs as 'the reptile house'. Would Joshua like to come?

Press gallery lunches were reserved for political

heavyweights; leaders of parties, chancellors of exchequers, ex-prime ministers and the like. Joshua had never spoken at one, but he had attended several. Eating in the canteen was not a gastronomic experience; the more sensitive of the scene-writers, employed by the editors of the nationals to amuse their readers, brought Fortnum's hampers with them filled with good things. Only the provincials braved the cod and chips. But Margaret had her attractions. How bitter was she? Was she dead but wouldn't lie down? How much of a danger was she to the Major Government? Joshua accepted White's invitation with pleasure and promised to meet him at five to one.

His post was more than usually dull. There was a death threat, but it was from the same anonymous Mancunian, written, as ever, in green ink. Joshua scribbled on it instructions to his secretary to forward it to the police. Another correspondent – this time the only clue was a postmark, 'Reading' – had sent him a printed form which purported to be a list of Great Bores, rather in the style of the top ten best-selling books, published each week by the *Sunday Times*. Top of the Pops was Clive James, followed by Roy Hattersley, Stan Gebler Davies and Robert Robinson, in that order. Tenth was Libby Purves. Joshua was in at sixth place, one below Dickie Attenborough. Joshua wondered why anybody would bother to go to the expense, and stuck it up on the wall. If he could discover who did for poor Emma he would go right to the top of the list.

There was a tap on the door and the Chief Whip's secretary entered carrying an assortment of files. She was a handsome dark blonde, the sort of girl who should be photographed standing next to a Range Rover, mused Joshua.

'I'm to sit here until you have finished looking through them, then I must take them straight back to Richard. It is all most unusual.'

The tightness of her lips suggested that it would never have been allowed to happen when David Waddington had been Chief Whip; but then nobody had been done to death and exhibited publicly when 'Wadders' was chief. No one would have dared. Circumstances, thought Joshua, alter cases. He waved her to his regulation armchair and passed her a copy of the *House Magazine*. She made a pretence of reading it.

There were five files. Peter Worthington Evans's looked particularly thin. Charles Harvey's was fatter, although on inspection the bulk was accounted for, not by reports of secret vice, but a copy of *The Economist* containing an article he had once written bitterly critical of Nigel Lawson. It was entitled 'Fiddler on the Roof'. Was Harvey anti-semitic? Grunte's contained an obscene photo; one bum, four feet and a terrible pair of grey shoes. Should he pass it to Miss Petersfield, who was showing signs of dissatisfaction with the *House Magazine*, a journal for which Joshua occasionally wrote the weekly diary column? On balance, he thought not.

The fourth file was that of Sir Tufton Bufton, who had died a year or so ago following Emma's maiden speech to the '22. Nicholas Soames had insisted that his last words had *not* been 'Damn fine woman', but 'Some speech, but that was no maiden.' As Soames had given Tufton the kiss of life, he should know. 'Why Bufton? He's dead.'

'The Chief says you must read it. It seems that he knew a good deal about "our Emma"; it appears she had a taste for blackmail.'

The fifth file was Emma's. Unlike the others it was tied with pink tapes.

Joshua returned to the first of the files, leaving hers for the moment unopened. There was really nothing very much to Peter Worthy Evan's dossier. He was a thoroughly decent if limited youngish man who had won his political spurs in and around Brum. He was married, but his wife seemed to play little or no part in his life. He had taken the newly elected Emma Kerr under his wing, and their love affair had been conducted (so said the author – Tim Renton?) with some circumspection. There was a copy of a profile of Worthy Evans written by the *Birmingham Post*, something about treading in Chamberlain's footsteps. Joshua, who had written many such profiles of politicians, thought that was pushing it.

A yellowed press cutting dated June 1976 fell out. It appeared that a Peter Evans had appeared in court on the charge of a drunken assault. The victim was Barry Kerr. He had been found guilty and sentenced to six months in jail, suspended. Joshua wondered if Emma knew. His voting record was exemplary and his loyalty had been given wholeheartedly to whomsoever happened to be the leader of the Party. David Waddington had written 'officer material' in green ink. Could be, thought Joshua; but Peter was no gentleman.

Charles Harvey's file was, if anything, duller than Worthy Evans's. There was a report from a recruiting officer of MI5 who had tried unsuccessfully to entice Charles to join the service when Harvey was at Oxford University. 'Nice lad,' the report had concluded, 'but he wants to become richer than he ever could working for us.'

Cecil Parkinson, who had been Secretary of State for Transport when Charles was given junior office, had written kindly of his Parly-Sec. He was 'as smart as paint', and would 'go far' – which was what one might have expected from a Minister of Transport. Harvey was said to possess a stable personality (was there a shrink in the whips' office?), a quick mind and to be happily married. Renton, who was not, had described him as 'A thorough-going Thatcherite, but pleasant with it'. Joshua laughed out loud. There was, sadly, nothing in Harvey's report to show that he was any more than a clever, youngish man of impeccably right-wing views and lucky enough to have a rich wife. The fact that he was a Roman Catholic was given as a reason for his hostility towards abortion and euthanasia. Joshua echoed a remark his daughters might well have made, 'boring'.

As much could not be said for Old Bufton's confidential report. Bufton had first been elected to the House in October 1959. There was a recommendation from Donald Kabery who had been the Party's Vice Chairman in charge of candidates. 'I knew his father during the first war and the son is a chip off the old block.' That could mean anything, thought Joshua: old Donald had been careful not to specify the wood.

More interestingly, there was a note marked 'Private and Strictly Confidential' which had been written by Martin Redmayne who had been Harold Macmillan's Chief Whip. Bufton, it turned out, was the 'Headless Man', the unknown Tory who had cavorted naked at the Astor/Profumo parties at Cliveden in the early 1960s. The press had set up a great hulabaloo. Who could it be? A senior Tory of impeccable credentials (could it have been Duncan Sandys?) was widely rumoured to have been the guilty man. To clear himself, the senior Tory had been obliged to send a photograph of his private parts to Lord Denning. 'I have spoken to Tufton', wrote Redmayne, 'and have told him that as far as the whips' office is concerned the matter is closed, but that he, Tufton, was to understand that all hope of promotion had gone, and that any recurrence of his outrageous activities would be passed on to the Chairman of the Nether Stowey Conservative Association.' Poor old Bufton, and poor old chairman, thought Joshua, for whom promotion had also been denied. At least I never danced naked *au bord du fleuve* in the company of Christine Keeler. More was the pity.

The reference in Bufton's file to Emma's blackmailing activities was skimpy enough. He had told his area whip when in his cups (it was two in the morning on the Report Stage of the Finance Bill) that Emma had told him that she knew of his Thames-side cavortings. She had been told as much by someone in the Lobby. I must ask Michael White, noted Joshua: perhaps he might know who it could have been? She had then suggested to the old man that she would not refuse a non-executive directorship in a company such as those owned by Tufton. She had told him that she was finding it hard to manage on her parliamentary salary, and that her worthless husband was running up debts. She had made no threats, but the inference was plain. Pay up if you want to keep your peace of mind. The whip had told his chief and Bufton had been invited to talk to Waddington, but, upon arrival in Waddington's office, the old man had clammed up and had claimed indignantly that he had said no such thing.

Miss Petersfield shifted uncomfortably in Joshua's chair. She, no doubt, had already read all the files. She refused to go away and drink a cup of coffee. In desperation, Joshua handed her his paperback copy of Marcus Aurelius's *Meditations*.

'Read me what he says about death on page ninety-seven.'

She did as she was told. 'Death: a release from the impressions of sense, from twitchings of appetite, from excursions of thought and from service to the flesh.' Joshua told her he had long wished he were a Stoic, but he was more of an Epicurean. Miss Petersfield looked quite mystified. Once released, she would no doubt take a surreptitious look at Joshua's file. What on earth did he mean?

As Joshua carefully untied the pink ribbons that bound Emma's confidential file, the telephone rang. It was 'The World at One'. Had Joshua heard that Sam Langford had said that he would stand as a stalking-horse candidate against John Major in November's leadership election? Would he care to comment? No, he would not. He gave Ryder's secretary the news but she was unimpressed. He then shook out the contents of Emma's file on to his desk. On top was a large photograph of a naked Emma standing beside a rose bush. She stood with one leg neatly in front of the other, a much younger Emma in an unflattering hair style. 'Her calendar picture,' said Miss Petersfield, unbidden. 'The one she posed for on behalf of the *Motor Traders' Gazette*.' So the rumour had been true after all . . . Joshua resisted the impulse to make a remark that might well have been judged facetious.

The whips' office clearly did not miss a trick. 'The Party's area office paid good money for that,' said Miss Petersfield primly. 'Norman Tebbit insisted when he was Chairman of the Party that we obtain the neg; you'll find it, too, among all that gubbins.'

Joshua thought the 'gubbins', as she liked to call it, pathetic. He could not help wondering what his own confidential file contained. A photograph of Felicity?

The notices of his several books published over the years? The telephone number of that interpreter in Milan? His bank statements? Joshua hoped he would never find out. Emma's remains lay scattered on his desk, so much flotsam. There was a copy of her election address ('Emma backs Maggie') with the obligatory pictures of candidate with spouse and candidate again with tame old age pensioner. I wonder if anyone actually reads election addresses? Joshua wondered. They probably went straight into the bin.

There was a sheaf of press cuttings culled from the provincial and national press: they were not so much political in content as social – Emma modelling an outfit designed for a woman MP, Emma on horseback in Hyde park in the company of Annie Heseltine, Emma attacked by that curmudgeonly old Scots swine John Junor in the *Mail on Sunday* for her 'frivolity'. Which of us would escape whipping? wondered Joshua.

There was a paragraph about the scene in the tea room the previous year when Langford and Emma Kerr had had a row. Emma, so it had appeared, had remonstrated with Langford about his attitude towards one of the black girls who man the urns. He had been rude to her. They had been standing in the queue at the time. Langford had then rounded on Emma calling her a 'tart', and claiming loudly that, given her reputation, she would get to the top on her back. Langford, in his turn, had been noisily abused by two Labour MPs, one of whom had prevented Emma from smacking Langford's face. When rebuked by the Chief Whip Langford had been unrepentant. He did not apologise to him or to her. 'Mark my words,' he had said, 'butter wouldn't melt in that bitch's mouth.' A note had been scribbled in the margin in Ryder's hand. 'Langford is the bloody end.' Joshua thought so, too.

There was a letter from the area agent to the chief whip at the time of the election suggesting rather coyly that all was not well in the Kerrs' matrimonial home. 'She's a pretty lady and fast with it,' had been the considered opinion of the Party's Midlands *apparatchik*. There was a report of the conversation between the chief whip and Old Tufton, and a copy of a letter warning Worthy Evans, in the nicest possible way, that dalliance sat uncomfortably with political ambition. Charles Harvey did not rate a mention. Emma Kerr, thirty-one, beautiful, married but fancy-free, who had once been tipped, albeit by the political correspondent of the *Express*, as the next woman Prime Minister but one, had been reduced to a handful of paper.

Joshua repacked the files and handed them over to their guardian. 'Will you thank Richard and tell him I would like a word later in the day?'

Miss Petersfield grimaced and left without a word. Thank God she doesn't work for me, Joshua reflected.

What had Emma been up to after she left Charles Harvey? If it came to that, what had Harvey been doing in the hours between two and eight a.m.? Could his fellow whips vouch for Worthy Evans? He had come off the bench at about one o'clock and returned to it at five, leaving for home at around eight. He had had more than four hours on his hands, although the autopsy report had suggested that Emma had been killed between five and seven on Tuesday morning. How well did Peter and Charles really know Emma? Was her rather clumsy attempt to persuade Old Tufton to put her on the board of one of his companies a true indication of her unscrupulousness? It was really very hard to believe that someone like Charles Harvey or Peter Evans would actually strangle the girl and then put her on show in that horrible manner. It was not

what the voter expected from Members of Parliament,
of whatever party.

A knock on his door heralded the arrival of Charles
Harvey, who was plainly not in the best of tempers.
The two men had had little to do with each other in
the past; in fact, they had barely exchanged a word.
'I'm told by Richard that I am to come and see you
about Emma Kerr. Better you, I suppose, than some
bloody policeman, although it is most extraordinary –
I mean, asking one Member to investigate the
behaviour of one of his colleagues. It is not as if you
were a whip or anything.'

Joshua said he knew that he was not kosher.

'Look,' continued Harvey, who had taken a seat in
the regulation armchair still moulded by the figure of
Miss Petersfield. 'I was having an affair with Emma. It
began last March or so. We slept together in Dolphin
Square. I tried to break it off, or rather to turn down
the heat, last night. We had a frightful row in my room
– I was hard at work on my boxes – about which
no doubt Peter Evans has told you. My wife had no
knowledge of our affair, and I hope she doesn't find
out. I most certainly did not kill Emma. You can't
seriously think I did, can you?'

Joshua shrugged. 'Someone did.'

Harvey jigged his crossed leg up and down and
peered impatiently at his wristwatch.

'Have you any ideas who might have killed her?'
Joshua continued unabashed.

'Norman Tebbit,' replied Harvey. 'Wasn't he known
as the Chingford Strangler?'

Joshua asserted gently that Norman had a sweet
disposition and, as far as he knew, had had no dealings
with Emma. 'Have you any better ideas?'

Harvey shook his head.

'Not even Worthy Evans?'

Harvey hesitated and then decided to bluff it out. 'I haven't the faintest idea who killed her. Worthy Evans is far too wet. God knows what a sassy girl like Emma ever saw in him. Anyway, your question is impertinent. Can you really suppose that I have come up to this remote corridor in order to finger a colleague?'

Joshua accepted the rebuke. No doubt the junior minister was missing an important engagement. He had heard how busy they were kept. 'Would you describe Emma as a nice person?'

'Very,' said Harvey, whose temper was clearly rising, his complexion matching his Leander tie.

Joshua tried another tack. 'Why do you think she was killed?'

'I have not the slightest idea.'

'Was Worthy Evans jealous?'

'Not enough to kill her.' Harvey, who was not afraid of Day and all the Dimblebys, was giving nothing away.

'Did Emma have any particular friends in the Press Lobby? Anyone in whom she might have confided? She was very much a media favourite.'

'I don't know of anybody. Emma was as keen as I am to keep her love life out of the papers. I do know she was being pursued for something by that shit Ron Barton of the *Brit*. He had invited her out to lunch. Should have been yesterday. She was worried about that, and possibly with good cause. You know what the *Brit* is like.'

'One last question.' Harvey winced. 'Can you account for your movements after the row with Emma in the early hours?'

Harvey thought for a moment. 'Not as easily as I would like. After Emma tried to kick my door down I stayed in my room working for a time. I was in a bit of a state. I then tried to find her. Try as I might I could not. I failed to spot her at the three o'clock vote and again at seven-forty. I have checked with David Lightbown in the whips' office; she didn't vote on either occasion. David was like a bear with a sore head. Said he hadn't seen her. I even came up here, or near here, to see if she was in her room, but there was no sign of her. I asked the policeman under the canopy in New Palace Yard after the last vote whether he had seen her, but he said not. Said something about being tucked up in bed, most likely – and leered as he said it. We are not getting the better sort of policeman nowadays.'

Joshua had no complaints: the hand-picked force of Metropolitan coppers called him 'sir', which was more than they could manage in the real world outside. He thanked Charles for his kindness and wished him well. Harvey, who was beginning to look slightly ashamed of himself, said, 'Good luck. I hope you find the bugger.'

What a cold fish, thought Joshua. But providing he's clean – and I haven't much to go on at the moment – he will probably rise effortlessly to the top. I suspect that he's quietly relieved by Emma's death; the affair had been on the brink of burning itself out, and he was running a risk. If they can't keep their pants on, Ministers of the Crown, however promising, are fair game for the press. Didn't the *Telegraph*, that organ of the respectable classes, now carry a 'Page Three' of its own, a sad record of sin in Scarborough, fornication in Frinton and buggery in Bude? Charles could well have found himself in that company.

Joshua took a piece of Commons writing paper, and with the help of his 1920s Parker Duofold – a gift from the Provost of Queen's – jotted down his thoughts. Peter Worthy Evans and Charles Harvey both had the opportunity; they were in or around the Palace of Westminster in the small hours of Tuesday morning; what was more, they both had a motive. Jealousy on the part of Peter, peace of mind on the part of Charles. But there was precious little to bite on.

Joshua left his office and walked along the Upper Committee corridor until he came to the parade of offices that had included Emma's. Her room was bleak save for a dozen rag dolls which were displayed on bookcase, desk and filing cabinet. Her room-mate, Annie Widdecombe, had abandoned it after she had been made a minister. A notice had been pinned to the door to the effect that the room had been 'done' for fingerprints. She had hung a print of Renoir's *A Girl on a Swing* on the wall above her desk. There was an unopened box containing a bottle of scent called 'Poison' and a photograph of a collie dog in a cottage garden. A copy of one of Joshua's favourite books, Sybille Bedford's *A Legacy*, was on the floor next to her desk. He picked it up and glanced at the flyleaf. Charles Harvey's name was neatly inscribed.

The telephone rang; Joshua hesitated for a moment before moving to answer it. As he touched the receiver the instrument went dead. He knocked on the door of the adjacent office which belonged to a Labour MP. It was empty. The office across the passage belonged to an old friend, Trevor Skeet. Joshua knocked and entered. Skeet was an active seventy-something with the brusque manner of the headmaster of a successful preparatory school. Joshua asked him whether he had heard anything unusual on Monday night.

'Noise Monday night?' he barked. 'You can say that again. And I was trying to kip. That frightful Lancaster and his research assistant. Shouts, screams, you know how shrill the female voice becomes in anger?' It was the disapproving schoolmaster again, for whom women are only relevant as matrons or producers of small boys.

'I'll show you what I did.'

Skeet seized a Victorian policeman's truncheon, the sort that has designs painted on it, and struck his door several times. The noise was deafening – so much so that a Welsh voice cried out plaintively from next door, 'Trevor, for Christ's sake, give over.'

Skeet gestured towards the wall with his thumb. 'Ex-miner. Salt of the earth.'

Joshua returned to his office. The red light on his telephone burned, a sign that there was a message for him in the Members' Lobby. It was to ring Sir Ralph Grunte, urgently. He duly picked up the phone and dialled four digits. 'Rafe?' said Joshua. He could not resist teasing Grunte. If Grunt could become 'Gruntey' at a whim, why shouldn't the plebeian Ralph become, overnight, the much smarter 'Rafe'? Knowing Grunte it could only be a matter of time.

'You wanted me to ring. Joshua Morris.'

Grunte was in one of his quarterdeck moods; he was not about to stand any nonsense. 'Now look here, Morris,' he began, 'I hear you're snooping about over the Emma business. The whips seem to think you are some sort of Sherlock Holmes. Just ran into Worthington Evans – never liked him much, I must say.' Joshua held the receiver slightly away from his ear. 'But that's not what I'm ringing you about. He says he has been interviewed by you. Trying to find out his whereabouts at the time of the crime. I hope you're not thinking of grilling me, because I'm telling you here and now that I won't have any part of it.'

Joshua felt his temper rise. 'Why should I talk to you, Ralph? It's common knowledge that you spent most of Monday night pissed as a newt. Didn't the unlucky Evans put you in a taxi, drunk and incapable? And, if it comes to that, have you paid him back the ten quid you owe him for the fare?' Joshua put the receiver back on to its rest and pushed the 'out' button. Grunte was really quite intolerable.

On his way to the press gallery lunch Joshua put his head into the smoking room. He was greeted with cries of 'it's a fair cop' and 'it weren't me, guv', so he did not linger. Why was it that there were no secrets in the Palace of Westminster? A messenger handed him no fewer than six pink slips: they included 'The World at One', Frank Bough and the BBC's World Service (five minutes talking to savages); it was almost as if there were yet another leadership contest. Mike White accompanied him along a maze of stairs and passages to the dining room reserved for the press lobby. It was to be a special occasion. Each member of the lobby had invited a guest, usually a politician.

The old regime was there in force: Sir Bernard Ingham, Mrs Thatcher's 'Rasputin' – the description was John Biffen's, who had, since the *putsch*, been working for the Pru.; Sir Charles Powell who, having been the possessor of Mrs Thatcher's ear in Downing Street, had just had his jabs; he was on his way, with the blessing of the Foreign Office, to Mongolia; and the egregious Sir Timothy Bell. Attracted to the presence of Mrs Thatcher herself, it was a meeting of a government in exile, or a Bourbon court.

Joshua put himself in the mood to be amused. He accepted a glass of sour white wine and watched the proceedings. Promptly at five to one, Mrs Thatcher made her entrance. She had a curiously unattractive, bustling walk, rather like a Jack Russell, but she looked her old combative self. She had worn well. Sir Peter

Morrison, as red as a turkey cock, was in attendance; so, too, was Jeffrey Archer. He carried a pile of his paperbacks: they were for sale after the speeches. Joshua asked Matthew Parris of *The Times*, standing nearby, who the speakers were. 'The Lady, of course, and then Nick Ridley.' Parris gestured towards a corner of the room where Ridley, partly obscured by cigarette smoke, was talking to Sir Peregrine Worsthorne. 'Perry' was in search of material for his next editorial. 'We have another treat,' said Parris, 'J. Archer is proposing the vote of thanks.'

Joshua asked if there were to be a raffle; as a long-serving Tory MP he could not bear there to be no raffle. 'Should it not be a copy of Mrs Thatcher's apologia?' asked Michael White. It was understood that the former Prime Minister had received two million pounds as an advance on her memoirs, to be called, or so White would have it, *Done Away With*, and published by The Crusader Press.

The company obeyed a request to be seated. Joshua, who had his host on his left hand, found that the place on his right had been reserved for Ron Barton, but of the intrepid investigator there was no sign. He was out somewhere, doggedly in pursuit of the truth, or something that approximated to it. White wanted to know about Emma.

Joshua knew that he would not be quoted. He told White that he had until the morning to come up with the culprit. So far, he had little to go on. Her lovers had both opportunity and motive, but the 'evidence', such as it was, was circumstantial. Joshua suggested that Emma might have been a nasty bit of work (he recounted the story of Tufton Butfon's confrontation), which, if true, could point discouragingly to other suspects as yet unknown. Her private life was in a mess and she was hard up. Worthy Evans had suggested as much to Richard Ryder.

'Doesn't the whips' office pay off the debts of Tory MPs?' asked White.

Joshua said he believed that it had occasionally happened, but not so much since Tim Sainsbury had left the office.

Lunches that combine politicians and political journalists are often fun. November's *Spectator* lunch at the Savoy, for example, was not to be missed. MPs and hacks fed upon each other, and the lobby rules encouraged indiscretion, which was more than could be said for the Muscadet. Its metallic taste invariably conjured up, in Joshua's mind, Tory Party supper club meetings in the home counties. It was wine with nothing to be said for it. There was also a refreshing cynicism which could not be found always in the Members' dining room. The titillating subject of Emma's murder battled for attention with the Tory Right's declaration of war on John Major's Government. A pansy young man, who worked for the *Mail*, declared to all and sundry that he thought Norman to be deliciously common. He was, or so the speaker claimed, embarking on a sequel to his book *Upwardly Mobile* to be called *The Sky's the Limit*, in which Cecil Parkinson finally gets the girl and lives happily ever after. This sally caused some merriment.

After a pink ice cream and a wafer biscuit, the Chairman of the Lobby called for silence. He then introduced Mrs Thatcher in glowing terms. Her rule, he claimed, had been a golden age. At this there were strident cries of 'hear, hear' from the journalists of the *Sunday Telegraph*. Sir John Junor tried to set off a standing ovation, but was told to sit down by the *hoi polloi*.

Mrs Thatcher looked around her. Was she among
friends? Her glance fell upon Colonel Mates, who had
been Heseltine's *chef du cabinet*. Her smile faded and
her eyes flashed. 'Mr Chairman,' she began. 'As you
can see, I'm not wearing my grey.' She was wearing
her blue, and everyone knew what that meant: another
good thrashing for someone. Would it be John Major?
The word 'grey' drew a laugh; no one could be as grey
as her successor. 'I'm delighted to see that my Bernard
is here.' This reference to her faithful press secretary
drew a second and louder laugh. There was a cry from
the *Daily Mirror* contingent of 'Take a bow, Rasputin.'
At this, Archer rose to his feet like a monkey on a
stick, and displayed across his chest a car rear window
sticker with the legend 'Come back, Maggie, all is
forgiven'. This display of obsequiousness was met with
rude noises. An anonymous voice was heard to ask
what happened to his peerage. Mrs Thatcher grasped
the microphone and continued. 'I am sure you would
all want to know that I am enjoying my retirement
hugely. Denis is playing a lot of golf.' Here there was
a scattered round of applause: Denis was a popular
figure. 'And I am keeping an eye on the shop.'

Joshua remembered a visit he had once made for a
newspaper to write a piece about the Roberts's corner
shop on what had been the A1 in Grantham. It had
been made into a shrine; the 1930s grocer's shop had
been recreated, even down to pots of 'Roberts's
Raspberry Jam'. The scales, before which the young
Margaret had learnt national housekeeping, were kept
burnished. He had given a present of a jar of the jam
to his local party's Christmas draw. It had been won
by a snobbish woman with a taste for writing offensive
doggerel. Serve her right.

Mrs Thatcher was getting up steam. 'As you will all

know, in my eleven and a half years in office, we always put the national interest first. At home, we rolled back the frontiers of socialism and encouraged the enterprise culture.' Here her voice dropped an octave. 'And we did not forget the less fortunate in society.'

Joshua, who had spent much of his time over the previous decade avoiding Mrs Thatcher's speeches, began to feel that he should not have come. It was appallingly familiar, Party conference oratory. John Major might be grey but at least he was comfortable. He did not hector. Nor did he boast.

'Abroad,' continued Maggie, warming to her theme, 'we re-took the Falklands, liberated Eastern Europe from socialism' – single-handed? wondered Joshua – 'and we refused to kow-tow to the bureaucrats of Brussels.' She was now almost shouting. 'We were all in favour of a European-wide free trade area, but we set our face against any political or monetary union. When I was in Downing Street, we did not sell our birthright for a mess of porridge. No. No. No.'

At this, there was a titter from the posher papers who recognised the solecism; several journalists, from sheets broad and narrow, slipped quietly out of the room. There had been nothing about selling birthrights in the official handout. The boat was well and truly being rocked. Joshua murmured his thanks to his host and left the room. Those who said Maggie was dead but would not lie down were right. Emma, however, *was* dead and, no doubt, would be buried before the week was out. And he still had no idea who had choked her to death.

14

The Minister of Posts and Telegraphs ran into David Lancaster in the Commons gym. 'I tried to reach you last night,' said Lancaster, 'but you were always engaged. What happened to you? Were you caught?'

'If I had been you would have heard about it by now. You're looking at a fully paid-up member of the Cricklewood Labour Party. A very nice class of person.' The minister fished out a five pound note and waved it. He recounted the story of his exploits. 'I shall give it to the charismatic church in my constituency. The wages of sin.'

Lancaster, in between press-ups, could not help admiring his friend's sang-froid. 'I spent the afternoon in the Gaumont State, Kilburn, watching a skin flick.' At thirty-nine, he could still manage thirty press-ups on the go. 'I can remember when there was an organist at half-time. The biggest cinema in Europe, or so it claimed.'

The minister no longer looked like a lumberjack; he had left his bobble-hat in the mini-cab. He was on his way to a cabinet committee. David Lancaster started to run on the spot. They were, once again, twin pillars of their Party. 'See you around,' said the minister.

'Not for some time. I'm not as fit as I was. I think I'll take things quietly for a bit. Too much excitement.' Lancaster began touching his toes. He could do so fifty times without losing his puff. There wasn't a copper in north-west London who could catch him; which was more than could be said for his Rt. Hon. friend.

Ron Barton was feeling a little fragile. Like most MPs that Monday night he, too, had been kept from his marital bed by affairs of state. He had not tramped through the lobbies on some desperate pilgrimage, but had been in hot pursuit of scandal. He had, it was true, caught up with Wayne Ellis who had, as he supposed, taken refuge in David Lancaster's room. Barton's membership of the Press Lobby did not permit him to range freely in those quarters of the Palace which were the preserve of the elected; nonetheless, he had taken the lift, Emma's lift, up to the second floor well after midnight, and had done so with impunity.

So large had the army of researchers and secretaries grown, to say nothing of the public on their way to various committees, that the attendants, who sit behind desks like so many Parisian concierges, found it hard to keep track. The man on duty recognised Barton's face from somewhere, and, satisfied, returned to reading a thriller by Douglas Hurd. That had been Monday night, or rather the early hours of Tuesday morning. Tuesday evening had been spent entertaining Barry Kerr to a late hour. Barry, with a cheque for £20,000 in his pocket, had wanted to paint the town. Not only had Ron been obliged to write up the sad story of Barry's blighted marriage for Wednesday's paper but he had had to act as chaperon as well. How hard is the life of those intrepid hacks who do not spare themselves in order to bring the truth to our tables! Ron was no stranger to the pleasures of the West End, but even he came to regard a tour that began with drinks at Harry's, followed by dinner at the Café Royal and ended at Raymond's Revue Bar as a calvary; so many stations of the cross. Finally Barry had picked up a 'bird'; Ron, who had a cold coming on, had not climbed into his Dulwich bed until three o'clock.

His editor had summoned him to his office at eleven. Ron made sure he arrived with several minutes to spare, and, finding the editor absent, sat down uneasily, reading and rereading his story. So Barry Kerr had been led a dance; so what? The paper's lawyers had toned down the references to Tory MPs who, by implication, might have enjoyed Emma's favours, and the story was, he had to admit, especially by the standards of the *True Brit*, a bit on the thin side. His editor, who had been trained in the hard school of the *Sun*, was not likely to be best pleased.

At eleven-twenty, the great man finally appeared. He had been playing squash and was wearing slacks and a sweater. A towel was wrapped around his neck. 'That was a fucking waste of twenty grand,' was his greeting. As he talked he strode backwards and forwards across the room, making forehand strokes with an imaginary racquet. 'So Emma spread it around "the colleagues". What's new? I want to know who bloody well did it. That sod Joshua Morris has been asked to find out, to keep the fuzz from treading on too many toes. Have you spoken to him?'

Barton said that it was his intention to try to do so the moment he got to the House.

'Good on you, Ron.'

Barton rose to his feet, ready to leave. The editor, who had begun practising his backhand, waved him down. 'What about that other sod? David Lancaster, and the wine waiter? Are you following that one up?'

Barton, eager to ingratiate himself, hurried to tell of his meeting with Wayne. 'There's something going on between them. I found the boy in Lancaster's room, in his room, mark you, and after two o'clock in the morning. The kid's a real bum-boy – pretty, if you like that sort of thing, but none too bright. He explained the wine incident as "a difference of opinion". You can't help but laugh. He had come to apologise to Lancaster because he was afraid of losing his job. Yes, they had been good friends. It seems they were going on holiday together on a Swan Hellenic cruise. You know the sort of thing, lots of wrinklies going around the Med. being lectured to on the pleasures of the ancient world.'

The editor, who had stopped playing squash, asked Barton whether this meant another large cheque drawn on the paper. 'You know what Rupe's like these days,' he warned. 'He's worried about the readies. But it seems a bloody good lead. Keep digging. And get hold of Morris. Give him the treatment. Set a thief to catch a thief, you know the line.'

Ron did. He made his excuses and left.

At two-thirty on Wednesday afternoon, the Government whips held their regular weekly meeting. The agenda was more than usually heavy. Besides deciding on the business for the following week, it was the whips' task to allocate one, two or three lines to the business itself, the number of lines indicating the seriousness of the matter under debate. Monday would be a one-liner; Tuesday was an Opposition Supply Day: the Labour whips had not yet told their opposite numbers the subject they would choose for debate, but that did not matter much. Whatever it was there would be a three-line vote at ten o'clock. Now is the time for all good men to come to the aid of the Party. Wednesday was the second reading of the Government's bill to legalise Sunday trading; another three-liner at ten, with a large number of Tory abstentions. 'We shall have our hands full, twisting arms,' said Ryder. Thursday, nothing very much, private members' motions, a one-liner, Friday, ditto. The dozen or so whips sitting in a circle before their Chief made a note of next week's business. So far so good. The meeting then moved on to 'any other business'.

'I have several items under any other business,' said Ryder. 'We shall be here some time. First, there is the sad, indeed shocking, matter of the murder of Mrs Kerr. You all know that John MacGregor and I have asked Joshua Morris to see if he can come up with the culprit. He has until mid-morning tomorrow to do so. I have had a word with him but he doesn't seem to have made much progress. We can only hope that he does so. We don't want Scotland Yard all over the shop. God forbid. Morris says that he has eliminated Grunte. Not too difficult. Pissed at the time. And tucked up in bed. Incidentally, I don't know what we can do about Grunte. His Monday-night nonsense was an embarrassment to us all. You know it is our policy to stick by Members through thick and thin, but Grunte's antics are getting to be too much of a good thing. And I understand he may be coming to us for money. Owes the Revenue sixty thousand quid.' At this there were groans all round. It was worse than being a member of Lloyd's.

'If Morris fails then the Leader of the House will have to make a statement on Emma's killing on Thursday afternoon after Questions. Has anybody anything they want to say on this matter?'

'What about the memorial service? Will it be at St Margaret's and when?' Alastair Goodlad, the Deputy Chief Whip, was suitably grave. 'Shall I go ahead and make the necessary arrangements, say for a month's time?' There was general assent. At this juncture, Peter Worthington Evans asked whether he could give the address. There was a general intake of breath. Had Peter gone off his head? Everyone knew that he had been in love with Emma; they also knew that he had been questioned by Morris in the course of his investigation. Ryder had said nothing about Peter being in the clear. He had not been pissed and tucked up in bed.

The Deputy Chief Whip, plump and stately, became even more butler-like. 'I am sorry to say that I have already had two letters making the same request, namely that they too, should give the address at Emma's memorial service.' All eyes turned towards Alastair Goodlad. 'They are from Charles Harvey and Sir Ralph Grunte.' There was a roar of laughter, a release of tension. 'Shall I read out his letter?'

Goodlad intoned: ' "Dear Goodlad" – I do wish Grunte would stop pretending to be a gentleman, when everybody knows he is nothing of the kind.' Tom Sackville laughed. Peter Worthy Evans who had, like most of the whips, failed to get the point (the bulk of the office not having been promoted by Hugh Montgomery Massingberd of the *Telegraph* into the top three social categories into which he had divided Tory MPs) cried out, 'Enough.' Not unreasonably, he felt that Emma's death was being turned into a laughing matter. Good-lad asked plaintively who then should be asked to give the address?

There was silence which was broken by David Light-bown. He was a burly man who had once been mis-taken for an off-duty policeman. He could be relied upon to call a spade a shovel. 'Look here, we can't have Bill Brewer, Dan Dailey, Uncle Tom Cobleigh, Charles Harvey, Ralph Grunte or Peter here. Do you want to turn it into a farce? We must ask Lord St John of Fawsley. He's safe.' A dozen heads nodded gravely. He paused. 'And he would do it very nicely.'

Richard Ryder brought the meeting to order and to the last item on the agenda. 'What do we do about Margaret?' He recounted briefly what the President of the Bruges Group and of the No Turning Back Group, the ex-Premier and the Rt. Hon. Member for Finchley had said to the press gallery lunch. It was not so much her text, said Ryder, which contained nothing new, but her statement at the onset that John Major had sold his birthright for a mess of pottage. That would grab tomorrow's headlines. The Party split, the Government in trouble. The boat was being savagely rocked; would it be able to stay afloat? After the recent *putsch* which had led to her downfall, there remained an element in the Party, both in the House and more especially in the constituencies, that had been scandalised by the way she had been treated. A majority, however, thought that she had destroyed herself. The 'irreconcil-ables', as they had become known, threatened to make the task of the Major Government very difficult indeed.

In an ideal world, ex-prime ministers should not stay in the Commons. Ted Heath had done so and made trouble for Margaret, now Margaret was about to do the same for John Major. The answer, if there was one, was to persuade them both to claim their earldoms and make tracks for the Lords. The soporific atmosphere of red plush and brass fittings, together with the company of clever old things, the occasional public platform and an inexhaustible supply of bread and butter pudding would turn down the flame that burned so fiercely within them. Lord Broadstairs and Lady Grantham – would that not be the way out?

It was decided that a delegation comprising Lord Whitelaw, Lord Carrington, Sir Georg Solti, Mr Norman Tebbit and the Chief Whip should call immediately upon them both. Not for the first time would the Upper House come to the aid of the Lower.

Joshua Morris returned to his room at three o'clock. It was Chancellor's Questions in the Chamber, and Norman Lamont was exercising dialectical skills picked up in Cambridge and honed in the House in defence of the Government's economic record. John Smith, for Labour, was at his Scottish best. How much more formidable would Kinnock be were he the son of the manse, thought Joshua; there was something both authoritative and comforting about an East of Scotland voice: all that rectitude. He collapsed into his regulation armchair, which he found hairy and angular; fifty years ago it might have been issued to the armed services, officers, for the use of. Sleep, which was becoming elusive at night, came swiftly by day. He was awakened by his telephone. Felicity was in the Central Lobby.

She spread her parcels on the floor of Joshua's office and chattered happily. 'What news of Emma?'

Joshua, who was dying for a cup of tea – there were no tea-making facilities in the corridors of power – brought her up to date. He was, he admitted, stuck.

There was nothing he could tell the police about Peter, Grunte or Charles Harvey that they could not quickly find out for themselves.

'We must think laterally,' said Felicity, who had recently read a piece by Edward de Bono in the *Spectator*.

Joshua said that under the old regime lateral thinking had been discouraged in the Tory Party; it seemed always to lead to yet another leadership election. 'Let's go and have a look at Emma's room. We should try and find out what she did after she flounced out of Harvey's room. How satisfying to have kicked his door.'

On the way Joshua regaled her with a description of his lunch and Mrs Thatcher's speech. 'Mrs T's problem,' observed Felicity, who remained one of her admirers, 'is that she never manages to speak softly altho' she's good with a big stick.'

'Talking of big sticks,' said Joshua, chuckling, and he told her about Sir Trevor Skeet and his Peeler's truncheon, and his headmasterly disapproval of noise.

'Wait,' said Felicity. 'Did you say a shrill female voice? I thought Lancaster was gay. He'd never employ a female researcher. Mightn't it have been—'

'Emma,' interrupted Joshua. 'Of course.'

'But why should Lancaster have been having a row in the small hours of the morning?' asked Felicity.

'Perhaps I have just had an inspiration,' said Joshua. 'I think I might know the answer. You remember I told you I had a glimpse of Emma on the terrace very early on the Tuesday morning. The moon was shining brightly, and she was standing by the parapet at the House of Lords end, talking to someone. They were alone. I had gone out for a breath of air. I didn't see who it was, but it was nobody I recognised. It could,

I suppose, have been Harvey – the figure was tall, taller than Worthy Evans. Evans and Emma were about the same height, you know, smaller than you.' Felicity stood about five feet nine inches. 'And, you know, it might just have been Ellis. But why should Ellis have spoken to Emma? Save perhaps for serving her a half-bottle, they would have had no contact whatsoever.'

'Who,' asked Felicity, 'was at the table on Monday night when Wayne Ellis poured a bottle of Blue Nun over Lancaster's head? Can you remember?'

Joshua reflected. 'Dame Elaine – she was magnificent; not the sort to stand any nonsense, Heseltine, Harvey – Harvey was next to Emma – Donald Thompson, the frightful Grunt and me. And the dripping Lancaster.'

'What happened to Wayne after he left the stage? Do you know?

Joshua said that he had inquired when he ran into Charles Irving, and had got the impression that he had been sent home with a flea in his ear.

'Have you spoken to Wayne?'

Joshua said that until this moment he had had no cause to. Queers might kill each other, but there was no obvious reason to link Lancaster, or Wayne, with Emma's death.

'We must find out whether Wayne met Emma later that night.' Felicity was on a high. 'Darling,' she said, 'you must make me the Secretary of the Sherlock Holmes Society of Great Britain. PLC.' Joshua kissed her. She was more likely to become its President.

'But why should Wayne have wanted to speak to Emma?' asked Joshua.

'A shoulder to cry on. Can't you see? Lancaster and Ellis had a row earlier that day. A lovers' quarrel. But it was bitter enough to make the silly boy do a daft and very public thing like pouring a bottle of wine over his lover's head. What was the row about? Did they kiss and make up? If, and I stress "if", Wayne sought out, or much more likely, ran into Emma, how much did he tell her? Perhaps Lancaster has a good deal to hide.'

Joshua felt that it was high time he made a contribution; he was playing the part of Watson to Felicity's Holmes. 'Have a look at this sketch map I've done.* Emma's room is on the same corridor as Lancaster's. She could have spotted Wayne coming out or going into Lancaster's room next door, or next door but one. An elderly Welsh labour MP has the one in-between. The "salt of the earth". And Wayne Ellis would have known his way around. He had, after all, been Lancaster's research assistant a year or so ago, if only for a couple of months, and must have spent a good deal of time on the Upper Committee corridor.' Charles Irving had told Joshua of this. 'Not very bright, spent his time addressing constituency envelopes. He had probably kept his researcher's pass in case he was challenged. The authorities are always complaining they can't get them returned.'

Felicity's face fell. 'Hold on, not so fast.' The injunction was as much to herself as it was to Joshua. 'Even were Wayne to have spilt the beans to Emma, he would have had to have told Lancaster that he had done so, or, if he thought it wiser to keep his mouth shut, Emma must have told Lancaster. Why should she have done that? Surely she would not have wanted to be that much involved? She had problems enough of her own. We have linked Wayne to Emma, and thanks to Skeet we can tie Emma to Lancaster, but why should a meeting between them give Lancaster a motive for murder?'

*Reproduced on page vi

223

'There's only one thing to do,' said Joshua, 'and that is to talk to Wayne, and to do so as quickly as we bloody well can. If what we suspect is true, Lancaster must be a very dangerous man.'

15

At four o'clock in the afternoon there was no answer from the refreshment department. It was siesta time. Joshua tried the reference room of the library once more, but they had no address or telephone number for W. Ellis. Would Charles Irving know? Joshua was uncertain how the Chairman of the Kitchen Committee would react to such a mundane inquiry. He thought better of it. The 'Gastronomer Royal' could hardly be expected to carry the telephone numbers of the kitchen staff in his head or on his person.

His telephone rang. It was the BBC, the 'PM' programme, Radio 4. Would he care to comment on Mrs Thatcher's 'mess of porridge'? No, he would not. Abandoning the telephone, he and Felicity determined to go downstairs and hunt for Wayne's address in and around the dining rooms. There must be somebody about, somebody serving tea.

When they arrived at the lift, Felicity refused to travel in it. It would bring them bad luck. She had made no objection to travelling up in it. Instead, they

plunged down the vertigo-inducing emergency staircase
that linked the Upper to the Committee corridor. The
second flight descended in marbled splendour. In the
Members' dining room, tea was being served to half
a hundred Tory ladies (Labour women do not wear
hats).

As Joshua and Felicity entered, the buzz of conversation stilled and, amid applause, Mrs Thatcher got to
her feet. Oh God, thought Joshua, not again. Standing
against the window and to one side of the speaker
was Catherine, the Irish waitress who had looked after
Joshua with great dispatch for the past two years. She
had served his table on Monday night. He caught her
eye and waved, beckoning her to come to the door
and speak to him. Mrs Thatcher saw the gesture and,
thinking it was aimed at her, brought her 'few remarks'
to a halt. She glared at Joshua. The look was of the
kind that had humbled Howe, crippled Kinnock and
destroyed Delors. Joshua smiled foolishly and pointed
rather desperately towards Catherine. Should he retire
swiftly? The audience had swivelled in their bentwood
chairs and were looking curiously in his direction. What
was going on? Mrs Thatcher, with pursed lips (Joshua
had campaigned for Heseltine), looked at Joshua and
said, 'Yes?' The tone was as if Mrs Fawkes had been
asked for a penny for the guy. At that, Felicity tugged
Joshua from behind, and they made good their escape.

The door that they had closed quietly behind them
opened and Catherine came out. She was beaming. 'Is
it me you're after?' Catherine did not have Wayne's
address – his mum, she thought, lived in Forest Gate
– but she knew a man who did. If they would kindly
wait a moment she would do her best to find out.

Holmes and Watson stood patiently in the corridor.
After a moment, the dining room door opened and a

large woman with a small hat and a Ronald Colman moustache emerged looking to her left and then to her right. She appeared agitated. After she had looked to her left again, Joshua, with a desire to please, spoke up. 'You'll find it there, the other side of the hall, behind where the attendant is standing.'

The dragon did not look him in the eye. As she strode past him, she hissed, 'Troublemaker.'

'Which is exactly what you are,' said Felicity primly. She turned to Joshua. 'And, if we don't talk to poor Wayne, I have a nasty feeling he may be in trouble, too.'

Catherine returned, a piece of paper in her hand. 'I've three numbers for him, which is two more than I hoped for. The head waiter – I woke him up – says he is expected in tonight, but he's on the washing-up. We can't trust him with the wine.' The accent was that of the Abbey Theatre. Having thanked her profusely, Joshua and Felicity ascended the marble staircase, passing as they did so the dragon, who gave them a filthy look. She stopped, as if to say something.

'Round to the right and first door on the left,' said Felicity quickly. There was no response.

They climbed the two flights of stairs. Out of breath, they made their way along the corridors, past Trevor Skeet's room, and the old Welsh Labour MP's. In Joshua's office they tried the telephone.

The first number they dialled rang and rang. Eventually it was answered by a woman with a cockney voice. His mum was, after all, on the phone. No, she did not know where her son was. He was an ungrateful boy and as far as she was concerned . . . Joshua replaced the receiver and dialled the second number. It was answered almost immediately. A rough voice said, 'The Importance of Being Earnest.' It turned out to be the name of a drinking club. No, he had not had sight nor sound of Mr Ellis. When the third number answered, Joshua gave his name and asked whether he might speak to Wayne Ellis. 'Who?' said a voice, which was somewhat familiar. 'Who is it who wants to speak with Wayne Ellis? Who did you say you were?' Unmistakably, it was the voice of David Lancaster. Before Joshua could say anything more, the line went dead. On his second and third attempt the line was engaged.

Lancaster put down Greg's telephone and sat with his head in his hands. He was alone in Sherwood Road, Wayne having left for work ten minutes ago, and Greg not expected back until late. Why in God's name should Morris want to speak to Wayne? What could the connection be? Morris wrote occasionally for the papers but he was not a foot-in-the-door journalist. He was not the sort to follow up the incident of the wine in order to make mischief. He must have discovered somehow that Wayne and he had met in his room at the House very late on the night of Monday/Tuesday. But how could he have learned of Wayne's meeting with Emma, at which the stupid boy had unburdened himself to her? Was it no more than an inspired guess?

Lancaster, who knew of Emma's promiscuity, thought that Joshua, and the police, would have their hands full as it was, what with a bevy of randy colleagues of the likes of Grunte, and that he, Lancaster, would not have come under suspicion. Morris could not know of his meeting with Emma in the middle of the night, for he had not told Wayne about it. Wayne, in his turn, had confessed to Lancaster that he 'had got things off his chest', and had told Emma the sad tale of their 'storm-tossed relationship'. (Wayne had taken to reading the works of Barbara Cartland after

228

the author had been made a Dame.) A repentant
Wayne had assured Lancaster only that morning that
he had not said a word about Lancaster's Cricklewood
escapade. 'You knew I would never do the dirty.' Lancaster feared that Wayne was lying. He might not have
bared his bosom to Ron Barton (was he offered money
by the poison dwarf?) but Emma knew almost everything there was to know, and she could only have
learned it from Wayne.

The bitch had had the nerve to call on him in his
Commons office in the dead of night and make him a
proposition. She could get £50,000 from the *True Brit*
for Wayne's story. She had every incentive, so she said,
to sell Barton a better story in return, not just for cash,
but for his silence about her affair with Charles Harvey.
All Lancaster had to do if he wished to keep his and,
more to the point, his friend's reputation intact, was
to pay her a pound more – only a pound more – than
the £50,000 she was confident she could squeeze out
of Barton. She was lunching at Bibendum with the
reptile on Tuesday. Lancaster should meet her in the
Central Lobby at midday; there would be lots of people
about so he could not make a scene. He could just tell
her whether he would play ball.

Lancaster had not got £50,000, and even if he had
he would not have given the money to Emma Kerr.
He had told her in no uncertain terms what he thought
of her. She was a blackmailing slut. She could ruin him
and his friend, bring the Government down if it came
to that, but she was not getting one filthy penny from
him. As for the *True Brit*, it could publish and be
doubly damned. Lancaster sat for an hour in his room.
The consequences of exposure would be appalling.
Were he to raise £50,000 by a second mortgage, the
interest burden would be crippling. Besides, why the

bloody hell should he pay danegeld? She would be back for more. Emma had left him with no choice. He closed his door and made quietly for Emma's room. With any luck she would still be there.

There were lights under few of the office doors; most were in darkness. Lancaster had not bothered to knock on Emma's door. He opened it quietly, to find its occupant asleep in one armchair, her feet up on the seat of another. She had covered her face with a copy of Monday's *Times*. The room was lit only by the blue reflected light of the television monitor, which bore the name 'Mr Robert Maclennan', and the time, twenty-five minutes past five. Maclennan was just the man for the watches of the night, thought Lancaster. He saw himself, strangely enough, as some sort of avenging angel. Emma was dirty. Emma would get what was coming to her. Emma was a bitch, like most women.

As he soundlessly closed the office door, he saw, hanging from a hook, a dark-coloured trouser suit, a top and trousers. He took his heavy silk handkerchief out of his top pocket, and, bending over Emma from behind, removed the paper and pinched her nose. Emma's eyes and mouth opened simultaneously. Lancaster thrust the large handkerchief into her mouth where it acted as a gag. He then pushed her head forward until it almost reached her thighs and looped a leg of the cotton trousers around her neck. He then pulled hard on both ends. He was a powerful man who had not wasted his time in Spicer's gym. He did not relax his grip for at least five minutes. Emma, who threshed about desperately, was never to see the face of her attacker.

After it was all over and Lancaster had taken refuge in his room (he was not to quit the Palace until the vote at seven-forty that morning), he could not explain even to himself why he had carried the body as far as the lift where he had hung it from a hook. He had been luckier than he had deserved. The concierge had fallen asleep at his post. The lift was already waiting on the second floor. He had rescued his handkerchief from her mouth and then, on impulse, replaced it with her knickers. The display had been an additional and unnecessary risk. He had not been fair to himself. He could only conclude that he must have been overdoing things; too much excitement, too many late-night sittings. He deserved a holiday, but of one thing he was sure: it would not be with Wayne.

Wayne Ellis, wine waiter extraordinary, washer-up to the tribunes of the people and the occasional light of David Lancaster's life, sat in the back of the mini-cab sent to pick him up from Greg's house in Battersea. He was en route for an evening's work in the Commons kitchens. He had made his peace with his lover. They had obeyed Greg's injunction to 'kiss and make up'. He had, naturally, been circumspect in telling Lancaster exactly what it was he had told Emma Kerr early on Tuesday morning. He had been very upset at the time and might have been less than wise. To Lancaster he had decided it wisest to be 'economical with the truth'.

Wayne had no idea who had killed Emma. A lovely lady, she had reminded him the other night so vividly of his sister married to an American working on the North Sea oil platforms. He supposed it had been one of Lancaster's fellow MPs; had not Dave said as much as he dried Wayne's tears? That Peter Evans, to whom Wayne had served wine, was the likely killer. The Swan Hellenic cruise around the Greek Islands for his mother and himself was once again 'on'. They would visit Delos and the Temple of Apollo, sail into the harbour at Rhodes where once stood the Pharos and visit the ruined temples of Anatolia. They would float like corks on a wine-dark sea. They might even dine at the captain's table. Wayne had left the comp. in Forest Gate with no 'O' levels, and, much to the secret relief of his headmaster, had never read a book with hard covers, and precious few with soft. He could not spell, but he craved affection. He had, on Wednesday evening, no idea of just how popular he had become. He was greatly in demand.

Ron Barton, who had received another bollocking from the editor of the *True Brit*, was hovering in the corridor outside the kitchens, waiting for Ellis to arrive. 'This time you'll *get* the story, for Christ's sake. Put a ferret up his bum. Fail and you'll be back on the free sheets.' His editor had told him to be generous. Although Rupe was 'rolling over' his debts, whatever that might mean, he was prepared to spend good money on a story which would embarrass the Major Government. Since Maggie's departure Rupert Murdoch no longer made for No. 10 Downing Street upon his arrival in Britain. Barton wanted to know much more than Wayne had been persuaded to tell him on Monday night. How did Lancaster spend his spare time, and with whom? Was it with a Minister of the Crown? Was it true what they say about Dixie?

Joshua said goodbye to Felicity, who was taking her daughter to the theatre. They would meet the next morning at eleven, before she returned to her cold house in Herefordshire. They would lunch together. He was to telephone her later that night. Joshua wanted a word with Wayne in order to find out just how much he had told Emma on the Monday night. If his hunch was right, and Wayne had really spilt the beans, Lancaster would have had not only the opportunity to kill later that night but the motive as well. Emma knew too much. But what should he do with the information? He had no proof that Lancaster was the murderer; he would just pass on his conclusion to the Leader of the House. It would then be up to the police. If he were right in his deduction, then Wayne was in very considerable danger.

The head waiter had said that Wayne was due to clock on at five and begin laying up the tables in the Members' and Strangers' dining rooms. 'We're keeping him off the wine. He'll be up to his elbows in Fairy Liquid.' The head waiter, who had a sense of humour, chortled merrily. 'Have no fear,' he told Joshua, 'I'll ring your office the moment the wandering boy shows.' Joshua told him that it was vital that he should; it was desperately important to have a word with Wayne. Not another admirer, thought the head waiter; what do they all see in the spotty little sod?

David Lancaster got into his hired car (his Scorpio had not been found, although the West Hampstead police assured him that they were making every effort to do so) and drove to the House. He, too, must have another word with Wayne, a brief yet final word.

Barton got to Wayne first. He took the waiter into the public canteen on the ground floor and told him to shut up and listen. They had been obliged to pass the kiosk that sold souvenirs of the Palace of Westminster. Ralph Grunte was buying a bottle of House of Commons aftershave and a pair of embossed cufflinks. He wanted to be at his best as he had been invited to dine

that evening at the Libyan embassy. At lunch he had
made light of it – 'Terrible people' – but he confessed
that he believed it his duty to break bread. 'Jaw jaw is
better than war war.' His neighbour, who thought the
saying to be one of Churchill's weaker contributions,
kept his silence. The Libyans and Grunte deserved
each other. With any luck Grunte would not come
back.

Barton wasted no time. 'How much money have you
got?' Wayne put his hand into his jeans' pocket. 'No.
How much are you worth? Do you own a house?'
Wayne said that he did not. He lived either with his
mum or he paid rent. He had a second-hand motorbike
but it was off the road. He had a ghetto-blaster, a
stolen video and the clothes he stood up in. He owed
Barclaycard seventeen hundred quid. 'Lancaster,' said
Barton, 'he doesn't look after you very well, does he?
See what we'll do for you.'

Wayne did not have to be carried very far up the
mountain in order to see the kingdoms of the earth.
He shopped David Lancaster and the Minister of Posts
and Telegraphs ('Once a week they do it, on the prowl,
that is. Filthy beasts') for the price of an artisan's
cottage in Charlton and a second-hand Porsche. It was
the Porsche that did it. Ron said that the paper would
also pay for his cruise ticket. And his mum's. Wayne
was to accompany him back to the offices of the *True
Brit*. 'We'll give you a bundle of the readies and put
you up at a hotel.'

They left the Palace by the factory exit and picked
up a cab in New Palace Yard. As they clambered into
the vehicle, David Lancaster, sitting in his motor car,
was undergoing the security check. It was at the
moment the guard lowered his bonnet that Lancaster
caught sight of them sitting in the back of the cab.

lovingly gathered under the expert eyes of generations of Tory knights, had been sold off thirty years ago by the then chairman of the Kitchen Committee, the young Robert Maxwell, since when his name had rarely been off the lips of MPs.

Under the influence of the *pinot noir*, Joshua began to take a benign interest in his neighbours. He was sitting opposite to Julian Brazier, one of the Party's keener subalterns, who asked Soames if he had ever been to Malta. 'On Malta, they speak Punic, or what passes for it. Bit like the Arab dialect in North Africa. Couldn't bear that fella Mintoff.' Brazier then inquired carefully whether that meant that the Maltese were Carthaginians; it was the second lieutenant speaking to the colonel of the regiment. Had he been speaking to Lord Hailsham, he would have said 'sir'.

Joshua, encouraged by the turn the conversation had taken, murmured, 'All them elephants,' an observation that was immediately taken up by Dame Elaine.

'I was once told that in Africa you can always tell if an elephant is nearby by the sound of its stomach rumbling.'

At this Soames was at his most magisterial. 'Went to Kenya on safari. Took my very nice secretary. We passed an enormous pile of dung. "What's that?" she said. "If Cyril Smith hasn't passed this way recently, my dear, it is undoubtedly elephant!" ' There was much laughter.

Not to be outdone, Joshua embarked on his Lionel Blue story. The rabbi/broadcaster had spoken at a literary lunch. He told of an American woman who had visited Rumania and had insisted on being taken to Dracula's Castle. At midnight there is a terrible clap of thunder and a flash of lightning. The bedroom curtains blow open and there, standing on the sill, is a frightful fiend. The poor woman plucks a crucifix from her bosom and holds it up before her. The fiend replies, 'Lady, is this your unlucky day . . .' The laughter would have been louder had Joshua's Jewish accent been better.

A Yorkshire knight who sat for Scarborough said, 'Dracula landed in Scarborough. There is a man who dresses up as Dracula and goes to parties; sometimes he is Dracula, sometimes he is Captain Cook.' Oh Harold Pinter, thought Joshua, if you could hear this.

After a cup of coffee in the smoking room, and demands from friends for news of progress of his enquiries ('Some, but you will have to wait and see what John MacGregor says tomorrow morning to the Lobby'), Joshua collected his executive briefcase from his room. His friend David Walder had once said that the custom MPs have of never being seen without their cases made them look like so many clandestine abortionists.

He walked the corridors to Emma's lift. The chemical smell still lingered. The hook, he noticed, had been removed and the screw-holes filled. What delicate susceptibilities on the part of the Sergeant at Arms. For a moment Joshua could not remember on which of Dante's circles he had left his car. It was not uncommon to see people wandering the spiral in a state of near despair. He found it and drove across the Elephant (no signs of 'Big Cyril') and down the Old Kent Road, past the boxers' pub. Millwall was playing at home. Cheerful yobs threatened to bring his Rover to a standstill. The flat was cold and in darkness; his daughter had gone to stay with her sister. Having turned on all the lights and heaters, Joshua took a bath and telephoned Felicity. She would be back from the theatre. After a moment she picked up the receiver.

'Darling, darling,' she said. 'Are you watching "Newsnight"? Switch it on.'

Joshua did as he was told. Peter Snow was interviewing Grunte, a Grunte who had squeezed himself into an elderly dinner jacket. 'Just said goodnight to the Ambassador – shifty fella – and there, bold as brass, and without as much as a "by your leave", was Lancaster, standing in the hall of the embassy clutching two suitcases. "Come for the night?" I asked him. I won't tell you what he said to me, except to say it was highly offensive. Not the sort of language one expects between colleagues. Not that we were ever close, you understand, and how could I know at the time that the chap had applied to the Libyans for political asylum? Bad show, if you ask me.'

The junior foreign office minister, who had been dragged from a NATO function where he had clearly dined too well, thought so too. 'Most irregular. Quite without precedent.'

At the stroke of eleven o'clock, on Thursday 10 June, 199–, the Leader of the House entered the Bernard Ingham Room, which is to be found with difficulty on the second floor at the back of the building. Few, if any, MPs can find it. But the Press Lobby, pencils in hand, were there in force. Ron Barton, who had taken the scalp of the Minister of Posts and Telegraphs, sat with a return ticket to Miami in his pocket. John MacGregor was at his most Scottish. He was wearing his trews. He was flanked by the Sergeant at Arms and the Chief Superintendent of Police. Joshua Morris went and sat at the back of the room.

'We have reason to believe,' said MacGregor, his Scots accent exaggerated by tension, 'that we know the identity of the murderer of Mrs Emma Kerr, the late

Member for Corve Dale. The police have informed me that they want to interview Mr David Lancaster, the Member for Nottingham South East, as a matter of urgency. They want him to help them with their enquiries. However, as you will all know by now, David Lancaster is presently inside the Libyan Embassy where he has requested, and been granted, political asylum.'

The questions came thick and fast. Would the British Government break off relations with Colonel Gaddafi? That was a matter for the Foreign Secretary, who would be making a statement in the House that afternoon. Had the wretched Minister of Posts resigned? He had: a personal tragedy. Would Joshua Morris be given a job? He would not. Not even the Ministry of Posts and Telegraphs? (Laughter.) MacGregor said it was not a matter for him, although he did say how indebted he was to Joshua Morris for his efforts. 'He was a great help. The Sherlock Holmes Society can be proud of him.' There was a muted cheer.

As the throng pressed to leave the room, Eleanor Goodman of Channel 4 News asked Joshua if he had heard the news. 'What news?' he replied sharply. 'Surely we have had more than enough news?' Joshua Morris, who had been elected to Parliament twenty years before in search of the quiet life, braced himself in anticipation of bad tidings.

Miss Goodman's rhetorical question held relish. 'Haven't you heard?' she said. 'Maggie Thatcher is going to stand for the leadership in November. It's on the tape.'

MAUREEN O'BRIEN
CLOSE-UP ON DEATH

A JOHN BRIGHT WHODUNNIT

A BOOK AT BEDTIME SELECTION

CLOSE-UP ON DEATH

Everybody loved Liza. Talented, pretty, popular, she had just landed a marvellous part in a new television series and her career was going from strength to strength. Then the bright flame of her life is cruelly extinguished and her hopes for a great future end with the shocking discovery of her corpse in an empty North London house.

There aren't any obvious suspects: Liza had no enemies. But Detective Inspector John Bright concentrates his investigations on her three closest associates – Liza's mother; her lover, Paul, and her best friend, Millie. Paul and Millie are also actors and find – ironically – that Liza's tragic death brings unexpected benefits to their careers. But it looks to John Bright as though everyone is performing a role and all the principal players find it hard to separate fact from fiction as suspicion mounts . . .

'More than just a crime novel – the love interest is beautifully handled, too, making this a gripping, almost hypnotic read' *Woman's World*

'A first-rate whodunnit – gripping, tantilising and with plenty of tension' *Best Magazine*

'Maureen O'Brien . . . is a dab hand at dialogue and also at thespian jealousies. A smashing debut . . .' *Evening Standard*

FICTION/CRIME   0 7472 3171 0

A selection of bestsellers
from Headline

FICTION

GASLIGHT IN PAGE STREET	Harry Bowling	£4.99 □
LOVE SONG	Katherine Stone	£4.99 □
WULF	Steve Harris	£4.99 □
COLD FIRE	Dean Koontz	£4.99 □
ROSE'S GIRLS	Merle Jones	£4.99 □
LIVES OF VALUE	Sharleen Cooper Cohen	£4.99 □
THE STEEL ALBATROSS	Scott Carpenter	£4.99 □
THE OLD FOX DECEIV'D	Martha Grimes	£4.50 □

NON-FICTION

THE SUNDAY TIMES SLIM PLAN	Prue Leith	£5.99 □
MICHAEL JACKSON The Magic and the Madness	J Randy Taraborrelli	£5.99 □

SCIENCE FICTION AND FANTASY

SORCERY IN SHAD	Brian Lumley	£4.50 □
THE EDGE OF VENGEANCE	Jenny Jones	£5.99 □
ENCHANTMENTS END Wells of Ythan 4	Marc Alexander	£4.99 □

All Headline books are available at your local bookshop or newsagent, or can be ordered direct from the publisher. Just tick the titles you want and fill in the form below. Prices and availability subject to change without notice.

Headline Book Publishing PLC, Cash Sales Department, PO Box 11, Falmouth, Cornwall, TR10 9EN, England.

Please enclose a cheque or postal order to the value of the cover price and allow the following for postage and packing:
UK & BFPO: £1.00 for the first book, 50p for the second book and 30p for each additional book ordered up to a maximum charge of £3.00.
OVERSEAS & EIRE: £2.00 for the first book, £1.00 for the second book and 50p for each additional book.

Name ....

Address ....

....

....